PERCEPTION

PERCEPTION

Alaric Albertsson

COSMIC
EGG
BOOKS

Winchester, UK
Washington, USA

First published by Cosmic Egg Books, 2013
Cosmic Egg Books is an imprint of John Hunt Publishing Ltd., Laurel House, Station Approach,
Alresford, Hants, SO24 9JH, UK
office1@jhpbooks.net
www.johnhuntpublishing.com

For distributor details and how to order please visit the 'Ordering' section on our website.

ISBN: 978 1 78279 261 1

A CIP catalogue record for this book is available from the British Library.

Design: Stuart Davies

Printed in the USA by Edwards Brothers Malloy

We operate a distinctive and ethical publishing philosophy in all
areas of our business, from our global network of authors to
production and worldwide distribution.

CHAPTER ONE

It was an afternoon like any other on Hugo Drive, and that was as it should be. After all, nobody was expecting humankind to topple from the apex of creation later that evening.

Dena Anderson set out two plates and two sets of silverware on the dining room table. She knew Michael would want to eat in the family room where he could watch television, but that was not going to happen. It had been a point of contention throughout their six years of marriage, leading to nightly arguments that had become an almost comfortable ritual. Dena would usually get her way, Michael would pout and all would be forgiven by the time they finished their salads. On rare occasions, when Dena was feeling magnanimous, she would let Michael win the argument and they would have their dinner on folding trays in front of their large, flat screen television. However, this evening was not going to be one of those occasions.

As she arranged Michael's silverware, Dena could hear him turn the television on – it sounded like a newscast. Michael liked to catch the news when he first came home from work.

The newscast was drowned out for a moment by the sounds of aircraft overhead. Dena glanced out the dining room window, but did not see any planes on that side of the house. Hugo Drive ended in a cul de sac and connected at the opposite end to an undeveloped stretch of Route 228 that ran east of Caldonia, Pennsylvania. Twenty years earlier a contractor by the name of Benjamin Hugo had built thirteen homes on a tract of land that he hoped would grow more valuable as Caldonia expanded eastward. But the town had not expanded eastward; all of its subsequent growth had been to the north and west. Other than the commuters on Route 228, there was very little traffic near Hugo Drive. The neighborhood was a combination of suburban ambience and rural quietude. Dena and Michael had moved into their home three years earlier, and Dena was sure she had never heard any planes or jets in all that time.

She went to the kitchen and took a head of lettuce from the refrigerator. Then Michael called out from the family room, "Have you seen this?"

"Seen what?"

"Come in here, Dena."

The ivory landline phone on the kitchen wall began to ring. It had to be either Dena's mother or Izzy Franklin from across the street. Dena started to reach for the receiver, but thought better of it. If Izzy was calling, it was undoubtedly about the new family that had just moved into the house between the Bouchards and the Inghams. Izzy Franklin was the president of the Hugo Drive Neighborhood Association. She was devoted to preserving their small enclave's heritage, which, to Izzy, meant keeping the neighborhood white and Protestant. When the Lewinbergs moved into Number Two Hugo Drive, not long after Dena and Michael had bought their own house on the cul de sac, Izzy Franklin had wanted to start a petition and was genuinely surprised to learn that the Hugo Drive Neighborhood Association had no authority to expel a Jewish family, no matter how many signatures she could muster.

The newest family on Hugo Drive was Indian. The moving van arrived yesterday, so Dena knew the Naras were still living out of boxes. She had met the husband, Rajinder Nara, earlier that day and he seemed very nice; but he was also very dark. He and his wife had a little boy. Other than that, she did not know much about them.

Dena decided that she did not want to risk the chance of being subjected to one of Izzy's racist rants. She really did not like Izzy Franklin very much, although Izzy's husband Jerry was all right. Ignoring the phone, Dena put the head of lettuce down on the granite kitchen counter and went to the family room.

She immediately took in the image on the television, but what she did not understand was why Michael was watching science fiction. Michael Anderson had very little imagination, and speculative fiction usually was not his cup of tea.

Dena asked, "What are you watching?" Whatever the plot, the setting was supposed to be St. Louis, Missouri. The wide television screen displayed the St. Louis Arch with an expanse of the Mississippi River behind it.

"It's a live broadcast, Dena."

She looked to her husband to see if he was joking, but from the expression on his face it was clear that he was not. "This has to be a hoax," she said.

Michael shook his head. "I don't think so."

Just behind the Arch and above the river was an enormous tear-shaped object. The tapered end pointed towards the Arch. Dena could not tell how large it was, but she thought it must be longer than a football field. The thing hung motionless in the air, or at least that is how it looked on the television screen.

Dena asked, "That's a UFO?"

"They don't know," said Michael. He ran his fingers through his thinning, blond hair. "I mean, of course it's unidentified, and it's obviously a flying object of some kind, but they don't seem to know what it is."

The phone in the kitchen stopped ringing. For a moment Dena wondered with a touch of guilt if the caller had been her mother. Or maybe her brother Dalton, although she had not talked to him in months. No, Dalton would have called her cell phone.

An announcer's voice came on, but there was no real information in his patter. The White House had not yet responded to press inquiries. The announcer speculated that the vessel – for it was surely a vessel of some kind – might belong to the military. Most of the announcer's talk was nothing more than an ongoing description of what Dena and Michael could see on their screen: the hovering UFO, the Arch, the river and an ever-growing crowd of onlookers. If the vessel belonged to the military, they obviously did not want anybody near the thing. A long line of soldiers in camouflage fatigues kept the crowd back from the Arch and its underground visitors' center. In addition to this, a unit of the Coast Guard was turning back all of the people who tried to approach the UFO by boat. Most of these were sightseers coming upriver in private speedboats and pontoons; from what Dena could see, none put up any argument or resistance.

Dena sat next to Michael on the striped loveseat. She saw how his hair was disappearing at the crown of his head, and thought to herself how odd it was to notice something like that just then. Michael had very light hair, with the reddish tinge that people often described as strawberry blond. His eyes did not leave the television screen as Dena sat down, but he reached out and took her hand in his.

Dena said, "It can't be anything really dangerous or those soldiers would have more than rifles, don't you think?" When Michael glanced at her, she added, "You know, like tanks or bazookas."

As if in response to her question, the announcer took a break from describing the riverside crowd to say that the Pentagon had issued a brief announcement. The Army and Air Force were both mobilized and standing ready, but keeping a distance to avoid creating a hostile situation. Dena thought this new development effectively obliterated the theory that the hovering vessel belonged to any branch of the United States military. The idea that a foreign power could penetrate the heartland of the nation was unsettling.

The announcer resumed giving another verbal sketch of the vessel and the crowd staring at it. Other than the vessel itself, the most amazing thing was the casual atmosphere that had come over the people gathered near the Arch. The initial surprise had worn off, and a festive ambience had settled through the crowd. Parents held their children on their shoulders to give them a view of the 'spaceship'. Some people had their dogs with them. A few placards had been hastily drawn up by people welcoming the 'aliens', if the vessel was indeed piloted by aliens, which Dena thought unlikely but not beyond the realm of possibility.

There was an insistent knocking at the front door. Dena looked to Michael, but his attention was glued to the television screen. With a sigh, Dena went to the living room to see who was knocking. She glanced back several times behind her at the screen as she walked, nearly tripping over the small Chippendale table next to the entrance of the family room.

She was not surprised to see Izzy and Jerry Franklin. Izzy was blond, but there was nothing natural about her hair color. She had an angular body with a thin, bony appearance that suggested borderline anorexia. Jerry Franklin, on the other hand, obviously had no difficulty eating. Dena thought he was probably medically obese. She sometimes wished that Jerry would stand up to his wife more often. The Franklins were nearly ten years older than Dena and Michael, and had two children who were both away in college. They often bragged about their son, J.J., but rarely spoke of their daughter.

It was Izzy who asked, "Have you seen the spaceship?"

Dena nodded. "Michael and I are watching it on television right now." The Franklins were looking at her expectantly, so she added, "Would you like to come in?"

Izzy Franklin pushed past Dena, with Jerry following along in her wake. Dena went with them into the family room, where Michael barely glanced up to say, "Hey Jerry…Izzy."

Jerry immediately sat down next to Michael, leaving Dena no choice but to share the adjacent couch with Izzy. Nothing had changed during Dena's brief absence. The tear-shaped vessel still hovered over the Mississippi River, and soldiers continued to hold the crowd back. The announcer's voice continued to drone on without telling them anything new.

Dena asked, "Do either of you know anyone in St. Louis?"

The Franklins both shook their heads. Jerry said, "I've met a few people from there, but I don't know anyone well enough to call."

Michael said, "I'm sure it's extraterrestrial. I didn't think so at first, but there's no other explanation."

"Why do you say that?" asked Jerry. "Just because they don't know where it came from doesn't mean there are Martians inside that thing."

"Not Martians, no," said Michael. "But they said the military is keeping its distance, except for the soldiers keeping that crowd under control."

Izzy said, "That's so the Army won't provoke a hostile situation."

Michael stared at her as if she had sprouted alien antennae herself. "When has our military ever worried about provoking a hostile situation? There should be tanks all around that thing, and somebody with a bullhorn ordering the ship to surrender." He let his attention return to the television. "Our government is afraid of these guys, wherever they're from."

They all watched the motionless vessel on the television, listening as the announcer gave the current temperature and humidity in downtown St. Louis. As if anyone cared.

Then the picture changed and they were looking at an astronomer, a Dr. Stephen Walsh, who admitted what everybody already knew on some level; the tear-shaped vessel was very likely from another planet. Dena listened attentively for a few minutes, but it soon became obvious that Dr. Walsh knew no more than anyone else. He was being interviewed by somebody offstage, reciting theoretical statistics concerning the likelihood of contact with intelligent extraterrestrial races.

Considering the fact that they were staring at the image of a UFO hovering next to the St. Louis Arch, Dena thought the chance of extraterrestrial contact was probably somewhere around one hundred percent.

Izzy Franklin said, "This is so exciting. Jerry and I were just getting ready to go out to eat when the newscast came on."

Michael glanced at her and Jerry. "Why don't you guys join us for dinner? Dena doesn't mind, do you, honey?"

Dena kept what she hoped was a smile on her face. There was no gracious way to say, yes, she really did mind. Instead she did a quick mental inventory of what she had in the kitchen that could possibly be stretched into dinner for four. It was Dena's habit to get all of her weekly grocery shopping done in one trip every Wednesday morning, and this was Tuesday. Her options were limited.

Izzy stood, saying, "Let me help you. It's the least I can do."

"Yes," said Dena. *It really is the least you can do.* She pushed her irritation with Izzy aside and followed her into the kitchen. It was Michael with whom she was really angry. Dena hated when he phrased something in such a way that she could not disagree without appearing mean or unreasonable.

In the kitchen Izzy looked around and asked, "What do you want me to do?" She spied the head of lettuce. "Can I make the salad?"

"Sure," said Dena. She opened a cabinet and surveyed her sparse collection of canned goods.

Izzy took a knife out of one of the kitchen drawers and found the cutting board that Dena kept in the cabinet under the sink. "This whole spaceship thing was beginning to bore me anyway," she said. "I wish the aliens would do something interesting."

Dena nodded absently as she chose a can of green beans, and another of new potatoes. She would mix them together, she thought, and add a little salt and tarragon. But she still needed to think of something for the main dish. The two chicken thighs she had planned to broil for Michael and herself would not stretch for four people.

Cutting up the head of lettuce, Izzy said, "I suppose you've heard we've had our own alien invasion here on Hugo Drive."

"What do you mean?" asked Dena. She knew exactly what

Izzy meant, but she was not going to play along.

"I mean the new family that moved into Number Fifteen. Have you met them?"

"I've met *him*, Rajinder. I haven't met his wife yet."

Izzy's eyebrows, much darker than her platinum hair, lifted ever so slightly. "And that doesn't bother you?"

"What? That I haven't met his wife?"

"They're black."

Dena opened the can of corn. "They're Indian." Like it made any difference.

Izzy put the chopped lettuce into a large wooden bowl. "I told everyone this was going to happen back when the Lewinbergs moved in. It's happening all over the country. First the Jews come, and then you get your colored. You mark my words, the next thing we'll see are the gays trying to buy a house here."

Feeling the flare of anger ignite in her stomach, Dena dropped the can opener on the counter and hurried from the kitchen. She passed the doorway to the family room, went quickly through the living room and stepped out through the front door. Once outside, after closing the door quietly behind her, she felt hot tears pooling in the corners of her eyes. At times like this she hated Izzy Franklin. Even worse, she hated herself.

The neighborhood was curiously quiet. Dena's home was one of five houses encircling the cul de sac. Evening shadows were beginning to reach across the lawns and gardens as night approached. Each of the five homes had a front lawn that tapered slightly as it came up to the pavement, and each had a mailbox standing at the end of its driveway. She saw that the door to the mailbox at Number Twenty Seven was hanging open. Either the mail carrier was getting sloppy, or Beaker was. Probably the latter, she thought. The side of the box was painted with the house number and the name R. K. Beaker in white, stenciled letters. Dena still did not know what the R. K. stood for. She and Michael had introduced themselves to the large, unkempt man when he moved in the year before, but all he gave them was his surname. They rarely saw Beaker. His large pickup truck was sitting out in his driveway as usual, so she knew he was home. Izzy had told Dena that the man was widowed.

Directly across the street was the Grahams' home. Like the Franklins, Dave and Lisa Graham were about ten years older than Dena and had grown children. Lisa had hinted to Dena more than once that she should think about a child of her own, tossing in the cliché about biological clocks, as if everyone's lifelong dream was to bear progeny. It was true that Dena had never tried to prevent a pregnancy after marrying Michael – she did not even use birth control – but it had never happened, and deep down in her heart Dena did not think she was missing out on very much. She did not mind other people's children, but she could not imagine taking on that much responsibility around the clock. On the other hand, she had always known that Michael dreamed of someday becoming a father, so she had left the matter up to God. At the age of thirty-two and still childless, Dena had come to the conclusion that God did not think she should be burdened with the responsibility of parenthood either.

Her home and the Grahams' bordered the entrance to the cul de sac.

Izzy and Jerry Franklin lived next to the Grahams, and the Martins' home – between the Franklins' house and Beaker's – completed the circle. The Martins were in their early seventies, and were the oldest couple on Hugo Drive. Jim Martin had paid for the centerpiece of junipers that stood in the hub of the cul de sac, and he personally tended the bushes with as much care as he lavished on his own lawn and garden.

On most evenings, even when there was nobody else to be seen from Dena's front yard, she could usually hear some kind of activity from elsewhere in the neighborhood: Jim Martin's lawn mower behind his house, the sound of the Bouchard children playing down the street or perhaps Stacy Cooper and Darla

Clark laughing about something over drinks on the Clarks' patio. That afternoon Hugo Drive was silent. There was not even much sound of traffic passing up and down Route 228.

The UFO in St. Louis had captured the world's attention.

The door opened behind Dena, and Michael leaned out. With an urgent tone, he said, "Get in here, now."

"Give me a few minutes, Michael. I can't face Izzy right now."

"Izzy? What about her?" He looked genuinely confused. "What are you talking about?"

"What are *you* talking about?"

"It's the UFO, Dena. It's moving."

CHAPTER TWO

Izzy and Jerry were both in the family room when Michael returned with Dena. The Franklins were now standing between the couch and the loveseat, their attention completely on the large television screen. Izzy Franklin gave no indication of being offended by Dena's sudden departure from the kitchen. In fact she gave no sign of noticing Dena at all.

The tear-shaped UFO had indeed moved its position. From what Dena could see on the television, it looked like the tapered end actually passed between the silver legs of the Arch. The bottom of the UFO hovered no more than twenty feet above the steps leading down to the visitors' center. The soldiers appeared to be trying to urge the crowd to move back, but with little success. The television announcer was describing the recent movement of the UFO with obvious excitement in his voice.

It was an hour earlier in St. Louis, but well past the time when most people had supper, and enterprising food vendors had arrived with carts selling hot dogs, burgers and canned drinks to the hungry crowd. The vendors on the television reminded Dena of their own forgotten dinner.

"We should eat something," she said. "I can put together those salads, at least."

Izzy started to follow her to the kitchen, but Dena said, "I don't need any help. I'll just be a couple of minutes."

As she left the family room, Dena caught Izzy's annoyed expression out of the corner of her eye. She ignored the look and went on to the kitchen where the bowl of chopped lettuce still sat on the counter. Dena took a tomato and a cucumber from the refrigerator and cut them into wedges and slices.

The next thing we'll see are the gays trying to buy a house here.

So what? How would it have any measurable, negative impact on the neighborhood? Dena did not often socialize with the Lewinbergs – they lived at the far end of the street – but they seemed friendly and agreeable. Despite Izzy's dire predictions, Jews had not destroyed the neighborhood. Dena thought Rajinder Nara and his family would make good neighbors too. Perhaps Hugo Drive would benefit from the addition of a nice lesbian couple. They could buy Beaker's house next door. He was not very pleasant company.

Hunting around for a bag of grated mozzarella in the refrigerator, Dena thought again of her brother Dalton and realized she had not spoken with him since the previous spring. She fished her cell phone from her pocket and found his name in her list of contacts.

Moments later the voice on the phone said, "Hey, Dena, are you watching television?"

"Right now I'm putting together a salad," she said, dropping a handful of the cheese into the salad bowl. "I assume you mean watching what is going on in St. Louis."

"Yeah, that's the only thing on all the channels. Bring it here, Spence."

Dena remembered that Spencer was Dalton's mixed-breed dog. She had never seen the animal.

"Well, most of the channels," he added.

"Michael and I have been watching it for a while now. We have neighbors here, the Franklins." Dena did not know why she added that last detail. Her brother had never met Izzy and Jerry Franklin.

"How's Mom?"

"She's fine. She and Dad bought a new car."

"Cool. Tell them I said hi."

"Yes, I'll do that." But Dena knew she would not. Her parents had disowned Dalton nine years ago. Since then they had not spoken to him and refused to speak about him.

There was an awkward pause, and then Dalton said, "They're having a dog show up here in Butler on Saturday. It's an informal thing, with some obedience and rally that Spencer is registered to compete in. You should come up."

"Maybe I will." She took a large spoon from a drawer and tossed the salad with her free hand. "Dalton, are you okay?"

"Why?"

"What do you mean, why? Do I need a reason to check up on my brother once in a while?"

"I'm still single, so I could be doing better in that department. But the business is picking up." Dalton groomed dogs for a living. The previous spring, when Dena had last spoken with him, he had moved to the town of Butler and opened his own grooming shop there.

Dena said, "You know, you might not be single if you spent more time with people and less with dogs."

She had intended that as a joke, but it was followed by another awkward pause. Then Dalton said, "Dogs love me unconditionally."

"So do I, Dalton. You know that, don't you?"

In the silence that followed, Dena knew what her brother was thinking. If she had really loved him unconditionally she would have invited him to the wedding. She would have asked him to dinner one evening, to come see her home there outside of Caldonia or perhaps even to stay overnight, but that had never happened either. Dalton did not know the Franklins, or any of their other neighbors, because he had never been to Dena and Michael's home. Dena did love him, but she was also ashamed of him, and to some extent blamed him for the disruption of their family. For nine years Dena's expression of love had consisted of little more than an occasional phone call.

She had time to think of all of this by the time Dalton said, "I'd like to believe so."

Dena took four salad bowls from a cabinet. "Dalton, I'd love to talk more, but I'm sure Michael is starving by now. I'll call you later this week and let you know if I can make it to the dog show."

"Okay." From the tone in his voice it was clear that he did not expect her to call.

"I mean it. If I don't call tomorrow, I'll get back to you on Thursday."

"Okay."

"Okay, then, I'll talk to you soon. Bye." Dena closed the phone and vowed silently to honor her promise and call Dalton back whether or not she could get up to Butler that weekend. And this time she really would try to get together with him. Butler was not that far a drive from Caldonia, certainly no farther than Pittsburgh.

She filled the four bowls with salad and placed them on a tray, along with bottles of Italian, French and Thousand Island dressings. It was dark now outside the kitchen windows. Dena carried the tray of salads into the family room.

Izzy looked up as she came in, saying, "You haven't missed anything."

Dena recognized the words as the closest Izzy Franklin would come to an apology. Izzy had recognized that she crossed a line and was trying to smooth things over with casual conversation.

Handing her the first bowl of salad, Dena asked, "The UFO hasn't moved anymore?" Apology accepted.

Bottles of salad dressing were passed around, and Dena explained apologetically that she did not have any croutons. Izzy mentioned running into Sara Lewinberg at the supermarket the day before, as if she and the Lewinbergs were now close friends, and Dena knew it was a continuation of the oblique apology. *No, you misunderstood me; I'm not anti-Semitic at all.* Michael then asked if anyone had met the new family moving into Number Fifteen. Dena said that she had met the husband. She made no further comment, and Izzy remained tactfully silent as well.

Jerry Franklin coughed, choking on a piece of lettuce and gesticulating wildly at the television screen. "Summons havenon," he garbled. Then, swallowing the lettuce, he said, "Something's happening."

The announcer's voice confirmed Jerry's observation, and now they could all see a small panel on the underside of the vessel detach and lower itself at an angle. The crowd around the Arch erupted in a cacophony of screams, cheers and exclamations. Only moments before there had been no visible indication of an entrance to the vessel.

Dena's fork paused between her salad bowl and her mouth. A drop of French dressing fell into the cleavage between her breasts, but she did not flinch or wipe it up. Her mouth, ready to receive the bite of tomato on the prongs of the fork, remained hanging open as she sat transfixed by the television broadcast.

A man-like being was stepping down from the UFO.

Although the creature was clad from head to toe in a protective suit, Dena could see immediately that it was not human. It was as large as a human, but its legs and arms were much shorter, and the torso noticeably longer. The hands and feet were shorter, too. Compared to a human, the person – if indeed it was a person – seemed to have incredibly tiny feet. It also had short, stubby gloved hands, and in one of those hands it clutched what looked like a wand straight out of the *Harry Potter* movies. The creature's suit was white, with a matching helmet that had an opaque visor obscuring its features.

Izzy asked, "What's that thing it's holding?"

The other three ignored her question. Now a second alien came out of the UFO, followed almost immediately by a third. All three were roughly the same height, and each held a wand. A quiet had settled over the crowd. Most of the soldiers had raised their rifles, but nobody seemed to know quite what to do.

"Jesus, I wish they'd put away the guns," said Jerry.

Michael said, "I guess they didn't get the memo about not creating a hostile situation."

Dena looked over at her husband. "That's not funny, Michael."

"You don't see me laughing, do you?"

The three beings from the UFO slowly turned right and left, shifting their positions on their short legs. They held the wands out, moving the devices slightly even as they turned.

"Are they looking for something?" asked Dena.

Michael shook his head. "I don't know."

All three of the creatures stopped turning. They were facing the same direction, ahead and a little to the right of the tapered end of the UFO. Then the creature standing in front of its two companions – Dena thought it was the one in charge – lowered its wand and held the device to the side of its torso. The wand disappeared into the suit. Dena noticed that the alien's arms were so short that its hands did not reach all the way to its waist.

Then it lowered itself to all fours.

"What the hell!" exclaimed Michael.

A similar sentiment was expressed by the crowd of onlookers on the television screen. The alien's movement was completely natural, as if it were as much at ease walking on four limbs as on two. Only now it looked far less man-like than its bipedal companions.

The alien lowered its chest all the way to the ground, its rump remaining up on the erect hind legs. In this odd position, it stretched out its right arm, sliding its hand and arm along the cement. Behind this display the other two aliens lowered their wands.

There was a sudden commotion in the crowd, and a dog, a German shepherd, burst through the line of soldiers. The animal ran towards the three aliens, but when it came within twenty yards of them a loud crack split the air. The dog jerked once, dropped to the pavement and lay still.

Dena leaned forward. "Did one of the soldiers just shoot that dog?"

The television screen burst into a brilliant white light, causing them to blink. Dena rubbed at her eyes.

And then there was nothing on the screen at all.

CHAPTER THREE

"What happened?" asked Michael. He picked up the remote and began changing channels. The only thing he could find was a black and white *I Love Lucy* rerun. All of the other channels displayed the same blank screen.

Jerry Franklin was running his fingers over his phone. "There's nothing about it yet on the internet. Nothing we haven't seen on television, anyway."

"Maybe we're being invaded," said Izzy, laughing weakly.

Dena glanced at her. "That isn't funny. I wish all of you would stop making jokes."

"Oh, I don't really mean it. Obviously something is wrong with your television."

"The television and my phone, both," said Jerry. He looked up at them with an annoyed expression. "I just lost my internet connection. And this piece of crap is supposed to be state of the art." Jerry Franklin, who worked in advertising, took pride in all of his electronics being state of the art.

Michael leaned closer to Jerry and looked at the phone's screen. "It isn't working?"

"The internet connection isn't." He pulled up his list of contacts, picked one and held the phone to his ear. "Hey, Bob, this is Jerry Franklin. I just wanted to make sure my phone is working. I don't have the internet now. Yeah, yeah, we were watching it, too. We're over at the Andersons' house. No, I don't think you know them. They're neighbors, great people. Yeah, same to you. Sorry to bother you. Love to Deb." He hung up.

"So it's just the internet," said Michael, stating the obvious.

Jerry nodded. "It looks that way. I'm going across the street to see what I can pull up on my laptop."

Izzy said, "If you're going to the house, leave me the phone. I want to call J.J. and make sure he's okay."

The phrase surprised Dena. It had not occurred to her that the

Franklins' two children might not be okay. She did not want to hear jokes about any kind of invasion, but Dena really had not thought there was anything wrong except for a television glitch. Now Izzy's words cast a cold shadow over her heart. She excused herself and went to the kitchen. Taking her cellular phone from her pocket, Dena hurried out the back door to the patio. It was dark outside, and she cursed as she kicked her shin against one of the wrought iron patio chairs.

She opened her phone. The display gave almost as much light as that coming through the kitchen window. Dena found her contacts and scrolled down to her parents' landline. Neither of her parents had a cell phone, but it took only a moment for her mother to answer.

"Mom? Are you guys okay?"

"Yes, Dena, we're fine." The sound of her mother's voice was comforting, like a warm blanket fresh from the dryer. "Why? You sound upset. You and Michael haven't had a fight, have you?"

So much for the comfort. Why did her mother always go there first, assuming there was some problem with Dena's marriage?

"No, we haven't had a fight. Haven't you seen what's happening in St. Louis? It was on all the television stations."

"But we weren't watching television," her mother said. "We've been watching a DVD of an old Bette Davis movie. Have you seen—"

Silence.

Dena took the phone away from her ear and looked at it. In the glow of the display she could see that the battery was still strong. Somehow she had lost her connection. That happened sometimes out on Hugo Drive. The Lewinbergs and the Kellers said they never had any problem with it, but they lived just off of Route 228 and received a stronger signal.

She tried calling her parents again, but the phone didn't respond. A third attempt elicited nothing either.

Going back into the house, Dena could hear a woman's voice

– and it was not Lucille Ball or Vivian Vance – coming from the television in the family room. She paused as she walked past the kitchen wall phone, thinking she could call her mother from there, but she was curious to find out why the televised broadcast had been interrupted. Her mother obviously did not know anything about the St. Louis situation, so it did not matter if a few minutes passed before Dena called her back again.

Besides, she thought, telephone service does work both ways. If her mother was concerned, she could call Dena as easily as the other way around.

Michael was alone in the family room. The woman's voice on the television had been replaced by that of a man. Michael was standing now, watching the oversized head of an announcer on the television screen. Dena recognized Phil Watson, an anchor on the late night news.

Phil was saying, "We have received word from the White House that the President of the United States will be making a statement shortly. We seem to have lost our connection with our St. Louis affiliates, possibly due to satellite interference from the UFO. A White House spokesperson has asked that everyone remain calm. Stay tuned to this station for further information as we receive it. I repeat, we have received word from—"

Michael said, "If we have to be told to remain calm it means that a lot of people aren't very calm at all."

"Where's Izzy?" asked Dena.

"She just now went home. She lost her phone signal, so she went to use her landline. I told her she could use ours."

"I'm glad she didn't," said Dena. "I want to use it to call my parents. I lost the signal on my cell phone, too." Dena turned and went back to the kitchen. Taking the receiver from the wall phone, she called her parents' number.

"Hi, Mom?"

"Sweetie, I told you that we're in the middle of—"

"Mom, turn off the damned DVD."

Michael came into the kitchen and said, "I'm going to make a pot of coffee. I'm guessing we're going to be up late tonight."

"Mom, just—" Dena held her hand over the mouthpiece and turned to her husband. "We're out of coffee. Sorry."

"How can we be out of coffee?"

"It's easy. I thought we had enough for the week, but obviously we didn't." Into the mouthpiece, she said, "Hang on, Mom." Then, back to Michael, "I know you think the coffee fairies deliver it, but I actually have to go out and buy the stuff. I'm going to the store tomorrow."

From the phone, Dena heard her mother ask, "Are you and Michael fighting again?"

She covered the mouthpiece more firmly with her hand. "If you need coffee right this minute, run out to the store and get some."

"I don't want to miss what the President has to say."

"For God's sake, Michael, you can be there and back in less than half an hour if you hurry. Oh, and get some milk. I assume you'll want milk in your coffee." Michael left the kitchen, and Dena turned her attention back to the phone. "We aren't fighting."

"It sounded like a fight," said her mother.

"Well it wasn't. We're just out of coffee. Mom, you and Dad need to turn off the DVD and watch the news."

"What channel?" Her mother's voice now sounded distant and metallic.

"*Any* channel. A UFO has landed in St. Louis. I'm not kidding."

Dena could hear her mother saying something to her dad. Then, still distant and metallic, her mother said, "Your father is turning on the news now." There was a sudden burst of static over the line. "Oh, it's that nice Phil Watson."

"We're watching the same channel. I mean, that's what's on in the family room."

More static came over the line, and then her mother was saying, "...always liked him. He says the President is going to be talking."

"Yes," said Dena. "We were watching a broadcast from St. Louis, but it was cut off." Static forced Dena to shout into the phone, "IT HAPPENED ON ALL THE CHANNELS, MOM."

Now there was nothing but a hissing, crackling sound.

"Mom? Mom, can you hear me at all?" It did not seem likely. Dena replaced the receiver. She looked around the kitchen. It felt curiously empty, although there was nothing physically different. "Michael?"

Dena went to the garage and saw that the BMW was gone. Michael had taken her advice and left to get coffee. Just then she wished he had ignored her and stayed home.

In the family room, Phil Watson was still sharing everything he knew with his viewers, which was next to nothing. No communication was coming out of St. Louis, even from the surrounding county bearing the same name, and the closest towns with radio and telephone connections were apparently as in the dark as the rest of the world.

Dena had always thought that the city of St. Louis was in St. Louis County, but Watson made it sound as if the city was separate.

News teams from St. Charles and Hillsboro had gone to the city in vans, but no word had come back from them yet. Phil Watson emphasized that it was a long drive for both of the news vans, and that their equipment was undoubtedly affected by whatever was disrupting communication in the city and county.

Then he had further news. Cellular telephone service was out across most of the United States, and landline service was intermittent in some areas.

Areas like western Pennsylvania, thought Dena.

But intermittent implied that the phones – at least the landline phones – could be on again. Dena went back to the kitchen and tried calling her parents once more.

The connection produced nothing more than static.

On a whim, she tried to call Dalton's landline. This time she got through, but it was only to hear a recorded voice telling her that the number was disconnected. Dena felt like kicking herself. Dalton had shut off his landline, or changed the number, and she did not even know about it. She did not know because they rarely spoke with each other anymore, and that was Dena's fault, not Dalton's. It had been easier over the years to distance herself from her twin. Dalton never mentioned it openly on the rare occasions when they talked, but he was not stupid.

She would have to get up to Butler for that dog show.

Dena looked at the clock on the stove. She was not sure when Michael had left, but she thought he would be home within the next few minutes. She checked her cell phone again. There was still no signal, so she could not call him. Not that she had any reason to call him, but it frustrated her nevertheless.

With nothing else to do, Dena went to the family room and tried to follow what the various announcers and experts were saying on television. Phil Watson had been replaced with a balding, freckled man from Carnegie Mellon University explaining how radio and satellite transmissions could be interrupted. Dena wondered if the man really believed what he was saying. She did not understand the details, but his lengthy monologue did not explain why news was not coming out of St. Louis through other sources: cars, trucks and buses.

She stretched out on the couch. Coffee sounded good.

* * *

The harsh sound of jets overhead pulled Dena out of her sleep. Phil Watson was back on the television screen. He looked disheveled. Dena rubbed at her eyes and sat up.

"...no contact since ten o'clock, Eastern Time," Watson was

saying. At first Dena thought he meant contact with St. Louis, although the television broadcast had broken off much earlier than that. Then Phil Watson's face disappeared, and his voice continued as the television screen displayed a map of Chicago and its surrounding suburbs.

Watson's disembodied voice said, "A team of reporters from Wheaton, Illinois have launched an independent investigation, but no word has been heard from them at this time." His face suddenly appeared on the screen again. "According to a source from Whiteman Air Force Base, a dozen B-2 Spirit bombers were sent to St. Louis after the televised transmission ended. There have also been reported sightings of military aircraft from other locations across the United States. There is no word yet on when the President will address the nation."

Dena shivered involuntarily.

"Michael?"

She went into the kitchen, calling Michael's name out again. A glance at the clock on the stove told her that she had slept for two hours. Two hours! Could Michael have been in an accident? It did not take two hours to drive into town to get a can of coffee and a gallon of milk. She picked up the receiver on the wall phone, but hung up when she heard the stream of crackling static.

Dena walked through every room in the house, as if Michael might have been hiding behind a bed or under the dining table. Then, to confirm what she already knew, she went to the garage and saw that the BMW was still gone. Her red Toyota Avalon on the other side of the garage looked as lonely as Dena felt.

Izzy and Jerry were home, she knew that. Dena felt an urge to run across the street and bang on their door, but going over to the Franklins' house would be admitting that something might have happened to Michael.

Hearing a vehicle coming up the street, Dena hurried to the living room and looked out the front window. A pair of headlights were coming up Hugo Drive. Before the vehicle reached the cul de sac she saw that it was Beaker's Silverado. The truck careened past the Grahams' and the Franklins' homes, bounced onto the edge of the Martins' lawn, and then circled into Beaker's driveway next door.

Through her window Dena could see the silhouette of the huge man as he climbed out of his truck. Beaker never kept the Silverado in his garage. Now he was walking over to the garage and opening the door. He went inside, returning a few seconds later with a wheelbarrow that he pushed over to the truck. Dena watched as the man pulled objects out of the bed of the truck and stacked them in the wheelbarrow. There were dark shapes that looked like a couple of large cans and several boxes. He pushed the wheelbarrow to the garage and disappeared in the deeper, blacker darkness. Then he was back outside and guiding the wheelbarrow back over to his truck.

This continued four times, filling the wheelbarrow and pushing it to the garage, and then Dena saw Beaker's silhouette close the garage door behind him. A light came on inside the house.

Knowing Beaker was home did not make Dena feel any better. She wondered what he was dragging into his garage. Dena was not usually judgmental or prejudiced like Izzy Franklin, but Beaker just acted so *odd* sometimes. And then there was his physical appearance. Dena thought he looked like the sort of man who might corner her in an alley and gut her open like a trout. Beaker's face was dominated by an aquiline nose, and that was not his fault, but it gave him a mean appearance. He was perpetually unshaven. Dena had never seen Beaker with a true beard, but she had never seen him with a clean jaw line, either. Somehow the man always managed to give the impression that he had last shaved two days earlier.

Beaker's odd behavior in the middle of the night pushed Dena to a decision. She could not stay in the house alone any longer.

Not with the phones out. Not with reports of Chicago and St. Louis being cut off from the rest of the world.

She opened the front door and looked around the cul de sac. There were no lights on at any of the houses other than Beaker's. The taller tree limbs at the far end of the street caught the lights of cars moving in both directions on 228. Dena could hear the cars, too, and sporadic angry honking. There was never so much traffic on that stretch of road. She wondered how Izzy and Jerry could sleep at a time like this, but Dena would have still been asleep herself if the jets had not woke her up. The jets were as much an anomaly as the inexplicable traffic. There were no airports near Caldonia; it took nearly an hour to reach Pittsburgh International Airport using the interstate. She wondered if she had been awakened by the military aircraft that Phil Watson had mentioned on television.

The windows at Dave and Lisa Graham's house were just as dark as the Franklins'. Dena was not sure if they were even home. Dave went out of town on business a lot, and Lisa often traveled with him now that their children were grown. The elderly Martins at Number Thirty-Two always went to bed early, so Dena was not surprised that there were no lights on at their house.

Farther down the street, beyond the cul de sac, Dena could see a light in one of the windows. She thought it came from the Inghams' house, but it was difficult to be sure. Anyway, she did not know the Inghams well enough to pound on their door this late at night. The thought was coldly amusing, almost causing her to giggle. Telecommunications across the whole damn world were falling apart and she was worried about being impolite!

This was not a time to think about etiquette. If Izzy and Jerry Franklin were asleep, Dena would just have to wake them up. She knew they were home, and the Franklins' house was much closer than the Inghams'.

Dena closed the door behind her and started across her lawn.

Then she froze as bright beams of light pierced the darkness. Another vehicle was coming up Hugo Drive. It moved slowly, and the headlights were at an angle, but Dena quickly recognized the blue-white lights of Michael's BMW.

"Michael!" She ran to the end of the driveway.

Instead of circling around the cul de sac like he usually did, Michael turned left and cut across the street directly to their driveway. Dena could now see why the car was moving so slowly. The right front tire was flat. In fact there was not much left of the tire itself, and she could hear a grinding sound from the rim of the wheel pulling the car along the pavement.

The garage door began to open, pouring a warm light across the driveway and front lawn. Michael had activated the door opener. The BMW limped forward, its tire-stripped wheel grinding, and pulled into the space next to the Avalon.

Dena walked up the driveway and followed the car into the garage. Then the door on the driver's side opened and Michael stepped out.

CHAPTER FOUR

"Are you all right? What happened to the car?" asked Dena, clutching Michael in her arms as if he might float away. Then she saw the back seat of the BMW. "What's all that?"

"It's everything I could get away with. There's more in the trunk."

The entire back seat was filled with boxes of cereal, jumbo packages of toilet paper, bags of potato chips, bottles of condiments, canned vegetables and more than a dozen plastic bottles of vegetable oil. It looked as if Michael had grabbed anything he could get his hands on, which, in fact, was exactly what had happened.

Dena asked, "But why did you buy this stuff? We don't need toilet paper, and one bottle of vegetable oil lasts us a couple of months."

"I didn't exactly buy it." He pulled himself away from her. "There wasn't any buying going on. People were just taking things."

"You *stole* this?" Dena stared at him incredulously.

"The store employees were gone." He opened the back door on the driver's side. "Hell, they were probably the first to start clearing off the shelves. It was insane, Dena. I ran into another car while I was trying to get out of the parking lot. The other driver didn't even stop, he just drove away."

"Where were the police?"

Michael took three packages of toilet paper from the back seat and tucked them under his arm. "I saw two officers trying to move people out of the hardware store on Main Street. Things were crazy there, too." He grabbed up two family-sized bags of corn chips with his free hand. "Caldonia doesn't have a very large police force. They don't usually need much protection over there. I'll carry all this inside. What I want you to do is clean out both bathtubs – get rid of any soap residue – and fill them with water."

"Why?"

"Beaker said to do it. He thinks our water could be shut off."

"Beaker was at the store?"

"Yes, thank God." Michael left the BMW open and carried his armload of chips and toilet paper to the door leading into the house. "I wouldn't have gotten out of there with all of these things if it hadn't been for him." Juggling the chips, he managed to open the door and go in.

Dena pushed the button on the wall to lower the garage door. Then she hurried inside to the downstairs bathroom. There were clean rags in the lower drawer next to the sink. She could hear Michael going from the kitchen to the garage and back as she began to wipe down the inside of the beige porcelain tub. She was rinsing it out when Michael came in.

"I tried to call you," he said. "My cell phone still doesn't get a signal."

"The landline is down, too. Michael, what's happening? Do you think this is related to what happened in St. Louis?"

He shook his head. "I don't know. A lot of people in town think we've been invaded by Martians. Maybe it's nothing. Maybe everything will have settled down by tomorrow morning."

"By this morning, you mean. You're going to have to get up for work in just a few hours." She turned on the faucet and let the newly scrubbed and rinsed bathtub start to fill with cold water.

"I've decided I'm not going to work tomorrow. Or today, depending on how you look at it. I'll take a sick day. How are your parents holding up?"

Dena shrugged. "I don't know. There was a lot of static on the line. I tried to call Dalton back, also, but his number has changed."

"Call him back?"

"I talked to him earlier on the phone, when Izzy and Jerry

were here."

"I don't remember that," said Michael.

"I was in the kitchen. He wants me to drive up to Butler this weekend."

Michael turned away from her. "You don't have to if you don't want to."

They rarely spoke about Dalton, and had not seen him in several years, but Dena knew that Michael was uncomfortable around her twin.

The tub was half full when Dena asked, "How long do you think we'll have to keep this up? We can't take baths if both of the tubs are filled with water. I assume this is supposed to be water for drinking or cooking with." She stared at the swirling water and the gushing stream pouring from the faucet.

Michael came up behind her and put his arms around her waist. "Maybe we should go upstairs and have a shower now, before filling the upstairs tub. That should do us for a few days, although I may have to use some extra deodorant after Thursday."

"Do you want to go first?"

She could feel his breath on her ear as he said, "Who said anything about one of us going first?"

"You mean both of us shower together?"

"It could be fun. When was the last time we did that?" Michael leaned over to shut off the faucet.

Dena smiled and turned to him. "How can you possibly be in the mood right now?"

He took her hand and led her into the hallway. "Call it desperation sex. Or stress-relief sex. I just know that I need it."

They went up the stairs and Michael turned on the shower in the second-floor bathroom. It always took a couple of minutes for the hot water to make its way up from the heater in the basement. While they waited, Michael and Dena stripped off their clothes and put everything in the laundry hamper.

"Maybe I should wash clothes in the morning," said Dena. "That could be important, too, if Beaker is right and we lose water for a while. I can get a load started while I run to the supermarket."

Michael shook his head. "You aren't going to the store tomorrow."

"Yes, I need to. I don't know what you thought you were doing, but that hodge-podge of sundries is not going to get us through the week. We need real food, not chips and—"

"I don't care." Michael stepped into the shower and pulled Dena in with him. Small pellets of hot water beat sensuously against their shoulders and arms. "I don't want you to go anywhere tomorrow."

"We're going to need groceries eventually."

He began soaping her back. "It can wait until all this craziness dies down. There probably isn't anything left at the store to buy anyway. You weren't there, Dena. The parking lot was full of cars, parked at all angles, ignoring the painted lines. Getting into the store wasn't difficult, but getting around after that was a nightmare. People were taking anything they could get their hands on. There weren't any employees, at least none that I saw. I thought about leaving some money at the checkout, but somebody else would have just taken it. We still don't have any coffee, by the way. Sorry. The coffee was all gone by the time I got there."

"And people were just taking things out of the store?" asked Dena.

"They're scared." Michael handed her the bar of soap and turned so she could get his back. "I saw Randall Fortune from down the street while I was there. He and Sue are leaving Caldonia tonight. Sue has family down in Pittsburgh."

"If we're being attacked by aliens, I don't know why they think Pittsburgh would be any safer." *Attacked by aliens.* It sounded so silly when she said it aloud.

"I don't either," agreed Michael. "I guess Randall and Sue believe there's safety in numbers. Randall's arm was bleeding where somebody had cut him."

"Cut him?"

"Yes, while fighting over a bag of potatoes. The produce was all gone when I got there, too. And as far as I could tell, Randall lost the potato fight."

"Is that how you got that bruise on your knee?" asked Dena. "From fighting?"

"No, nothing that glamorous." Michael turned back to her and grinned sheepishly. "Somebody had spilled a gallon of milk in one of the aisles, and I slipped in it. I didn't get much on my pants, but I came down hard on my knee." He ran his hands over her breasts, the bar of soap clutched in his left hand. "I may need you to kiss it and make it better."

"I was worried about you, Michael. I know what time the store closes." Caldonia was a small town, a bedroom community, and did not have an all night supermarket.

"Tonight it didn't close at all. There are still people over there, scrounging whatever they can. Not that there's much left. I just hope the owner of the store is heavily insured."

"Well you could have left some of that vegetable oil for them. We sure don't need that much."

"I wasn't thinking; I was just getting whatever I could and trying not to get hurt doing it. Then a couple of punks tried to take my carts."

"Carts?" She took the soap from him and rubbed it over his chest. "You had more than one shopping cart?"

"I wasn't the only one. I was trying to manage two carts, and so were some of the other people. As soon as I got into the store, I knew it might be closed down for a while after tonight. I wanted to get as many supplies as I could get my hands on."

"So you managed to fight off the punks." She wondered what Michael meant exactly by punk.

"No, I couldn't have handled them by myself. I thought they were going to get one of my carts, but then Beaker showed up out of nowhere and started to beat the crap out of one of them."

"Beaker? R. K. Beaker, from next door?"

"The very same. I don't think the guy has said a dozen words to me since he moved in last year, but he was right there when I needed him. I landed a couple of punches myself on the other kid, but I couldn't have fought off both of them if Beaker hadn't been there." He shook his head. "Don't even think about going into town tomorrow, Dena. For that matter, I don't think driving up to Butler this weekend is a good idea either."

Dena found the idea of her husband fighting valiantly over a shopping cart mildly arousing. She lowered the bar of soap, working a lather over his genitals.

Michael inhaled sharply. "Keep that up, and you're going to get something started down there."

"It looks to me like I already have," she said. She continued to stroke him. "Maybe I've misjudged Beaker. We should invite him over."

"Now?"

Dena laughed. "Not right this minute, no. I had something else in mind now, unless you're too tired. That was the whole point of taking a shower together, wasn't it?"

"Yeah, but let me rinse off so we can take this to the bedroom and do it properly."

They both rinsed, turned off the shower and then took turns drying each other. Michael led her to the bedroom, and their lovemaking was as he had predicted, desperation sex, urgent and forceful. Dena fell asleep almost immediately after. Michael pulled her to his chest and then fell asleep himself.

Neither of them woke when the power shut down throughout the house. The digital display on Michael's alarm clock went out. Down in the kitchen, the hum of the refrigerator came to an abrupt silence.

CHAPTER FIVE

Dena woke to the distant sound of knocking on the door downstairs. She looked over at Michael's alarm clock almost instinctively and immediately saw that there was no digital display. The sunlight streaming through the bedroom windows told her that they had slept much later in the morning than usual.

"Michael, wake up!" She pushed at her husband's shoulder. "The alarm didn't go off. You're late for work."

Michael pulled himself out of bed and stumbled towards the bathroom. His hair stood up in a ring around his head, giving him a clown-like appearance. Dena went to the dresser and found her hairbrush. She looked around for her robe.

"Wait, I'm not going to work today, remember?" Michael called from the bathroom. "Is something wrong with the power, or is it just the alarm clock?" This was followed by the sound of him urinating.

"I don't know," said Dena. She pulled on her robe and listened. Other than the splashing of her husband's urine, the house was completely still. "I think it's the power. Somebody's at the door."

Hurrying down the carpeted stairs, Dena pulled the brush through her dark brown hair. Yes, she thought, it was definitely the power. The silence told her that much. She could hear none of the quiet background humming, thrumming and clicks that normally emanated from various thermostats and appliances throughout the house.

She went across the living room and opened the front door. Whoever had knocked was no longer there, but Jim Martin was trimming the juniper bushes in the center of the cul de sac. He was dressed in khaki slacks, a dark green cotton shirt and canvas loafers. Dena was not sure if the elderly man had noticed her, but she waved and called out, "Morning, Jim."

Looking around, Jim nodded to her and said, "Jerry Franklin was just at your house. He's gone down to the Coopers'. It seems Izzy wants a neighborhood meeting today at noon." He grinned and shook his head, as if to say there was no telling what Izzy Franklin would be up to next.

"Is it about the UFO?" asked Dena.

Jim slowly lowered his shears. He came across the street to her, a frown creasing his brow. "Did Jerry and Izzy already tell you about this notion of theirs?"

"It isn't just a notion, Jim. It was on television last night. I'm surprised you didn't see it."

"So there really are spaceships out west?" He rubbed at his jaw. "I'm not saying you're lying, Dena, but that's hard to believe."

"I know." She nodded.

"Do you think there's some connection between the spaceships and this power outage? Our phone is down, and I don't think anyone on the street has electricity."

Dena did indeed suspect there could be a connection. Perhaps not a direct connection – she had no reason to believe the aliens were closing down power plants in Pennsylvania – but she remembered Michael's description of the looting at the supermarket and hardware store the night before. The Tuesday evening news seemed to have thrown the entire area into chaos.

Jim said, "I'd better gather up Mrs. Martin and run over to Caldonia. We should stock up on groceries."

"No!" Dena grabbed his arm, startling the elderly man. "You don't want to do that."

He stared at her with a surprised expression. "Folks in town may know more about what's going on than we do, Dena."

She told him then about Michael's attempt to drive into town for coffee and milk. She told him about the crowd Michael had described to her, and about how people had been fighting for whatever they could find on the shelves. She told him about the two youths who tried to take one of Michael's carts. Jim Martin listened solemnly, and he seemed to age a little as he took in what she was saying.

When Dena got to the part about Beaker fighting off Michael's assailants, Jim said, "You mean the fellow who moved in last year." He nodded to Beaker's house, between their two homes.

"Yes," said Dena.

"Barbara has talked to him more than I have. I've only seen him at the Association meetings. I don't really know him very well."

"We don't either," Dena said. "He keeps to himself. But promise me that you won't go into town by yourselves until people settle down. If you or Barbara need anything—" She saw Jerry Franklin walking up the street, and suddenly she was acutely aware of standing in her front yard with nothing on but a terrycloth robe. She waved to Jerry self-consciously, while to Jim she said, "Michael is taking off work today. Tell Jerry we'll both be at the meeting."

Turning abruptly, she hurried back into her house.

* * *

Nearly thirty people gathered in the Franklins' spacious living room. Jerry excused himself for a minute after Dena and Michael arrived. He went next door to let the Martins know that it was noon. Jim and Barbara Martin did not have cellular phones (Barbara was afraid they could cause brain cancer) and of course the electric clocks in their house were not working. Missy Bouchard introduced Dena to Rajinder Nara's wife, a tiny woman named Asha who seemed even more nervous than the rest of them. Dena wondered if Izzy had been openly rude to the Nara family. Asha wore a crimson saree, giving her a more exotic appearance than her husband, who was dressed in casual clothes similar to what the other men wore. Their little boy, as dark-skinned as his parents, was playing in the next room with Missy's youngest son, Logan. The two eight-year-olds seemed to be having a better time than anyone else.

The power had not been restored to any of the homes on Hugo Drive, but the entire western wall of the Franklin's living room consisted of glass panes that welcomed in the midday sunlight. Izzy had set out a bowl filled with semi-soft lime sherbet, reasoning that they might as well eat it before it melted. She was spooning sherbet into her mouth while listening to Darla Clark's concerns about the fish in her fifty gallon aquarium.

"Toxins are going to build up in the water if the aeration doesn't start working soon," Darla was saying. "And the temperature dropped into the low seventies this morning. My fish are tropicals; most of them can't handle cold water."

Dena and Michael were cornered by the Grahams, who had been visiting friends over in Cranberry Township the night before. Rather than coming home, the Grahams stayed the night with their friends and drove back to Caldonia early that morning. Apparently the situation in Cranberry was just as bad. Dave Graham described the broken store fronts they saw as they drove past Cranberry Mall. Farther down on Route 19, a police officer had shot at them.

Michael asked, "Why did he do that?"

"I didn't stop to ask," said Dave. "I guess he thought we were looters. It scared the hell out of us."

Lisa Graham nodded. "Dave said we should stop at the store in Caldonia and buy some supplies, but I wanted to get back here as soon as we could."

Michael said, "It's just as well. There's not very much left at the store, if anything at all. Some of us tried to get groceries last night. I was there, and Randall Fortune and Beaker."

At the mention of Beaker's name, Dena looked around and saw the large man sitting by himself in a corner. Somehow Beaker had managed to find the single spot in the Franklins' vast living room that was shrouded in shadow. He sat in an upholstered recliner, wearing a stained, sleeveless tee shirt and sweat pants. His arms were folded across his chest. The usual carpet of dark stubble covered his jaw and cheeks.

Jerry was ushering Jim and Barbara Martin in through the front door, but Dena knew Izzy would give the older couple a little time to settle in before opening the meeting. She excused herself and went over to scoop some of the rapidly melting sherbet into one of the porcelain bowls that Izzy had set out.

Walking to Beaker, Dena held out the bowl to him. "Care for some sherbet?"

The man's dark eyes turned to meet her own, but he said nothing and did not reach out to take the bowl. Even sitting, his head was nearly even with hers.

The moment that passed between them grew uncomfortable. Dena took a bite of the lime sherbet, as if she had intended it for herself all along, and had only offered it to Beaker as an afterthought.

Glancing around at the other people in the room, Dena hoped she did not look as foolish as she felt. From all appearances the gathering was just another monthly meeting of the Hugo Drive Neighborhood Association, which had always been more of a social organization than something with any real purpose. Adults were grouped in twos and threes, either speculating about the UFO they had seen on television or complaining about the inconvenience of losing their phone service and power. Missy Bouchard's daughter Emma sat by herself, displaying the extreme *ennui* that only a seventeen-year-old can muster. Asha Nara still looked nervous, but was engaged in conversation with her husband and Don Cooper.

Making a second attempt at breaking through Beaker's wall, Dena said, "It was nice of you to help Michael last night."

Again she was met with a cold stare.

"He told me what you did," she added lamely.

"Yeah, well, it was nothing." The response was gruff and abrupt. Beaker then punctuated this by scratching at his armpit and examining his fingernails as if he might have extricated something from the underbrush.

"Okay, then." Dena nodded and walked back to Michael. A bowl of sherbet and a thank you were her entire repertoire of friendly overtures that day. She had made the gesture.

Izzy Franklin went to the chrome and glass coffee table near the center of the room and stood next to it, looking pointedly at each person who was still standing. This included Dena and Michael, who found a place to sit on the step to the small landing at the front door. They were both well familiar with Izzy's somatic signal for beginning the business portion of an Association meeting. Not that the Hugo Drive Neighborhood Association often had much in the way of business to discuss. This day was an exception.

When everyone had settled into chairs or on the floor and given Izzy their attention, she said, "The fact that so many of us could attend a weekday noon meeting tells me that you are all aware of why I have asked you here. Last night on television – and this could have been a hoax – we saw what looked like a spaceship or flying saucer in St. Louis."

Alan Clark interrupted, saying, "It was a hoax. Must have been."

"Maybe, but let me get to the point, Alan. Since then we have all lost phone service, both cellular and landline, and the power has gone out." Izzy glanced over at Beaker, still sitting in the shadowed corner of the room. "I also understand that there has been looting at most of the stores in town, and that it might be dangerous for any of us to drive into Caldonia right now."

"I don't think it's just Caldonia," said Charlotte Keller. "People were speeding up and down the highway all night. Andy and I didn't get hardly any sleep at all."

"How could you?" asked Ben Lewinberg. Like the Kellers, the

Lewinbergs lived just off Route 228. "I know we've only been here for a couple of years, but I have never heard such a ruckus. You would have thought the Steelers were going to the Super Bowl again." That elicited a brief round of laughter from everyone but Izzy, and even she managed a tight smile.

Stacy Cooper said, "The school bus didn't come this morning, either." She looked over at Missy Bouchard, who confirmed this with a nod. Stacy went on to say, "I was going to keep Connor home anyway, but I thought it odd that there wasn't any bus."

"What are the police doing?" asked Dolly Ingham.

Michael said, "From what I saw last night, there were too many looters and not enough officers."

"And the police could mistake us for the looters if we try to go into town," added Dave Graham. "One of them shot at Lisa and me when we drove through Cranberry Township this morning."

That elicited gasps from some of the others. Apparently most of them had not yet heard this news. Even Emma Bouchard momentarily dropped her expression of teenaged boredom.

Dolly asked, "What about the military, then? Shouldn't the mayor be asking for state or federal assistance?"

Jerry shook his head and said, "There isn't any military base in western Pennsylvania. The closest we have to something like that is the Ninth District Coast Guard up in Cleveland. And they probably have their hands full with Cleveland."

Alan Clark said, "There's the Oakdale Support Facility."

"That hardly counts as a military base," said Michael. "Anyway, the military may already have its hands full. We know that St. Louis was cut off from the rest of the world last night, and from what my wife saw on the news – before the power went out – it looks like something similar may have happened to Chicago."

"So what are we supposed to do?" asked Missy Bouchard. "Just sit here and wait for Caldonia to get back on its feet? I have three kids to feed, and right now it looks like we're going to lose everything in our refrigerator."

Izzy said, "Maybe each of us should take inventory of what we have in our pantries. We should be able to get through the next few days without too much trouble if we pool our resources. Just until things are under control again."

"I have plenty of vegetable oil if anybody needs some," said Dena.

"That's what I mean," said Izzy, smiling broadly. "Most of us probably have something we can share with others. Except for the Naras, here, since they've just moved in."

Rajinder Nara spoke for the first time, saying, "We have food, too, that we can share. We did not move in without provisions."

"Great!" said Izzy.

Dena stared down at the floor and tried unsuccessfully to suppress a smile. She saw the venom in Izzy Franklin's eyes, and knew how much it annoyed the woman to think that she might need to accept assistance from the newest and only non-white family on the block. But Izzy's voice was light and friendly. She was the sort of woman who most often preferred her victims to look the other way when she pushed her knife into their backs.

Ted Ingham said, "The Fortunes are gone, you know. They packed up their car and left late last night."

"I saw Randall at the store in Caldonia," said Michael. "He told me they were going to stay with Sue's family down in Pittsburgh."

Izzy ran her fingers through her platinum hair. "That's ridiculous. We're perfectly safe here."

Ben Lewinberg cleared his throat and said, "Sara and I are thinking of leaving, too. We might stay with my brother and his wife and kids in Squirrel Hill. I don't know that it's any safer, but I'd like to be close to family. You are all welcome to whatever we have in the refrigerator."

Izzy nodded slowly. "Well, we understand, Ben. You have to go where your heart leads you." She certainly did not have any issue with the Lewinbergs leaving the neighborhood, even if it would only be for a few days.

Rajinder asked, "Does anyone know if Trenton has no electricity also?" When most of his new neighbors stared at him blankly, he said, "Trenton, New Jersey. It is where we moved from."

It was Michael who said, "We don't even know for sure what's going on over in Caldonia. How would we have any information about New Jersey?"

Dena pushed her elbow into his ribs. He looked at her with an expression of confusion, and she tried to tell him with her eyes that he was being rude and unfeeling, but of course he was not psychic and had no idea why she was glaring at him.

Izzy then said, "Let's all go to our homes this afternoon and make lists of what we have. Not only food, but also things like toilet paper, soap, laundry detergent and so on. List anything you might have that somebody else might need. And nobody should leave Hugo Drive until the power is back on and we hear that things are under control."

Dena was not sure how Izzy Franklin was defining control, but she shook her head and said, "I can't do that. I need to make sure my parents are okay." She turned to Michael. "It won't take more than an hour or so if we take the turnpike down to Monroeville like we usually do."

Izzy said, "We need you to make your list."

"Oh, screw the lists!" Dena rose to her feet, feeling a little embarrassed for her outburst. "Look, I can tell you right now that we have extra vegetable oil and toilet paper that we can share, and very little else. I wasn't planning on the grocery store being looted last night or I would have been better prepared for this."

Izzy was shaking her head. "There may be other things you aren't thinking of. We've decided to stick together, Dena, and you can't just—"

In a small but clear voice, Barbara Martin interrupted, saying, "I don't remember 'we' deciding anything, Isadore Franklin." The old woman walked over to Izzy, pointing at her with one finger. "If our Dena needs to see if her parents are all right, it is not your place to tell her that she can't. This is a neighborhood association, not a dictatorship, even though you seem to forget that sometimes."

Izzy's mouth opened and closed twice while she gathered her wits. "I only meant that we should—"

"I know what you meant, and I know you meant it with the best intentions." To Dena, the older woman said, "Go ahead, honey. Make sure your parents are okay, and then come back to us. Bring them with you, if you want. I know if our daughter lived closer, I'd want her to come check on us."

It occurred to Dena that she did not even know that the Martins had a daughter. She asked, "Where does your daughter live, Barbara?"

"Sue and her husband are in Seattle. Jim and I don't see them often. But never mind that, you go ahead and do what you have to do."

Dena nodded both to Barbara Martin and the other neighbors, and then left the Franklins' house with Michael following close behind her.

CHAPTER SIX

When they reached the turnpike, the car ahead of them drove through the toll booth without paying. It did not even slow down. Michael, however, stopped and tried to take a ticket from the automated dispenser. Nothing was dispensed. The red light telling them to stop and get their ticket was also off. Like the homes on Hugo Drive, the toll booth had no electricity.

"Well, I tried," said Michael. He started driving forward onto the turnpike without the requisite ticket.

"You're bothered about breaking the law?" Dena grinned at him. "That's ironic, coming from a guy who burgled the grocery store last night."

Michael shrugged and hit the accelerator. As the Avalon picked up its speed, he said, "The way I see it there are two possibilities. If the Department of Transportation is still functioning, we may have to pay a fine, but that can't be helped."

"And what's the other possibility?"

"The government is completely gone."

Dena looked at him, searching for a hint of a smile or some other sign indicating he was on the precipice of delivering a punch line. But when the line came it was delivered earnestly.

"And if there's no government, then the money I would have paid the toll with is worthless anyway."

Dena felt her stomach tighten. "It's not a permanent thing," she said, more to herself than to Michael.

"I hope you're right." He jerked the wheel suddenly, causing the Avalon to lurch to the left, barely missing two smaller cars that had collided earlier on the turnpike. A man was lying prone on the hood of one of the cars. It looked like he had come completely through the windshield. Bits of glass from the windshield and one headlight were scattered across the pavement where they sparkled like jewels in the afternoon sunlight.

"Michael, stop! Those people are hurt!"

"Call 911," he said grimly. He kept his eyes on the road. The Pennsylvania Turnpike wound through steep hills on the western side of the state, giving a relatively short line of vision for a highway that ran all the way from Ohio to New Jersey.

Dena slouched down in the passenger seat. "I cannot believe you left those people. If the phones are down we have a responsibility —"

"To do what?" Michael hit the steering wheel with the palm of his hand. "We have a responsibility to do exactly what, Dena? I don't think anyone was alive back there. And even if somebody was, neither of us has any medical training. And we can't call the police, or a hospital or even the fucking Boy Scouts. What do you think we could possibly do?"

"I don't know." Dena shrugged. "Something."

"Honey, I wasn't kidding when I said the government may have shut down. Think about it. We don't have any electricity or phone service. Hell, the water and gas could be out by now. People are taking whatever they can from the stores, and the police can't seem to restore order. And two large American cities were suddenly cut off from the rest of the nation last night." He shook his head and began to drive faster. "Whatever's happening, it's big. It isn't just something that has affected our neighborhood, or the town of Caldonia. This is something that's happening all over America."

"America?" Dena repeated.

"Or maybe even beyond that."

She stared at a pickup truck that had been abandoned at the side of the highway. "So you really believe we've been invaded by space aliens?"

"I don't know what to believe," said Michael. "What I'm saying is that it looks to me like we are in a survival situation. I'm sorry for those people we passed, but my priority is keeping you and me safe."

There was a sound of a distant gunshot, but Dena could not tell where it came from. The sharp report seemed to emphasize what her husband was saying. She watched the trees, turning gold and red with the onset of fall, as they drove down the highway. The idea of an alien invasion sounded so silly, but she could not forget the huge tear-shaped object she had seen on television the night before.

Michael said, "Look at this. Have you ever seen the turnpike with so little traffic at this time of day?"

"I want to bring them home."

"Bring who home?" He glanced at her. "Oh, you mean your parents."

Dena nodded. "We have plenty of room to put them up. And Barbara said I could bring them home with me."

"I'm sure not going to argue with that old lady," said Michael. "Did you see how she shut Izzy up? I think Hugo Drive may have a new alpha female."

Dena smiled. "Maybe, but I don't think Barbara Martin will stand up to Izzy unless it's something that really matters to her. It was sweet of her to take my side; I think she really misses her daughter right now." After a brief pause, she said, "We can put them in the blue room."

"Sure," said Michael, knowing Dena was referencing her parents again. The blue room was the larger of their two guest rooms. Dena had decorated it completely in shades of blue: the curtains, the walls, the bedding and carpet.

They said nothing else as they drove the rest of the way to Monroeville, both lost in their thoughts. Dena still felt guilty for not stopping to see if somebody in the collision needed help. But it was Michael who was driving; there was nothing she could have done. She was sure Michael was exaggerating their situation. As extraordinary as the UFO had been, it was in St. Louis, hundreds of miles away. She found it hard to believe that there could be a direct connection between that and what was happening in Pennsylvania. Everything would be all right after people settled down and the power and phones were restored.

Michael, for his part, was thinking of how much it was going to cost to fix the right front fender and wheel on the BMW. No matter how dark his worst fears were, there was the possibility that Dena was right, that the sudden loss of electricity, phone service and government was 'not a permanent thing'. He wondered if the Beamer would be down in Sewickley the following week, undergoing what would certainly be expensive repairs.

As they came to the Monroeville exit, they saw black smoke billowing over the buildings to the east. There was no need for a toll ticket, because the booth at the exit was empty, its gate smashed. Michael drove through and took their car down Route 22. The absence of traffic was even more obvious here than on the turnpike.

"Where is everybody?" asked Dena.

A Ford Fiesta drove up the street, travelling well over the speed limit as it passed them. Its tires squealed as it turned down a side street.

Michael said, "Obviously some people are still moving around. I guess most are hiding out in their homes. And I don't blame them."

None of the shops and restaurants along Route 22 were open. They drove past a supermarket and saw that the front glass doors were shattered. From what Dena could see, the shelves inside the store were bare. There was a crumpled pile of clothing in the parking lot, and Dena gasped when she realized it was a body. The discount store in the next building had also been broken into.

Flashing lights of a police car appeared in their rearview mirror. Michael slowed the Avalon and started to pull over to the side of the road, but then the police car shot past them and continued on towards whatever it was pursuing.

At the next intersection Michael had to drive around a three car collision. There were no people in or around the cars, but Dena thought all three vehicles were probably totaled. Hanging directly over the intersection was the cause of the accident – the dead, blank orbs of a traffic light.

They saw very few people as they made their way to the residential neighborhood where Dena's parents lived, and most of those few were in cars, driving quickly to some refuge. As Michael drove the Avalon down a tree-lined street between two rows of upper-middle-class homes, they saw an elderly woman face down on a sidewalk, obviously dead. He slowed the car, and they saw the old woman's blank, dull eyes staring at a line of ants parading past her face and into the grass next to the sidewalk. It was impossible to know the cause of the woman's death without stopping to examine her, and Michael had no intention of doing that.

When they turned onto Peterson Street, Dena felt her chest tighten. The street was too calm. Peterson Street had become quieter, more gentrified, since the days when she and Dalton had played tag and four-square here with their friends, but today an unnatural silence hung over the houses. Michael seemed to notice it too as he pulled into the driveway and turned off the engine. Dena opened the car door and looked at the house she had grown up in. A little wooden sign engraved with *The Holts* hung over the steps leading up to the porch. The mailbox next to the door was empty.

She started walking to the porch, but Michael clamped his hand to her shoulder.

"Wait," he said quietly. "This isn't right."

"What isn't right?" asked Dena.

Then she saw what had caught Michael's attention. The front door was not completely closed. It hung slightly open, leaving no more than a couple of inches between the door and its frame.

Michael ran up the steps, turning to her quickly and using his hand to silently signal for Dena to wait. Then he cautiously opened the door and went inside.

Dena did wait for a minute, but it was her house, the home she had grown up in. If her parents were in trouble she needed to go to them. She walked up to the porch and went in after Michael.

The living room had a reassuring familiarity. A mahogany coffee table stood in front of a sofa upholstered in brown corduroy. Next to this was the fireplace, rarely used anymore, with her mother's favorite kitten statuettes arranged in a row across the mantel. Dorcas Holt had acquired an extensive collection of porcelain kittens and cats over the years, but only a few claimed the coveted space over the living room fireplace. The rest were in a large glass cabinet in the master bedroom upstairs.

Sunlight came through the windows, but Dena turned on the light switch anyway. There was no response.

Michael came from the back of the house. His face was pale, and all he said as he pushed Dena to the door was, "Let's go."

Pulling back from him, Dena said, "Go? We just got here."

"And now we're leaving."

"No, I want to see my parents." She turned from him, but he took her by the arm.

"They're dead, Dena!"

"Dead?"

"You don't want to see it. It looks like they were stabbed to death. There's blood everywhere."

"But why? Why would anybody do that?" She tried to pull away from Michael, to go to her parents and see for herself if what he said was true, but he held her firmly.

"I don't know why. For money, probably."

"How can all of this be happening, Michael? It's just a power outage, for Christ's sake!" Warm tears fell across her cheeks.

"It's not, and you know it. It's much more than that. People have panicked. The good people are hiding out, and the bad people are taking what they can." He shook his head grimly. "I guess I'm one of the bad guys. Any way I look at it, I stole all of those things from the store last night."

"That's not the same thing at all. You didn't *kill* anybody!" She leaned against him, letting the tears stream over her face and fall into his shirt. "I didn't even get to say goodbye to them, Michael!"

"I know, honey." He stroked her hair. "I'm sorry, but there's nothing we can do for them now."

"I want to go home." And by 'home' she meant their Caldonia home. Her parents' house was a place of death now. There was no longer anything familiar about the furnishings and knick-knacks. "I know how awful that sounds."

"It doesn't sound awful at all," said Michael.

"But we're just leaving them here." Dena glanced to the doorway that led back to the kitchen. "Don't we need to bury them?"

"We'll do that if order is restored. I mean, just as soon as order is restored."

"Can you…cover them or something? I can't stand the thought of us leaving them without doing anything for them."

Michael nodded. "You wait here. Promise me you won't come to the kitchen." He released her then and went to the back of the house.

Dena walked around the living room, looking at the framed photographs, trinkets and pieces of furniture, trying to imprint them in her memory. She felt as if a part of herself had been killed, a part of her past that could never be reclaimed. Going to the mantel, she examined each of the feline statuettes, at last choosing a calico cat playing with a porcelain ball of yarn. It was one of the oldest figurines in her mother's collection and, from its position on the fireplace mantel, it had been one of her mother's favorites. She decided that she would take it with her.

Michael returned to the living room. "Okay, they're decently covered," he said.

"With what?" asked Dena. "The sheets and blankets are kept

upstairs."

"I used two of your mom's tablecloths. The nice, big linen ones she keeps in the bottom of the china cabinet. Aren't those good enough?"

Dena did not really think so, but she also could not think of any reason why the tablecloths were inappropriate. After a quick mental debate, she nodded. "That's fine."

"Good," said Michael. "Let's get back up to Caldonia, then, okay?"

They turned to leave, but stopped abruptly when they saw the man in Army fatigues standing in the doorway. The man was young, probably in his early twenties. He held a pistol in his hands, aimed directly at them, and from his stance Dena knew that he would not hesitate to shoot.

"Where are the Holts?" he asked in a hard, angry voice.

CHAPTER SEVEN

Dena noticed the name on the man's fatigues. *Rutherford.* "Jimmy?" she asked. "Jimmy Rutherford?"

The soldier hesitated. He looked closely at Dena, but continued to aim his pistol at them. "You know me?"

"It's me," said Dena, pointing to herself, as if the young man did not know the meaning of 'me'. She tried to smile, which was difficult while staring down the barrel of a pistol. "I used to babysit you, remember?"

At last he lowered the handgun. "Dena Holt?"

"Yes." Dena nodded emphatically. "Well, it's Dena Anderson now. This is my husband Michael."

The young soldier nodded in Michael's direction. He returned the pistol to the holster hanging from his belt. "Sorry if I scared you, but I thought you were breaking into your parents' house. There have been some murders here on Peterson."

Michael nodded. "We know. Mr. and Mrs. Holt are dead."

"We just now found them, Jimmy." Dena slid her arm around her husband's waist, taking comfort in the warmth of his body. "Or Michael did."

The young man said, "It's just Jim now. I haven't been Jimmy since I was fourteen. I'm really sorry, Dena. The Richters are dead, too, and Mr. Visconi. I think a gang came through here early this morning and shot anyone who got in their way. I found Mr. Visconi in his back yard. It looked like he was trying to climb over his fence."

Michael said, "I don't think Dena's parents have been dead very long either. And they weren't shot – they were stabbed."

Dena felt sick to her stomach. If only she and Michael had left a little earlier, perhaps they would have been driving back to Caldonia with her mom and dad before the assailants broke in. She sat down heavily on the corduroy sofa and placed the calico cat figurine on the coffee table next to it.

"Is it this bad all over?" asked Michael.

"I don't think so, sir." Jim stepped to the window and glanced out. "There's rioting in some places, and I passed what looked like a hundred or so people in a prayer group on my way here. Most people seem to be staying indoors, waiting for somebody to come by and tell them that everything will be all right. Poor suckers."

Jim Rutherford had black hair and pale blue eyes. Dena pulled herself out of her despair and looked into those eyes, and beneath the soldier she saw the little boy she used to babysit twenty years earlier.

"Jimmy? I mean, Jim," she corrected herself. "Didn't your family move to New Mexico a few years ago?"

"Yes, when I was a senior in high school. Then I went to college for a couple of semesters, but that wasn't for me so I worked at a few minimum wage jobs and eventually enlisted in the Army. Last month I was transferred to the Oakdale Support Facility." He shrugged. "Basically, I'm a filing clerk in a uniform, but I like that better than dodging bullets in the Middle East."

Michael said, "I don't mean to sound rude, but none of that explains why you followed us to the Holts' house."

"No sir, it doesn't," agreed Jim. "Everyone, the officers and enlisted men, left the Facility this morning after everything fell apart. I didn't know where to go, so I thought I'd make my way here to Peterson Street and see if I could stay with one of our neighbors. Almost made it here, too, but a cat ran out in front of my Malibu and I drove right into a maple tree."

"Were you hurt?" asked Dena.

Jim Rutherford shook his head. "No, but I had to walk the last couple of miles to get here. I found the Richters dead in their living room and Mr. Viscoli in his back yard, and then I noticed a car parked in the Holts' driveway that hadn't been there before."

Michael's eyes narrowed and he sat next to Dena. "What do you mean exactly by everything falling apart?"

"You don't know, sir?" asked Jim. "There isn't any government left, at least not on the federal level. The military is pretty much gone, although there are probably some units still trying to fight. From what I've seen it looks to me like the state and local services have also collapsed."

"But what caused this?" Dena asked, surprised at the high pitched, plaintive tone in her voice.

"The aliens." Jim said this to her as if explaining the most obvious thing in the world. Then, more gently, he said, "You really have no idea of what has happened?"

"We have our suspicions," said Michael. "We know that something big happened in St. Louis, and then in Chicago. The lack of phone and internet service makes me think that we've lost the use of our satellites. But I'd like it if you would fill us in with what you know."

Jim glanced out the window again.

"Sir, I didn't know any more than you did until the St. Louis ship descended yesterday at 1600 hours."

"St. Louis ship? There's more than one?"

"Nine, sir. I guess there could be more, but the military only identified nine. The others were about 200,000 kilometers from earth. All branches of the military were alerted, but for the most part the Army was keeping its distance. I guess the Marines and Navy were doing the same."

Dena said, "We heard that on television."

Jim nodded. "The aliens launched their attack without any warning. We heard that nearly three thousand people in St. Louis were killed instantly, but that couldn't be verified. The aliens took out our satellites, just like you said. Then the other ships began descending. They were moving faster than anything we've got. One was approaching the Great Lakes region, and the others went towards South Africa, India, mainland China, Japan, the U.K. and Russia. Oh, and Argentina. Without satellite communication the Facility was already losing a lot of its connections with other Army installations."

Michael held Dena close to him. "You said the Great Lakes region. Is that why communication with Chicago was cut off?"

"I think so, sir. All we heard was that Chicago was under attack."

"Well, what were you guys doing? Why weren't we fighting back?"

"Sir, the Army did fight back. We threw everything we have at them. So did the Marines, the Navy and the Air Force; or at least that's what I was told. Nothing touched the ships, not even nuclear missiles. We might as well have attacked them with sling-shots." Again the young soldier glanced out the living room window. "We lost New York City this morning at zero-dark-thirty. By that time we knew about the Pittsburgh riots, but every-thing was confused at the Facility. We should have responded. Not that it would have made much difference. Communications with the Pentagon were cut off at 0500 hours. That's when we knew we'd lost to whatever this is we're fighting."

Michael frowned. "So two extraterrestrial ships are taking out all of our cities?"

"No sir, only one. The Chicago ship. The intelligence we were receiving at Oakdale indicated that the St. Louis ship was moving into rural Missouri."

A loud but distant explosion forced a scream out of Dena. Jim Rutherford dropped to the ground and rolled across the living room floor, rising into a crouch behind the front door, his pistol drawn.

Michael peered out the window, but Peterson Street looked no different than it had on any other afternoon when he and Dena had visited her parents. When it was apparent that they were not in immediate danger, he turned to Jim and asked, "Was that the aliens?"

"I don't know, sir. We didn't learn much about them, other than that they are hostile." Jim slowly stood. "But, no, I don't think that was the aliens."

"Why not?"

The soldier shrugged. "When the Chicago ship moves into an urban area, suddenly everything goes quiet." He returned the pistol to its holster.

Michael also stood, drawing Dena to her feet as he did so. "I want to get you home," he told her. "We'll be safer there than here in Monroeville."

Dena looked over at Jim Rutherford. "What about you? Where are you going?"

"I don't know." As he spoke the words his features took on a vulnerable expression, reminding Dena of the child who grew up down the street from her. "I don't even know why I came back here. Everyone is either dead or has left."

Dena said, "Come back to Caldonia with us." She glanced in Michael's direction, to silently ask him not to protest, but she saw in his eyes that there was no need. Michael was in complete agreement with her. For a moment she was surprised that he did not object to her bringing home another mouth to feed, but then she understood. Michael saw Jim Rutherford as an asset. Trained in combat and survival, it was possible that he could more than earn his keep.

It was not the most compassionate reason, but Dena was glad there would be no argument.

To Jim, she said, "You don't have anywhere else to go. You've practically said as much. We don't live in Caldonia itself, our house is east of town, but we have plenty of room for you." *Now that my parents are dead.* She did not give voice to the thought, but it gnawed at her heart.

Jim shook his head. "I couldn't impose on you."

Michael said, "One thing my parents taught me when I was a boy was to obey the babysitter." That elicited a weak smile from the soldier. "You won't be an imposition. And Dena won't stop worrying about you if we leave you behind."

"Thank you, sir."

"There's one condition, though. You have to stop calling me 'sir'. I'm not your superior officer, I'm just a friend."

"Yes, s..." Jim caught himself. "All right, Mr. Anderson."

They left the house and Dena locked the front door after closing it firmly behind them. Michael led them over to the parked Avalon, but Jim stopped him before he could walk around to the driver's side.

"Sir? I mean, Mr. Anderson? How much gas do you have in the tank?"

"I'm not sure, but I can check. I think we still have about a quarter of a tank, and that's more than enough to get us back to Caldonia."

"But then you'll be nearly empty." Jim nodded to the Visconi house. "I saw Mr. Visconi's car in his garage. I was thinking about looking for the key and taking it. I know that sounds wrong, but it's not like Mr. Visconi has any use for it now."

"You want us to steal his car?" asked Dena.

"You can't steal from the dead," said Jim. "But, no, you already have a car. What you don't have – or won't have – is gasoline. I think it might be a good idea if we drive out of here with a full tank."

Dena said, "Then let's just fill up at a gas station." She glanced briefly at her parents' garage door. Her dad's new Chevrolet Impala probably had a full tank of gas, but to take it would be an insult to her parents' memory.

"No, Jim is right," said Michael. "If a station still has gasoline, somebody may be protecting it. And after what I saw at the store in Caldonia last night, I don't think they'll be interested in sharing."

Michael drove their car across the street while Jim and Dena opened Mr. Visconi's garage door. Dena was pretty sure that taking Mr. Visconi's gasoline was wrong, too, but it did not bother her quite as much as the idea of taking it from her dad's new car. The Camry inside the Visconi garage had a full tank of gas. Michael was not sure how to go about transferring it into their own tank, but Jim Rutherford wasted no time cutting a short length of garden hose. Using the hose, he siphoned gas from the Camry into a bucket, and from there into Dena's car. Within ten minutes the Avalon's tank was full.

Dena gave him a sideways glance. "Do you do this often, Jimmy?"

He laughed and said, "Only when necessary."

Michael drove, with Dena in the front passenger seat and Jim Rutherford in the back. The drive back up Route 22 was much the same, although now they saw fires to the west.

The same three cars were still sitting at the intersection where they had collided with each other. No tow trucks had come to move the cars out of the street. Dena was sure that no police officers had come to make a report.

The dead body was still sprawled in the parking lot in front of the supermarket. A middle-aged man ran out of the supermarket and dashed around to the side of the building. In his arms he clutched two bags of flour and a box of salt, clinging to them as if he were making away with the Crown Jewels.

"People have gone crazy," Michael muttered.

From the back seat, Jim said, "It's only going to get worse."

Dena looked back at him. "Worse?"

"They've cleaned out the supermarkets, so everything will probably quiet down for a while," said Jim. "But that food isn't going to last forever."

"Maybe not, but when the government—" Dena stopped. The fact that a soldier was sitting in the back seat of her car was evidence that the government was not going to be doing much of anything. At least not for some time. "What I don't understand is how all of this is happening here, in Pennsylvania. We haven't seen any aliens or spaceships."

Michael turned off of Route 22 and drove up the ramp to the

turnpike.

Jim said, "Most power plants stopped functioning within a few hours after the first attack in St. Louis. Nobody knew how the aliens did that. We had our own generator at Oakdale, of course, and batteries still work okay."

"The phones are down, too," said Dena. "Not just cellular, but also the landlines."

Jim nodded grimly. "I know. The aliens were familiar enough with us to kill all of our communications."

They had driven a mile up the turnpike when Dena remembered that she left the cat figurine on her mother's coffee table. She felt a pang of regret, but said nothing to Michael. They would have enough to worry about without fretting over sentimental losses.

A convoy of three minivans, a pickup and a brown Toyota Corolla passed them. The bed of the pickup truck held stacks of plastic totes and suitcases, and one of the minivans had more luggage strapped to its roof with bungee cords. All of the vehicles had Pennsylvania plates. Then from the other direction, on the opposite side of the concrete median wall, an even larger group of cars and trucks came down the turnpike.

There were two more collisions that Michael had to drive around. Dena did not see any bodies in or around the cars, and she silently prayed that none of the passengers had been seriously injured.

From the back seat Jim said, "That's why people have panicked so badly, you know."

"Why?" asked Dena. She turned to look at him. "What do you mean?"

"The aliens took out the internet and telecommunications. It might not have mattered so much when my dad was a kid, but now it does. No phones, no Facebook, no email." Jim stared out the window at the trees whipping past them as the car sped along the turnpike. "Most people don't even know their neighbors' names anymore. We only connect over wires, and the wires are crap now."

Dena said, "That's not true, Jimmy. I know all of my neighbors' names."

"Then you're lucky."

Michael glanced at her and risked a smile. "Sort of makes you appreciate Izzy, doesn't it, Dena?"

"Who's Izzy?" asked Jim.

Looking at him in the rearview mirror, Michael said, "Isadore Franklin is the grand matriarch of Hugo Drive. She organized a neighborhood association before we moved in, and holds a meeting every month. Attendance is voluntary, but only if you don't mind Izzy shredding your reputation."

Jim frowned. "Why do you put up with that?"

"She means well." Michael shrugged. "I guess over the years Hugo Drive has become something like a hobby for her. Anyway, it's largely because of Izzy that the rest of us all know each other."

Dena opened the glove compartment and fished around until she found the travel package of facial tissues. She could not quite accept that her parents were really dead. She remembered when her mom and dad had first come up to Caldonia, a few months after Michael and Dena had bought their home, and how Izzy had shown her parents around the neighborhood. Michael was right. Had it not been for Izzy Franklin and her Hugo Drive Neighborhood Association, Dena would probably not know many of her neighbors. She often saw Jim Martin out in his yard or caring for the bushes in the center of the cul de sac, and she spoke to him at least a couple times every month, but she had met most of the other neighbors at the Association meetings.

Even so, she barely knew the Kellers or the Inghams. Beaker, living in the house next door, was practically a stranger.

When they came to their exit Michael quickly drove to Route 228 and turned down the long stretch of road towards Hugo

Drive. A small silver van passed them going the other direction.

Michael asked, "Wasn't that Don Cooper's Odyssey?"

Dena looked back at the van, now shrinking in the distance. "It could have been. I wasn't paying attention."

"Well if he's driving into town, I sure hope he has somebody with him," said Michael.

She raised one eyebrow. "So you took me along with you to Monroeville for protection?"

"This was your expedition. It's Jim who I've brought along for protection."

Dena smiled in the rearview mirror at Jim, but she knew her husband was only half joking.

Michael slowed the Avalon as they came up to the entrance to Hugo Drive. He turned onto the isolated residential street. Sara Lewinberg was putting a suitcase in the trunk of her car. She looked up as they drove by, but did not wave. Across the street, Andy Keller was putting a padlock on his garage door.

Just before they came to the cul de sac Dena saw Stacy Cooper hugging Missy Bouchard in the Bouchards' front yard.

"Michael, something's wrong." She pointed to the two women. Missy was sobbing into Stacy Cooper's shoulder. Eight-year-old Logan Bouchard stood next to his mother, staring up helplessly at her.

Michael drove past them and took the car around the cul de sac, passing the Grahams' house, and the Franklins', the Martins' and Beaker's, and then pulling into their own driveway at Number Twenty-Two.

Dena pushed open the Avalon's front passenger door. She caught an acrid scent of smoke as she climbed out of the car and hurried down the street to the Bouchards' house.

Missy was making wet choking sounds as she pressed her face into Stacy Cooper's shoulder.

Stacy caught Dena's questioning look. She was gently rubbing Missy Bouchard's back. "It's Emma," she said quietly. "She has gone for a drive."

Missy lifted her puffy, tear-stained face long enough to say, "She was kidnapped!"

"Kidnapped?" asked Dena. She saw Michael and Jim coming up to them.

Missy Bouchard nodded, but Stacy shook her head as she said, "Come on, Missy, there's nothing you can do right now. Let me get you a glass of water."

"I don't want water! I want my goddam daughter!"

"I know you do," said Stacy.

Looking to the west, Jim Rutherford asked, "What's that smoke?"

Dena saw that he and Michael were both staring at the same thing. She looked in their direction and saw dark clouds of smoke rising in the west. That was where the burning smell was coming from. It was not the pleasant, warm scent of wood smoke, but a combination of burning oil, rubber, wood and plastics.

"That looks like it's coming from Caldonia," said Dena. Then she turned her attention back to the two women. "What do you mean Emma was kidnapped?"

Stacy said, "A boy who Emma goes to high school with drove over here this afternoon. They were talking, and apparently they've gone for a little while."

"He took my daughter!" screamed Missy.

Stacy rubbed the other woman's back with renewed vigor. "You don't know that. They probably just want some privacy. This has all been stressful on everybody."

Logan reached up and touched his mother's arm. "Mommy, Emma's coming back."

Just then Don Cooper's silver Odyssey came up the street, its tires screeching as the van stopped at an angle in the middle of the road. The driver's door opened and Don stumbled out.

"Caldonia's burning!" he shouted.

"We can see the smoke," said Michael. "What part?"

"The whole damn town." Don leaned against the side of the van and clenched his eyes against tears that refused to be held back. "I think it started at the Handi-Mart, but it doesn't matter. The whole town is burning."

CHAPTER EIGHT

They all watched the rising dark smoke.

"So the fire department is gone, too," said Michael.

Don Cooper shook his head. "No, the firemen were doing what they could, but the fire had already spread too far by the time they were alerted. The police are also trying to contain it." He finally noticed Missy Bouchard. "What's wrong with her?"

Stacy said, "Emma's gone." In response to Missy's renewed wailing, she added, "I didn't say she was gone forever. Hush, now."

Izzy Franklin came running from the cul de sac with Jerry puffing along behind her. She wore a violet jacket over a matching beige blouse and slacks ensemble. Her eyes darted repeatedly to the western sky as she approached and called out, "What's on fire?"

"Caldonia," said Michael. "According to Don, here, the entire town is burning."

"Is it under control?"

"Obviously not."

Jim Rutherford said, "The wind is blowing south, so it's unlikely to spread this way."

Izzy stared at him as if he had suddenly popped in out of nowhere. "Who are you?"

"This is Jimmy," said Dena. "I mean Jim...Jim Rutherford. We both grew up on the same street down in Monroeville." She tactfully did not mention that she used to babysit him.

Satisfied with the answer, Izzy looked from Michael to Don. "Is he right?" she asked. "Could the fire spread all the way to Hugo Drive?"

"I said it's unlikely," said Jim.

"Unlikely, but not impossible," replied Izzy. "That's what you meant, isn't it?"

"I suppose—"

Izzy cut him off, turning her attention to the other men as she said, "We need to wet down all of the back lawns on the west side of the street. Michael, Don, soak your lawns thoroughly. Use sprinklers. We'll need to get Alan and Mr. Beaker to do the same. Jerry, have the Lewinbergs left yet?"

"How should I—"

"Then run down there and see. It would be just like them to run off when we need them. Hurry up, Michael, are you waiting for an engraved invitation?"

Michael hurried to his house. Dena went after her husband, signaling Jim to follow her. Izzy Franklin was in her organizational element, which meant for the time being she would be even more annoying than usual. As they left, Dena heard Izzy barking orders to Stacy Cooper and the distraught Missy Bouchard. A missing teenager would not deter Izzy just then.

As Michael led them across the street to their own lot, Dena said, "I hope Emma's okay."

"She's as okay as any of us right now," said Michael tersely. "Besides, you heard Stacy. The girl is just out for a while with her boyfriend. Missy's making a mountain out of a very small molehill."

They went around to the side of their house. The gate to the cedar privacy fence surrounding their back yard clattered as Michael pulled it open. Dena remembered seeing Andy Keller securing his garage with a padlock and wondered if they should not do the same with the fence gate. But what would anyone want to take from the back yard? She did not keep bundles of cash or boxes of jewelry out on the patio, and it seemed unlikely that a thief would be interested in their wrought iron outdoor furniture.

Did they even have a padlock?

Jim looked around the spacious back lawn that sloped down from the patio. "Nice place," he said.

Michael was already at the outside faucet next to the patio

where a length of green garden hose was rolled around a plastic holder. He pulled the hose free and screwed one end to the faucet. The other end was already connected to a lawn sprinkler.

While Michael pulled the sprinkler out onto the back lawn, Dena pointed out the neighbors' houses. "Mr. Beaker lives there," she said, pointing to the north. "And that's the Coopers' house, just south of us." Because of the slope of the land she could see most of Beaker's lawn over her fence. As usual it was overdue for a mowing and dotted with dead, brown patches of grass. The Coopers' yard was completely obscured by the privacy fence. Dena had often wished it were the other way around, with the fence affording more privacy from Beaker and less from the Coopers and their twelve-year-old son Connor.

Michael set the sprinkler on the grass. "Okay, honey, turn it on," he called.

Beaker came out and stood by his back door as Dena began turning the faucet. He stared at her silently, like a surly golem, his dark hair clipped almost as short as the stubble across his jaw.

Streams of water shot up from the sprinkler, arching to the west and catching the sun's late afternoon rays.

After no more than fifteen seconds the watery arches faltered. As one, they lowered, diminishing in both size and strength until there was only a trickle rippling over the sprinkler head. Then the trickle became a dribble, and then there was nothing. Beaker turned and went back into his house, letting the screen door slam shut behind him.

Michael sighed. "Perfect. The water's gone."

* * *

That night Dena, Michael and Jim sat on the patio and watched the Caldonia fires light the western sky. Over the next few evenings the glow gradually faded. The acrid smoke permeated everything, but the flames never traveled as far as Hugo Drive.

Michael thought the fires might have been cut off by Pine Creek.

As the evening skies changed, so did the neighborhood. The magnanimous spirit of sharing evaporated as each family realized they had limited resources that would be depleted rapidly enough without being divided with needy neighbors. Worse was the realization that people displaced by the fires in Caldonia could come to Hugo Drive looking for food and supplies. The Kellers boarded up their windows, and Andy kept his fiberglass recurve bow by the front door. He was an amateur archer but, as he told Michael one morning, even a target arrow can do serious damage if it hits the right spot.

The Inghams had also boarded their windows, but they had no means to defend themselves if someone were to try to break in.

Farther up the street people were less cautious, however Dena kept the curtains closed at the front of the house. There was no point in inviting trouble. The Franklins obviously felt the same, because one morning Jerry painted a coat of white primer over all but the top two feet of the plate glass around their living room. That by itself made the cul de sac look less like a neighborhood and more like a war zone.

Everyone had filled tubs and containers with water before the supply shut off, but some people had more than others. Water, the most essential of resources and, until then, one of the least expensive was now a priceless commodity. Dena thought of Darla Clark's large aquarium and wondered how long the needs of Darla's tropical fish would outweigh her family's need for drinking water.

Nobody was doing much cooking. All of the homes on Hugo Drive were built for electric stoves. Now Dena's stove was little more than an uneven countertop; the electric oven was just extra cabinet space. The microwave, the toaster and the coffee maker were equally useless. For several days Don Cooper used his charcoal grill on his patio next door and the smell was delightful, but soon the Coopers, like everyone else, were subsisting on cans of beans, fruits and cold soups.

Despite Stacy Cooper's reassurances, seventeen-year-old Emma Bouchard did not return home.

Even the elderly Martins, who Dena thought were the most level-headed couple on Hugo Drive, disappeared behind curtained windows and locked doors. Within days their yard acquired a rough, unkempt appearance. Most of the residents up and down Hugo Drive were staying in their homes as much as possible, but there was something especially odd about not seeing Jim Martin out mowing his lawn or carefully trimming the junipers in the center of the cul de sac.

Dave and Lisa Graham left the same day that the batteries in Dena's cell phone finally gave out. Dena did not hear them go, but Michael later saw that Lisa's SUV was gone. His own phone battery had died the day before. Their cell phones, of course, had become nothing more than portable clocks, and time did not seem so important anymore.

CHAPTER NINE

The muscles throughout Dena's body tightened when she heard the knock at her front door. After what she had seen in Monroeville, every disturbance and sound had become a source of anxiety for her.

Two weeks had passed since they had seen the televised arrival of the UFO in St. Louis, but that former life was rapidly becoming little more than a memory. Between Michael, Jim Rutherford and Dena, they had used half the water in the downstairs bathtub. Jim was wearing Michael's clothing, which fit remarkably well, but all of their clothes reeked of sweat and body odor. They could not afford to waste water on washing anything other than dishes. Their food supplies were also low, and Dena envisioned the three of them eventually drinking cups of vegetable oil for sustenance.

She was frightened, not of the aliens she had yet to see, but of her own neighbors. The fear tightened around her heart as the knock sounded again on the door.

Then Jim was at her side in the dark living room, in a print shirt Michael had bought in Hawaii and a pair of cargo shorts. The young man had his pistol in hand. Dena looked down at the gun and nodded grimly.

Michael came into the room and silently walked to the window. At the third knock, he peered carefully through the narrow space between the curtain and the window frame. The morning sunlight seemed like a bright beacon where it striped his face. "There's a yellow Civic in the driveway," he whispered. "It doesn't belong to anyone we know, that's for sure."

"How can you tell?" asked Dena. She could not think of anyone who owned a yellow Civic, but any of their friends could have bought the car recently.

"I can tell by the paint job. It looks like the car has been painted by hand. Maybe it's stolen. Wait..." He held up one hand, cautioning them. "There's something in the car. An animal. Yeah, it's a dog."

Dena stepped over to the door and looked back at Jim Rutherford. "Be ready, but don't shoot unless you have to." It seemed unlikely to her that anyone planning to attack them would have brought a dog along in the car.

Jim raised the pistol with both hands. "I understand."

Michael said, "Dena, you don't know who it is."

"And I won't unless we open the door," she whispered. "I have an idea of who it might be, though."

"Don't open it."

Michael stepped back almost instinctively as Dena turned the lock and pulled the front door open. Sunlight streamed into the room and she found herself looking at a reflection of herself, but this reflection had much shorter hair and wore a tee shirt, cut off jeans and canvas running shoes.

"Dalton!" Dena threw her arms around her brother. "Come in!"

The reflection that was not a reflection pulled away from her and went to the Civic in the driveway. "Let me get Spencer," he said.

Dena stepped out and looked around the cul de sac but, as usual, there was nobody outside. The Franklins' house, its glass front painted with primer, was silent. So were the other homes. Weeds grew among the junipers in the center of the cul de sac, and the surrounding lawns were shaggy and brown.

Dalton pulled open the back door of the Civic and a medium-sized dog bounded out. Any intentional breeding in its pedigree had clearly taken place generations earlier. The dog was light in color, but its coat was dotted with black and dark brown hairs along with the predominant white and blond. The hair was not short, but neither was it notably long; the ears were neither standing nor floppy. Dalton tousled the dog's head and beckoned it to follow him as he turned to walk back to the house.

Behind her, Dena heard Michael say, "Not the dog."

"Michael!"

"We don't have enough food for ourselves, much less for a dog."

Dena had not considered that this might be more than a visit, but she realized Dalton probably intended to stay. With no police or communications, people were not making social calls. Certainly not all the way from Butler.

Dalton said, "It's all right. Spencer has his own food." He stopped, and the dog sat on the cement walk next to him. "He won a year's supply of kibble in an agility competition. I have all the rest of it in the trunk. It's enough to feed him for a few more months, at least."

"And then what?" asked Michael.

Dena said, "And then we'll figure out something else. Come on, Dalton, you can bring the dog in with you. He's housebroken, isn't he?"

Michael stepped to one side, letting Dena's brother and his dog come into the house, but he was obviously not happy about this newest development.

Dalton said, "Of course he's housebroken. Spencer's a great dog. I told you, he won—" He stopped when he saw Jim Rutherford. The young soldier was lowering his pistol now that he could see that the newcomer was not a threat.

Darkness fell across the room as Dena closed the front door and locked it. "Jimmy, you remember my twin brother Dalton."

Jim shook his head. "Not really."

Dalton looked the man over. In the darkened room he could barely make out the young soldier's features. "You're Jimmy Rutherford, from down the street."

"I've grown some," said Jim.

"I'll say you have." Dalton nodded. He turned to his sister and asked, "Are you guys okay?"

"I've had better days," said Dena. "Dalton, come into the

70

family room and sit down. I hate being in the front of the house even with the curtains drawn. I know it's silly."

"It's not," Dalton countered. He and the other two men followed her to the family room, with the dog staying close by Dalton's side. The flat screened television stared at them like a dead rectangular eye. Dalton sat on the couch, and the dog sat quietly next to his feet when he made a subtle gesture with his hand.

Dena and Michael took the love seat, while Jim stood behind them with his hands clasped behind his back.

Looking over at the dog, Dena said, "He really is well trained."

"I don't know what I'd do without Spencer. I think he has some border collie in him, but it's hard to tell." Dalton reached down and scratched Spencer behind the ears. "You're right about staying away from the front of the house. Up in Butler some of the road wolves are shooting through windows to see if people are home."

Dena glanced at Michael, but he obviously did not know what Dalton was talking about either. "Road wolves?" she asked.

Dalton nodded. "That's what I've heard them called, people who come down the road looking for houses they can rob or just scavenge from. I guess that's why that crazy guy down at the end of your street shot an arrow at my car."

"That's Andy Keller," said Dena. "I'll have to let him know you're staying with us."

Michael asked, "For how long?"

Dalton looked from Michael to Dena. "I don't know. I hadn't really thought about it."

"We don't have much food left," said Michael. In response to Dena's angry look, he said, "Honey, even with just the three of us it isn't going to last more than a couple weeks."

Dena could not help the tears that came. Her parents were both dead, and now her husband wanted to turn her brother out.

It was Jim Rutherford who said, "Michael, it might be a good idea to have somebody else here. What he's telling us sounds a lot like what happened down in Monroeville, don't you think?"

"But the food..."

"We're going to run out of food soon whether or not Dillon is staying with us."

"It's Dalton," said Dalton.

"Yeah, okay." He looked back to Michael. "Anyway, Dalton staying here is not going to change that. Pretty soon we're going to have to go out and find more supplies, whether we're feeding three people or four. I think we'll be safer with another person here. And if the dog comes with its own food it could be useful as a watchdog."

Michael shrugged. "Okay, then, he can stay. Dalton, you can sleep in the blue room."

"Where's that?"

Dena remembered that her brother had never been to their house before. "It's upstairs. I'll show you. Did you have a hard time finding Hugo Drive?"

"It wasn't easy," said Dalton. "I didn't know you lived out in the middle of nowhere."

Dena said, "We're lucky to be out here. There was a big fire over in Caldonia."

"I know. I saw what's left of the town, and it isn't much. Do you know how Mom and Dad are doing?"

In a quiet voice Dena said, "They're dead, Dalton. Michael and I drove down there when all of this started. That's how we found Jimmy."

"I'm sorry." Dalton caught the brief look of skepticism in his sister's expression. "No, I really am. I'm not going to pretend that I'm going to miss them, not after all these years, but I hoped that we could mend that bridge someday."

Jim said, "We should get your dog food in the house. I can do that if you'll give me your key, Dalton."

Dena knew Jim Rutherford wanted to see exactly how much food there was for Dalton's dog. There was no reason otherwise why the dog food needed to be brought into the house right away. The likelihood of somebody breaking into the trunk of Dalton's Civic to steal kibble was very slim. At least she hoped so, although, another part of her argued, dog kibble could soon become a delicacy as food supplies were depleted.

Dalton stood up. "I'll go out with you. The trunk sticks."

All four of them went outside, with Spencer following along. The dog left Dalton's side only long enough to lift its leg on the spirea bush next to the porch. The trunk did stick, as Dalton said it would, but yielded when he hit it just to the right of the lock with the heel of his hand. Inside the trunk were four large bags of kibble and a canvas duffle.

Jim Rutherford took out one bag, threw it over his shoulder and then pulled out a second. Dalton took a third bag of kibble, which was all he could manage. Michael took the last bag of dog food, leaving the duffle for Dena. She could tell from the feel and weight that it was stuffed with Dalton's clothing. Clean clothing, she hoped. She had grown used to body odor, but she was pretty sure Dalton had bathed no more recently than the rest of them had.

Walking between Jim Rutherford and Dena back up to the porch, Dalton asked, "What smells so bad out here?"

Dena looked at him. "I think you're smelling us."

"No, it's something else."

"That rotted smell? I don't know, it could be anything. We haven't had trash service for the past couple of weeks."

Dalton said, "It isn't the smell of garbage, not unless somebody is stockpiling it. It's coming from that house over there." He nodded in the direction of Number Thirty Two, two doors around the cul de sac. The Martins' home.

Dena stared at the Martin residence. "I don't know what it is. I guess we're accustomed to the smell. Everything stinks now."

They went through the front door and carried the bags of kibble and Dalton's duffle through the living room and into the kitchen. The dog food was stacked in one corner on the floor. Dena put the duffle on the counter.

Michael said, "I want to check on the Martins and make sure everything is okay over there." He caught Jim Rutherford's eye. "Do you want to come along?"

"Sure." Jim nodded.

"I can go, also," said Dena.

Michael shook his head. "No, this isn't a three-person job. Show your brother his room and get him settled in. We'll be right back."

Dena picked up her brother's duffle again. "Michael, ask if there's anything they need."

Michael started to speak, caught himself, and then said, "Okay, honey. I'll ask them." Then he and Jim left the kitchen.

Dalton took the duffle bag from his sister. "I can carry my own stuff." He glanced to the front of the house where Michael and Jim had gone. "I didn't mean to cause you any trouble, Dena."

"Everybody is on edge, I think, and frightened by the aliens." Dena led him through the hall and up the stairs to the second floor. "Not that we've actually seen any aliens out here. It's still hard to believe that they took us down so quickly."

"I don't think they did," said Dalton. "Not really. Most of what's happened is our own doing."

"Do you know something I don't?"

"Probably not." He followed her into the blue room, with its blue walls, blue curtains and blue carpeting. As with rest of the house, the curtains were drawn, filtering the sunlight to cast an even deeper blue throughout the room. "But, like you said, the aliens haven't been in this area."

"I only saw what was televised. You saw that, didn't you? The ship that came down in St. Louis?"

Dalton dropped his duffle on the blue bedspread. "Yeah, I

probably saw it before you did. There was a big dog show going on in St. Louis that day. They say the attendance was almost as large as that at Westminster."

Dena gave him a perplexed look. "And the aliens came down to watch dogs walk around in a show ring?"

That made Dalton smile. It was the first time she had seen him smile since he arrived. "No, of course not," he said, "But I'm pretty sure the channel I was watching was the first to show the ship lowering next to the Arch. A lot of the dog shows in St. Louis are held out at Purina Farms, but this was in the downtown area of the city itself. Of course it was only a few minutes later when most of the television stations were broadcasting the same thing." Dalton started to pull several tee shirts out of the duffle, but he stopped and asked, "Are you sure I'm not causing you trouble?"

Spencer was sniffing at Dena's hand. She stooped and petted the dog. "No, you're not. I'm glad you're here."

"I didn't have anywhere else to go." His voice cracked. "My power went out that night, both at my apartment and the grooming salon. Not that any of my appointments showed up the next day, or could even call to cancel. The phones and email didn't work."

"I know," said Dena. "It was the same here."

"At least you weren't alone."

She stood up, hugged him and held him in the embrace. "You're here now. It's going to be okay."

Dalton pulled away and stared at her with an expression of incredulity. "Okay? How is it going to be okay?"

"I don't know." Looking into a face that was so much like her own, she said, "That's just what people say, isn't it?"

Then they both laughed, and for a few moments it felt as if everything really would be okay, but the severity of their situation quickly intruded again. Dalton's laughs faded away.

Dena helped him put what little clothing he had brought into the bureau drawer that she kept empty for guests. The shirts, shorts, cotton briefs and jeans were clean, as she had hoped, and she thought they were probably the last of the clean clothing he owned. As they put his things away, Dalton told her a little more of his experiences since that fateful day when the aliens made their presence known. He said nothing that surprised her. The reaction in Butler had been the same as in Caldonia: the looting of supermarkets and hardware stores, the police fighting a hopeless battle against a panicked population, the immediate loss of power and phone service, and not long after that the loss of water.

Dalton said, "I heard that the Chicago ship took out New York City and is moving from one urban center to another, but the St. Louis ship stayed in Missouri."

"That's what Jimmy told us, too," said Dena. "Washington D.C. is also gone. Oh, by the way, he doesn't like to be called Jimmy now. It's Jim. I just keep forgetting."

"Got it." He sat on the bed, and reprimanded Spencer when the dog tried to jump up with him.

"It's all right," said Dena. "Spencer is probably cleaner than any of the rest of us."

"Okay." Dalton nodded to the dog and patted the bed. Spencer jumped up on the bedspread again and settled next to him. "It doesn't make any sense, though, Dena. If the aliens are trying to wipe us out, why aren't both of the ships going from city to city? Or is there some kind of mineral or other resource that the St. Louis ship is looking for in Missouri?"

"I don't know, Dalton."

He put his arm around Spencer. "They must want something."

"You're tired," said Dena.

"Exhausted. I was trying not to let it show."

"I'm your twin. I can tell these things. Lie down and take a nap. We only eat twice a day now, to conserve food, but I can wake you in time for dinner."

Dalton nodded and reclined on the bed. In a softer voice he said, "I really didn't mean to get Michael upset with you."

"He's not upset with me. He's just worried, like we all are." Dena sat on the bed and looked at Spencer. The dog watched her cautiously, but then seemed to understand that it was all right for him to be there.

Dena reached out and rubbed the dog's belly. "Dalton, you've never done anything to be a problem. It was our parents' problem, and I was stupid to go along with them. I can't do anything to change the past, but things are going to be different from now on. I love you, Dalton. I hope you can believe that. Dalton?"

She looked over at his face and saw that he had fallen into a deep sleep. Giving the dog a final pat, she stood and left the room, closing the door softly behind her.

CHAPTER TEN

Michael looked sick to his stomach as he staggered into the living room. Jim seemed grim, but it was more difficult to read his emotions, partly because Dena had not seen him since he was a boy, but partly because Jim Rutherford's military service had hardened him beyond his years.

"The Martins are dead, Dena. Both of them." Michael stumbled and leaned against the sofa for support.

Jim said, "I'm sorry, Dena." He handed her a sheet of lined notebook paper. "This was on the table next to their bed."

Dena had rarely seen Barbara Martin's handwriting, and then only on Christmas card envelopes and a petition that Izzy Franklin had taken around the neighborhood earlier that year, but she immediately recognized the strong, blocky letters.

May God forgive me, the letter began. *I know that I have done the right thing, no matter what the law or the Bible may say about it. I have prayed every day for the past four days that we would hear something or the power would at least come on, but when I found out that the medical center burned down I knew that I could not let this go on any longer. It might have been different if I had kept up with Jim's meds, we might have had time to wait and see if things would turn around. But I will not sit by and watch him suffer. God has blessed us with a long and happy life together. I can only hope that we will continue to know happiness in the life after this.*

Dena looked up at Michael. Her hands shook.

Michael pushed himself away from the sofa. "She used sleeping pills," he said. "From what we found in the kitchen and bedroom, we think she dissolved the pills in some canned soup, fed him and then put him in bed. They were both in the bed when..." He clamped his mouth shut, holding back the sickness that threatened to erupt.

"I didn't know he wasn't well," said Dena.

"I didn't either."

"But...he was always so active."

"He was probably fine with medication. Think of all the diseases that are controlled but not cured. Asthma. Diabetes. He could have had any number of things that we didn't know about."

Jim said, "It's not healthy to have their exposed cadavers two houses down. We should bury them. Can Dalton help?"

"Dalton's sleeping." Dena folded the paper. It was all she had left of the Martins. A final memory, horrible as it was. "I can help, though."

Michael said, "Jim and I can do it. I'll get a couple of shovels. I think that I have a level somewhere, too. I can probably find it if I open the garage door and let some daylight in. I want their graves to be nice."

Dena looked into his eyes. "We should have buried my parents."

"It wasn't safe, honey. You know that." With a sigh, he left for the garage.

Dena sat on the couch. "I can't believe that I won't see Jim Martin working in his yard anymore." She looked up at the young soldier in his cargo shorts and Hawaiian shirt. With a grim smile, she said, "We've lost a Jim, and gained another Jim. I'm glad we found you when we went to Monroeville."

Jim Rutherford nodded, but his thoughts were elsewhere.

"Are you okay?" asked Dena.

"Yeah," he replied. Then, "Is he gay?"

"Dalton?" When Jim nodded, Dena said, "Yes, he's gay."

"That's cool." Jim shrugged. "I mean, I was all for letting gays serve in the Army."

"Jimmy...I mean, Jim—"

"It's okay, Dena. I don't care if you call me Jimmy." He grinned. "So long as you let me stay up late and watch television."

"You can stay up as late as you want, but I can't promise

much in the way of television. It's hard not to think of you as Jimmy. How did you know Dalton was gay, anyway? Is it that obvious?"

Jim said, "No, it was just the way he looked at me."

Dena nodded. She knew the Look, the brief flicker in someone's eyes that acknowledged her sexuality. Usually that person was a man, but there had been a lesbian who regularly shopped at the grocery store over in Caldonia, and Dena had recognized the woman's sexual orientation by the Look she had received. Although she did not know the other woman's name or anything about her, Dena wondered if she was okay. If she was even alive.

The emotion caught in her throat. "Jimmy, I don't think we're going to get through this."

He sat next to her. "Don't say that. We're going to fight one battle at a time, and we're not giving up until we have to. For all we know, the aliens may be gone."

"Do you believe that?"

"Sure, if that makes it easier for you. I'll believe anything I need to believe if it helps us get by." He reached out and gently rubbed her back. "Dena, what I believe most of all is that life is too valuable to just throw in the towel."

They heard footsteps on the second floor and then Spencer dashed down the stairs and into the room, his paws dancing as he turned in a circle.

"Dalton?" Dena called out. "You're up already?"

Dalton walked barefoot into the living room, rubbing at his left eye. He still wore the same tee shirt and cut-off jeans. "Spence needs to go out."

Dena said, "He peed on my spirea when you let him out of your car. How often does he need to go?"

"I think it's the stress," said Dalton.

"You can go through the kitchen to get to the back yard. You know where that is."

Dalton nodded and went to the kitchen with the dog following. They heard the back door open and close.

"That dog is amazing," said Jim.

Dena nodded. "Dalton has always been good with animals, especially dogs. I think he likes them more than people." She looked at the soldier. "What do you really think, Jimmy?"

"About your brother?"

"About the aliens. Do you think they could be gone?"

"I don't know, Dena. Nothing they've done has seemed to have any purpose. Washington was the third city they took out. Why wasn't it the first? Why did they target St. Louis?" He shook his head. "You can't chalk it up to incompetence. The way the aliens shut down power and communications across the whole nation is proof that they know what they're doing. The trouble is, *we* don't know what they're doing. So, yeah, I think they could be gone, or they could be heading here right now. Or they could be playing the slots in Vegas. I have no idea."

They heard Spencer barking in the back yard.

"Well they must want something," said Dena.

"If they do, nobody knows what that is. Why did the first ship head for a rural area? What happened in the cities that we lost contact with? I can tell you whatever you want to hear about the aliens, but anything I say will be a complete guess. We never had a chance to learn anything about them."

Spencer yelped, and a moment later resumed barking, but this time with more urgency.

"What's wrong with that dog?" asked Jim.

"I don't know." Dena slowly rose to her feet. "It sounded like Dalton kicked him, but he wouldn't do anything like that."

Then they heard voices in the garage. One was Michael's.

Jim was on his feet and had his pistol in hand when Michael came into the living room. Another man, clad in oil-stained coveralls, thin and missing several teeth, walked just behind him holding the business end of a shotgun at Michael's back. Now the dog's barking seemed to come from the front of the house. Outside the fence.

Dena inhaled sharply when she saw the man coming in behind her husband. She started towards Michael, but the man with the shotgun said, "Stay where you are, sister."

Jim kept his pistol aimed at the man. "Just lower your gun, sir. Nobody has to get hurt."

"And nobody's gonna get hurt, kid, unless you keep pointing that pistol at me."

Dena looked from Michael to Jim. "Please, Jimmy…"

Jim seemed unsure of what to do. His eyes darted to Dena.

The man with the shotgun said, "We just want to see what food you have."

Jim shook his head. "We don't have anything extra."

"This ain't a request, kid. Now drop the fucking piece."

"No, sir, I can't do that."

From the kitchen, a deeper voice said, "Drop the pistol, or your buddy is going to eat a bullet."

A heavy-set man with a full, dark beard came into the room with Dalton. The stranger had one arm around Dalton's neck. In his other hand he held a large frame revolver with the end of the barrel shoved into Dalton's mouth.

Defeated, Jim lowered the pistol and dropped it to the carpet.

"That's right," said the bearded man. He nodded to Dena. "Kick that over here, lady, and don't even try to reach down for it."

Dena kicked the pistol in the man's direction.

Looking closer at Dena, and then at Dalton, the bearded man said, "You two must be related."

The man with the shotgun said, "Let's get the food, Frank."

"We'll get it." He looked over at Michael. "You sit down there on the couch. You too, kid," he added, nodding to Jim. To Dena he said, "Is this your brother?" He indicated Dalton by pushing the barrel of the revolver even deeper into the frightened man's mouth.

Dena was too scared to answer. She couldn't even bring herself to nod.

"No matter," said the bearded man. "After I have you, maybe I'll see if this guy wants to suck on something other than a gun."

The man with the shotgun pushed Michael towards the couch. Shaking with fury, Michael sat next to Jim Rutherford. He looked up at the bearded man and said, "Don't you dare hurt her."

"I don't see that you have much to bargain with, buddy." The bearded man grinned and stepped towards Dena. He kept one arm wrapped around Dalton's neck, but lowered the revolver. With one foot he kicked the pistol to the other side of the room.

The other man said, "Come on, Frank, let's just load up and go."

"We'll do that," growled the bearded man. "But this chick is prettier than the last two."

"Then take her with you."

The bearded man looked at his friend. "If I take her with us, we'll have to feed her. I just want to fuck her; I don't want to marry the bitch." He grinned at Dalton. "Get over there on the couch with your boyfriends." He pushed Dalton roughly to the couch.

Dalton stumbled and fell against the side of the couch. He clung there, half on the couch and half on the floor.

"Keep your gun on them," snapped the bearded man, indicating Dalton, Jim and Michael.

The man with the shotgun said, "If you're going to fuck her, then do it quick."

"Or what?" asked the bearded man. "Is somebody going to call the cops? Is one of their neighbors going to come to the rescue? Nobody around here is going to do anything. These fat cats are nothing but a bunch of chickenshits in their big, fancy houses."

Michael said, "Please...we'll give you anything."

The bearded man looked at him. "You her husband? Her boyfriend?"

Michael nodded. "She's my wife."

"So what are you going to give me?"

"Anything," said Michael. "Anything you want."

"But you see, that's the problem here." The bearded man sneered. "I can already take whatever I want. I'm gonna take any food you have stashed away here. I'm gonna take the kid's pistol, and any bullets if I can find them. If you have water, I'm taking it. If money was still worth anything, I'd take that, too. What is it that you have that I can't just take?"

"Anything..."

"You don't have shit, buddy. We have the guns, so anything you have, we can take." He turned to Dena. "And the first thing I'm gonna take is the little woman here, while the three of you watch."

Dena tried to back away, but the bearded man's hand snapped out and grasped her wrist. "Come on now, lady, let's give a good show for your husband. And your brother." He grinned at Dalton.

An explosive shot split the air. Dena screamed as the man in coveralls dropped his shotgun and fell forward, landing heavily on the carpet. The bearded man turned quickly, throwing Dena to the floor as he did so.

"What the—" His words were cut off as a bullet went through his skull and implanted itself in the wall behind him. With an angry, surprised look on his face, the bearded man also collapsed.

Dena crawled towards the couch, wondering what just happened. She could see a pool of blood staining the carpet where the man with the shotgun was sprawled. The bearded man's revolver had fallen not far from him, and Jim's pistol was still on the floor on the opposite side of the room.

Standing in the doorway to the kitchen was a huge, unshaven

man holding a Browning rifle in his hands. It was their next door neighbor, the man who Dena knew only as Beaker. Nodding curtly to Dena and the others, Beaker lowered the rifle and stepped into the room.

CHAPTER ELEVEN

Dalton's dog Spencer ran in from the kitchen just then, darting under Beaker's legs and launching himself onto the couch. Dalton grabbed the dog and hugged him weakly, receiving a sloppy bath of saliva in return.

Michael rushed across the room and knelt next to Dena. He stared at Beaker as the large man walked to the couch, eyed Dalton curiously and then turned his attention to Jim Rutherford.

"Who're you?" Beaker asked. He pointed to Jim with the tip of his rifle.

Dena pulled herself into a sitting position, holding Michael's arm for support. "He's a friend of ours. And this is my brother Dalton," she added.

Beaker gave Dalton another curious look.

Michael said, "Thank God you came when you did, Beaker."

Scratching his belly, Beaker looked at the two dead bodies. He walked over and nudged the body of the bearded man with his foot. "I saw this guy kick the dog out through your back gate. Didn't think the dog was yours, but I knew this fucker was up to no good."

Dalton sat up, pushing Spencer away from him. "Spencer, off," he said. "Sit." The dog leaped off the couch and sat next to Dalton's bare feet.

Beaker looked at Jim Rutherford. "You got a name?"

Jim started to rise, but sat back down on the couch when Beaker lifted the rifle. "Private James Rutherford, sir. United States Army."

"There's still an army?"

The soldier stared up at the much larger man. "I was stationed at Oakdale, sir. Nobody's there now. I didn't desert my post. Colonel Manning closed us down."

Dena and Michael stood up. Rubbing her wrist, Dena said, "Mr. Beaker, if there's anything we can do to repay you, just let us know."

"Gotta get rid of these bodies."

"What?"

Beaker pointed with his rifle. "These two bodies."

Dena said, "I guess we have two more graves to dig then. Mr. Beaker, Jim and Barbara Martin are dead."

The man nodded. "Yeah, I know."

For a moment Dena thought she must have heard him incorrectly. She looked at Michael, and from the expression on his face she knew that Beaker had said exactly what she thought he said.

"You know?"

Beaker parted the living room curtain with the barrel of his rifle. A slice of sunlight came through the opening. He looked out at the house at Number Thirty-Two and said, "Martin had problems he didn't let on about. Barbara said he needed his drugs, so after the fire I drove over to the Caldonia Medical Center. It was gone. So were both of the pharmacies. Barbara was real upset when I told them."

"Did you know she was going to give him sleeping pills?"

He shook his head and let the curtain drop to shroud the room again in darkness. "Found them later."

It occurred to Dena that Beaker had spoken more words than she had heard from him over the previous year. The Martins' deaths must have affected him, and yet he had left them lying in their bed.

"Why not them?" she asked harshly. "You say we need to bury these men, but not Jim and Barbara?"

"I didn't say we need to bury them, I said we need to do something about them." Beaker looked down at the body of the bearded man. "Jim and Barbara Martin aren't lying on your living room floor."

It was hard to argue with that. The other dead man, the one who had held a shotgun on Michael, had bled considerably into the carpet. The pool of blood had stopped expanding, but Dena suspected the stain and the memory would never completely come out.

In a more gentle voice, she asked, "What was wrong with Mr. Martin?"

"He didn't tell you?" asked Beaker.

"No."

"Then I reckon he didn't want you to know."

Dena started to protest, but Michael said, "It doesn't matter now. We have work to do, Mr. Beaker, could you help us dig the graves? And do you have an extra shovel? We only have two."

Beaker nodded. "I have three. Enough for all of us."

"One's fine," said Michael.

The larger man looked around at everyone. "I count five people here."

"You, Jim and I will be digging the graves."

Dena said, "I told you that I can help, Michael." She turned to Beaker. "If you don't mind loaning me a shovel, I mean."

Beaker pointed his rifle at Dalton. "What's his problem?"

"He's tired," said Dena.

"No." Dalton stood, but the top of his head barely came to Beaker's chin. He looked up at the tall, unshaven man. "I'll dig too."

"You bringing the dog?"

"Is that okay?"

"If he doesn't get in the way."

Jim Rutherford stood also, holding his hands up, respectful of the Browning rifle that Beaker still held. "Sir? Is it alright if I get my pistol?"

"That might be a good idea, son."

They decided to bury all of the bodies in the Martins' back yard. Michael thought it was what the elderly couple would have wanted, to be interred near their home. Dena did not think either Jim or Barbara would have wanted the other two men buried there, but the bodies had to go somewhere. After Beaker retrieved his three shovels they all walked over to the Martins' house. Beaker and Jim Rutherford began digging two graves for the Martins with straight, smooth sides. Their shovels bit into the soil with practiced efficiency as they worked.

Michael helped Dena and Dalton dig a second, larger grave for the two intruders. There was unanimous agreement that Frank and Shotgun Guy were not worthy of individual graves. The appearance of their joint grave was not as important either, and this was a good thing because Dalton and the Andersons could not have dug a sharp, straight grave like the ones Beaker and Jim were digging even if they had wanted to. The grave they dug was more of a hollow, shallow depression scooped out of the Martins' back lawn.

The act of digging graves near the marigolds in the back garden at Number Thirty-Two Hugo Drive had a feeling of permanence. Dena did not think Jim and Barbara Martin would be exhumed later and moved to a proper cemetery. No Pennsylvania state official would be coming around with a complaint about health code violations or breaking local ordinances. This would be the Martins' final resting place, there in the yard with the two burglars. Dena was almost sure of it. The challenges they were facing were not, as she had hoped and believed, a temporary thing.

While they were digging, Spencer began to bark at something they could not see. The dog started to run to the side of the Martins' house, but Dalton called him back. Returning to the dig, Spencer kept looking to the house.

"What is it, Spence?" asked Dalton.

Beaker set his shovel down. He had brought his rifle with him, but had put it aside when they began excavating the graves. Now he stooped and took it, releasing the safety. Jim also had his pistol out and ready. Both men had stepped out of the graves they were working on.

It was Dena who saw part of a face peering through the

overgrown forsythia next to the Martins' house. "Jerry, is that you?"

Jerry Franklin stepped out from behind the forsythia. He wore polyester slacks, a white undershirt and bedroom slippers. His belly hung over the waist of the slacks.

Beaker lowered his rifle. Following his example, Jim Rutherford put the safety on his pistol. Dena felt her muscles relax.

Jerry said, "We heard gunfire." He looked around at the three large holes they were digging. After a moment he walked over to them. "I just wanted to see if you were okay."

"That was an hour ago," said Michael. "We could have used a little help then."

Jerry was staring at Dalton. "You are…?"

Dalton stepped forward, holding out his hand. "Dalton Holt," he said. "I'm Dena's brother."

"I didn't even know Dena had a brother," said Jerry, shaking Dalton's hand.

Dena couldn't think of anything to say. Jerry and Izzy did not know about Dalton because she had not wanted them to know.

Her brother broke the awkward pause, saying, "I don't get down here very often. I own a grooming salon up in Butler." His smile faltered as Jerry Franklin suddenly released his hand and took a step backward. "For dogs, you know. I guess I should say I used to own it. I'm not sure what anybody owns now."

Jerry turned from him abruptly and held his hand out to Jim. "I'm Jeremy Franklin, from across the street." He glanced at Spencer and frowned as the dog sniffed at his leg.

"James Rutherford, sir." Jim shook his hand firmly.

Jerry looked over at Michael. "I'm sorry, but Izzy and I don't keep any firearms. I wasn't about to leave the house while we could hear shooting."

"That was me," said Beaker. "Two men broke into the Andersons' house. They aren't going to be a problem anymore."

Jerry glanced towards the Martins' house and the cul de sac beyond that. "There's a black van parked in front of the Coopers', and an old Civic in your own drive, Michael."

Michael said, "The Civic belongs to Dalton."

Dena grabbed Michael's arm. "The Coopers! We need to make sure they're okay. Those men wouldn't have come to our house first. They must have been to the Coopers' and the Clarks'." They had probably burgled the Lewinberg and Franklin homes, too, but those houses would have been empty. There was no way of knowing if the men had hit the houses on the opposite side of the street.

Jerry looked up at Beaker and asked, "You killed the two men? Why are you burying them in the Martins' back yard? Do Jim and Barbara know about this?"

Dena took a step towards him. "Jim and Barbara are dead, too. I'm sorry, Jerry, we just found out ourselves."

"They've been killed?" he asked, his eyes widening in alarm.

She shook her head. "Overdose of sleeping pills." It seemed kinder and more respectful than telling him that Barbara Martin had killed her husband and then committed suicide. Out of the corner of her eye Dena saw Beaker nod almost imperceptibly.

Michael said, "They've been dead for a while now. It's not pretty. But we need to check out that van, and we need to see if the Coopers are okay. Come on, Jerry."

He hurried around the side of the house with Beaker and Jerry Franklin close behind him. When the three men were almost out of sight, Dena noticed Jerry split away from the other two men and head across the cul de sac to his own house. That meant Michael was alone with Beaker, and Beaker had a rifle. That was unnerving. Dena silently told herself that Michael was no match for Beaker even if the man did not have a weapon, and Jerry Franklin certainly would not level the playing field if Beaker wanted to do harm to her husband.

She silently told herself to stop thinking of Beaker as the

boogie man. An hour earlier he had saved her from a potential rapist.

Dalton asked, "Should we go with them?"

"No." She reached down and scratched Spencer's head. Glancing at Jim Rutherford, she said, "No, they'll be fine. We'll probably be more help if we can get some work done on these graves before they get back."

They took up their shovels and resumed working; Jim Rutherford digging a final resting place for Barbara Martin, and the twins enlarging the hole where the two intruders would be buried. Spencer explored the yard, sniffing at the birdbath and at the flower garden that Barbara had always taken such pride in. Now the marigolds and zinnias were overgrown with weeds.

The grave that Jim was digging was soon deep enough that he had to jump down into it to continue working. Standing waist deep in the hole, he threw several more scoops of soil onto the adjacent dirt pile before stopping to take off his shirt.

Dena looked over at him. "It's not *that* hot. Or are you just showing off?"

Jim laughed and tossed the shirt onto the grass. "I don't want to get it any dirtier than I need to. I stink enough already."

"Good point. Dalton, why don't you do the same?" When he shook his head, she said, "We don't have enough water for washing anything more than the dishes."

Dalton ignored her, seemingly focused entirely on digging the larger grave. Dena glanced again at Jim digging the smaller but better constructed grave, and she thought that she understood her twin. Jim Rutherford had defined muscles, with a visible six pack beneath his well-toned pectorals. His biceps knotted as he lifted another large scoop of earth out of the grave. Dalton had a slender build, and even with his tee shirt on Dena could see that he did not have anything resembling Jim's sculpted torso.

Michael and Beaker were gone longer than Dena had expected, and she was starting to worry again about her husband when they finally came walking back between Beaker's house and the Martins'. Michael did not look happy.

"You were right," he said. "They got both the Coopers and the Clarks. They were tied to chairs, in both houses, and Connor Cooper was beat up pretty bad."

"He's only twelve!" said Dena.

Michael nodded. "I think we're going to lose the Coopers. Don says they're going to try to get to his brother's house in Harrisburg. The van had a lot of food in it – more than what we have left – but Don and Alan say it's all theirs." He looked at Beaker. "I think they were lying. I think some of the food came from other houses. I know for a fact that Randall Fortune loved to snack on fried onion rings, and I saw eight cans."

Beaker shrugged.

"I tell you, I'm pretty sure some of that stuff was taken from the Fortunes' house."

Beaker set his rifle on the ground and took up his shovel. He shrugged again and then resumed digging the grave for Jim Martin.

Michael and Dena exchanged a glance. Beaker was back to being his uncommunicative self. Michael came over to the hole that Dena and Dalton were digging. "The Inghams, the Kellers and that Indian family are still here on the other side of the street," he said. "I think Andy Keller is losing his mind. He wouldn't let us come up to the door, even when we said that Beaker would put down the rifle."

"What about the Bouchards?" asked Dena.

"They're gone." Michael took his shovel and began digging. "I don't know when they left, but I found a note for Emma in their mailbox. It didn't say much, only that they were going to Emma's grandmother's house. I left it there, in case she comes back home. Maybe we should leave a second note to let her know she can come over to our place."

Without looking up from his work, Beaker said, "The

Bouchards left two nights ago."

"Why didn't you say so?" asked Michael.

"I just did." He kept digging.

Nobody spoke for a while. Each was lost in thought. Dena could not help but wonder what had become of Missy Bouchard's daughter Emma. That led to memories of Missy's other two children, both boys. Thirteen-year-old Aidan Bouchard had been close friends with Connor Cooper. Missy and her family were gone, and the Cooper boy had been beaten up – Michael only described it as 'pretty bad' – by two strangers. And Dena was digging a grave in her neighbors' back yard.

Even though Michael, Dena and Dalton were all working together to dig the hole where the two intruders would be buried, it was Jim Rutherford who finished his grave first. He pulled himself out of the open grave, wiped his muddy palms on the grass and stepped over to the grave that Beaker was digging.

"That's good work, sir."

Beaker glanced up at him. Without replying, he threw a scoop of dirt out of the grave. Jim went over to get his shovel and then jumped down to join Beaker. They dug for a few more minutes, and then Jim said, "You've been going out at night, haven't you, sir?"

The only response was a sullen shrug.

"That's how you know that other family left. You go someplace after dark." When Beaker still didn't respond, Jim said, "I noticed that your truck isn't always parked in the same place. Close, but not exactly. Sometimes it's all the way up to your garage door, and sometimes it is barely in the driveway. That's because you go out at night."

Beaker slowly turned to face him. From where they stood Michael, Dena and Dalton could see no more of Jim Rutherford than his head. Being a much larger than the young soldier, Beaker's head, shoulders and part of his chest were visible.

In a low voice Beaker said, "What of it?"

"Where do you go, sir?"

"Out."

"But where?"

Worried that Jim was pushing the man too far, Dena called out, "Mr. Beaker, could you come over here for a minute? I think we've dug a deep enough hole, but I'm not sure."

Beaker started to say something to Jim, but instead he pulled himself out of the open grave and strode over to where the others had dug the third grave. Dena was standing at the rim of this grave. Michael and Dalton were both standing inside.

"It's good enough," said Beaker. "I don't reckon any dogs or other animals will dig that deep."

As if responding to the mention of his species, Spencer trotted over to Beaker and sniffed at the fresh dirt around the edge of the pit. Beaker leaned down and reached out to the dog. Dena suppressed a gasp when she thought, for just a moment, that the man was going to grab the dog by its neck and strangle it. But instead Beaker rubbed his hand over the animal's shoulders. "What do you think, little buddy?"

Seeing the huge man who rarely spoke to anyone address Dalton's dog like that was almost absurd. Dena would have laughed if their circumstances were not so dismal.

Jim finished the last grave by himself while Michael, Dalton, Dena and Beaker went to get the bodies of the two dead intruders from Dena's living room. They dragged the corpses to the Martins' back yard, holding them by the ankles and wrists, and dumped both into the large, shapeless grave. Dena insisted that she did not want to handle the bodies of the elderly couple who had been her neighbors, so she and Dalton filled in the grave while Michael, Jim and Beaker went back into the Martins' home.

Jim Martin and his wife had a relatively decent and respectful burial. The men wrapped each body carefully in a sheet and a blanket. Barbara Martin was buried with her Bible, Jim Martin with his pruning shears.

Dena broke down crying when Beaker began to shovel dirt over Barbara Martin's wrapped remains. Michael and Dalton took her back to her house while Beaker and Jim Rutherford finished filling in the graves and covered them with sod.

CHAPTER TWELVE

Two days had passed since they buried the Martins, but Michael Anderson could still smell the scent of death on his skin and in his thinning hair. He had changed out of the clothes he was wearing as soon as they had returned home, and that helped a little but there was still a residual scent, almost like a lingering memory that refused to go away. Today Michael wore a pair of swimming trunks, an old Steelers tee shirt and flip flops. Neither the trunks nor the shirt were really clean, but they did not smell too terribly bad. Or maybe he was just getting used to his own body odor. Dena had started hanging their clothes on a line in the backyard. It did not help much – the clothes were certainly no cleaner when she took them off the cotton line she had found in the garage – but it was the best they could do.

Even without washing their clothes or their bodies, they were running dangerously low on water. Bringing home Jim Rutherford was probably a good idea, Michael thought, but Jim consumed as much water as either he or Dena did. In Michael's opinion letting Dalton move in with them was not such a great idea, but that was Dena's twin brother, so what could he say? It was sharing their water with the damn dog that annoyed Michael more than anything. If they did not have enough water to bathe themselves, then they did not have enough water for Dalton's dog.

Shotgun Guy's blood was still a dark stain on the living room carpet. They could not waste any water on that problem either.

Michael stepped over the stain, opened the front door and looked around carefully before going outside. After having a gun pressed into his back and nearly seeing his wife raped, he no longer viewed Hugo Drive as a haven of safety.

Nothing looked amiss, and yet at the same time everything was wrong. Most of the houses that Michael could see from his front porch were vacant. The Bouchards down the street had left home earlier that week, and now the Coopers were gone. In the cul de sac, the Grahams had left and the Martins were both dead. Even the occupied houses had a vacant look. Izzy and Jerry Franklin were hiding out behind their painted windows, and Beaker's curtains were perpetually drawn.

Blinking in the afternoon sunlight, Michael hurried across the lawn to the house next door. If Jim Rutherford was right about Beaker's nocturnal trips, the man probably slept most of the day. It was late enough in the day now, though, that Michael thought Beaker would be up. Of course there was no way for Michael to know the exact time of day. When Michael was young he had had a wristwatch that kept time by winding it up, but that had been years ago. The electric clock on the stove, the digital display on the VCR, his alarm clock, and even the time display on their cellular phones: all had become useless.

It was late in the afternoon, the position of the sun told Michael as much, but he could be no more precise than that.

Remembering the Browning rifle, Michael stood to one side of Beaker's front door as he reached out and knocked on it. He thought he heard movement from somewhere inside the house, but he could not be sure. Knocking again, he called out, "Beaker! It's me, Michael Anderson." A third series of knocks also produced no response.

He was knocking a fourth time when the door opened a crack. From inside he heard Beaker say, "Yeah?"

Although he did not like to admit it, Michael found Beaker as unnerving as his wife did. He knew the guy was widowed and felt sorry about that, but everything about R. K. Beaker was strange. The man did not have a regular job that Michael was aware of. He kept to himself and he never had house guests. It was as if Beaker had some dark secret, and after seeing the man's skill with a rifle Michael would not have been at all surprised if Beaker's secret involved bodies under the cement in his basement.

But Beaker had rescued Dena. He had rescued all of them, really.

"Hey, Beaker, can I come in?"

"What do you want?" The voice behind the door was almost a growl.

Okay, this was not going to be a neighborly social call. Michael took a deep breath. "We wanted to know if you'd like to come over and have dinner with us tonight."

"I have food here."

"I'm sure you do, Beaker. It's just that Dena feels really bad that we've never had you over, and after the other day..." Michael cleared his throat. "It's not really dinner, of course, but we have some canned peaches and I think there's still a partial bag of corn chips that aren't too stale."

"You don't have to feed me. I just did what I had to do." The door started to close.

Michael put his palm firmly against the door, but then pulled it back quickly, afraid that he might see the barrel of the rifle come through the narrow opening. "It would mean a lot to Dena if you would come over. Is it because of Dalton? Believe me, I know how you—"

"Okay, fine."

"—probably feel about...fine? You mean you'll come?"

"Yeah, I'll come. Let me get a couple of things done here and then I'll be over."

"Great! We'll look forward to seeing you." Michael was talking to a closed door. He heard the lock click on the other side. "Nice talking to you," he muttered.

He returned to his own house to find Dena in the kitchen trying to wash that morning's dishes with sand. Her long, dark brown hair was held in a ponytail with a rubber band. Dena had read somewhere that some culture had once scrubbed their dishes with sand, and Michael had come across a large bag of sand in the back of the garage. From the look of things, the result was not very satisfactory.

She looked up as he came in. "Is he coming over?"

"Yeah." Michael nodded. "But I hope this isn't going to be a weekly ritual. I shouldn't say this about someone who very well may have saved our lives, but Beaker is not my favorite person. Where are the guys?"

"They're both out back. Jim got the Coopers' charcoal grill and brought it over here. Now he's trying to break off some limbs from one of the oak trees at the back of the yard to use as firewood. The limbs are green, but they'll dry."

Michael said, "Somebody on Hugo Drive must have an axe or a saw."

"Dalton is back there, too. He's working with Spencer while there's still some daylight." She scraped sand off of a plate with the side of her hand.

"That's great," said Michael. "New dog tricks will be very useful."

"Oh, for God's sake, Michael, can't he have a hobby? You know how much Dalton loves Spencer. And you have to admit, the dog is very well-behaved."

Michael shrugged. "I'm just saying that Jim is contributing a hell of a lot more around here than Dalton is."

"What is your problem with Dalton?" Dena put the plate firmly down on a stack she had been trying to clean. The remaining grains of sand on the plate made a scritchy sound. "It's not because he isn't doing enough. Is it because he's gay?"

"No." The response was a little too quick.

"Michael, you knew I had a homosexual brother before we were married. If it bothered you so much, you should have said something then."

"You're the one who took his name off the invitation list."

"Yes, and I've had to live with that for the past six years." Dena looked to the back door, wondering if her voice was loud enough for Dalton to hear. "He can't help who he's attracted to."

"Dena, I don't care if he's gay. I've never had anything against gay people, you know that. Hell, before I met your brother I never even thought much about gays."

"Then what is it?"

"It's because….it's…." He turned away from her. *"He looks like you."*

"Dalton and I are twins, Michael."

"Yeah, fraternal twins. You shouldn't look any more alike than other siblings. But Dalton could be you with a sex change, or vice versa."

"So?"

Michael walked over to the window and looked out at the back yard where Dalton was throwing a ball for Spencer, but making the dog wait until he gave permission to retrieve it.

"Dena, when I look into your brother's eyes, I see your eyes. His lips are your lips, and the smile and pout the exact same as yours. His voice is baritone instead of alto, but it's close enough to the sound of your voice to make me think of you whenever he speaks."

She wiped sand from her hands. "Are you saying that you want to have sex with my brother?"

"No! Well, not really. I'm saying that sometimes when I'm around him I have the same feelings that I do for you." Michael shrugged. "Yeah, I guess I'm aroused a little. And I hate myself for those feelings; I hate him for making me feel that way, even though I know the attraction would end once we got our pants off."

Dena went to him and put her arms around him. "I don't see anything wrong with that. It's flattering to think that you're turned on when you see a resemblance of me, whether it's in a photo, or a mirror or in my brother's face."

"I've never thought of myself as bisexual."

She chuckled. "I don't think you are, Michael. Not until you actually have sex with another man. Anyway, the idea of a bisexual husband sort of turns me on. Let's go upstairs."

Michael kissed her. "That might not be a good idea. I haven't had a bath or shower since that night." He did not have to elaborate on which night he meant. "I'm pretty ripe."

"I'm not exactly a gardenia myself," said Dena. "But it's not going to get any better soon, I don't think, and we also haven't had sex since that night."

They heard a knock at their front door.

Michael sighed. "That's Beaker. Can I get a rain check, Stinky?"

He went to the living room to let Beaker in. Behind him in the kitchen Dena opened the back door and called for Dalton and Jim. There was no need to call Spencer. If Dalton came into the house, the dog was certain to follow unless told to do otherwise.

In the living room, Michael unlocked the front door and opened it. He was surprised to see Beaker holding a large corrugated cardboard box in his arms. The man was wearing a clean shirt and slacks.

"Come on in," said Michael. "You didn't have to bring us anything."

"Nope," Beaker acknowledged. "I didn't. Where can I put this?"

"Dena's in the kitchen." Michael led the man through the living room. He was not sure where Beaker should put the box because he had no idea what was in it, but the kitchen seemed as good a place as any.

Dalton and Jim were coming in through the back door even as Beaker set the box down on a kitchen counter. Spencer also came in and pranced around Beaker's legs until Dalton told the dog to sit.

"What's this?" asked Dena, looking at the box and wiping away a few stubborn grains of sand caught between her fingers.

The big man opened the box. "I don't much like peaches by themselves," he said, pulling a canned ham out. "I thought this might go with it. And here's some water." He took out three unopened plastic gallon jugs of spring water.

Michael stared at the jugs of water as if they were bottles of Dom Perignon. "Beaker, you didn't have to do this," he said again.

"I know." Beaker began pulling other cans out of the box. "I have some more stuff, too. Some cans of corn; those will be better if you can warm them up somehow. Some pears. Here's a jar of maraschino cherries. Oh, and I didn't forget about you, little buddy." He took two cans of Blue Buffalo dog food out of the box and held them down for Spencer's inspection.

Michael raised one eyebrow. "You have canned dog food?"

Beaker said, "When the human food runs out, this will start to look like filet mignon."

Dena shook her head. "We can't take this from you, Mr. Beaker. We're already in your debt."

"You can take it, and you will." He pulled the tab on the canned ham. "You people don't seem to get how bad off things are."

Dalton said, "We know exactly how bad it is out there. My sister was almost raped."

"Yeah," said Beaker. He glanced at Dalton briefly and then turned away from him. "As I recollect, I'm the one who stopped that. You got a plate, Dena? No, not one of those, something without sand on it."

Dena and Michael tried to set a decent table in the dining room, but without much success. Beaker would not let them put out paper napkins ("You might need those for kindling or cleaning") or light more than one candle ("We don't need any more than that to see by"). Their dinner consisted of chunks of canned ham, slices of canned peaches and for each of them a handful of slightly stale corn chips. To wash that down they had wine glasses filled with the bottled spring water. For Michael the crystal clear water was the nectar of the gods compared to the stagnant water they had been scooping out of the upstairs bathtub.

The flame of the candle in the center of the table cast a dim, flickering light over their faces as they ate. Dalton (looking even more like his sister in the faint glow) was quiet and subdued. Michael wondered if it was because of Beaker's rebuke. Now, over dinner, their reclusive neighbor was more outgoing than Michael had ever seen him. Beaker seemed almost jovial, in a gruff sort of way, as he cut chunks of ham and passed them around.

Beaker explained that the feast's ham and spring water were part of the bounty that he had been collecting at night while they slept. "Yeah, I've been trying to stockpile what I can," Beaker said, scooping peach slices onto his plate. "We can't sit here on Hugo Drive waiting for the cavalry to come. It isn't going to."

Dena frowned. "Where are you getting...I mean..."

"I'm not breaking into occupied homes." Beaker shook his head. "I do go into houses, but only if nobody is there anymore."

Michael asked, "Are there that many empty houses?"

"More than you'd think. Some houses are just vacant, where folks have packed up and gone somewhere else. At others..." Beaker stared down at his plate. "There are people who've gone the way Jim and Barbara did."

Michael swallowed a piece of ham that had suddenly lost its flavor.

"Anyway, I take what I find if it looks like it will be useful. There are others doing the same, collecting whatever they can. Some will kill you as soon as look at you, so you have to be careful. Other people are decent enough. I hear things, most of it rumor."

"You mean about the aliens?" asked Michael.

Beaker nodded. "There's a church over in Wexford where people are trying to organize. I don't know how long they'll last, they argue about every little thing, but they told me about what's happening to the Amish."

Jim Rutherford looked up from his plate. "The Amish, sir?"

"One of the ships has moved into Pennsylvania and has been taking out some of the Amish communities."

Michael said, "That sounds a lot like what happened in Missouri, but I don't think it was the Amish there. Was it the same ship?"

"I don't know."

Dena said, "Are there a lot of other people? I mean other than the church you mentioned?"

"Of course." Beaker scratched at his belly. "Most of them are hiding out. I've tried to help a few of them. Nothing much, just sharing some food, you know. Then Michael came over and invited me here, and I thought maybe I should be helping you folks."

Jim Rutherford chewed thoughtfully. "If one of their ships is in Pennsylvania, maybe we should move out. How long do you think it will be before they get to this part of the state?"

"Where do you plan to go?" asked Beaker. He pointed his fork at the younger man. "If the aliens set their sights on us, we're goners. They've taken out our military, our power plants, our satellites – hell, they've thrown us back into the Stone Age. You know that. There's nothing much we can do except hope the fuckers either leave or let us know what it is they want."

Michael said, "And so far they haven't shown any interest in communicating with us."

Beaker shook his head. "We don't know that. They may be screaming at us for all they're worth. Just because we aren't hearing a message doesn't mean there isn't one."

"Fair enough. But we can't communicate with them, and I agree there probably isn't any safe haven, so what do you propose we do, Beaker?"

The big, unshaven man looked around the table. "We need to organize ourselves a little better. I'll move in here tonight."

Dena quickly said, "We don't have any extra beds." She could not meet Beaker's eyes. "I'm sorry, but we just don't. Jimmy is in one guestroom and Dalton in the other."

There was a long, uncomfortable pause, and Michael knew what Beaker was probably thinking. There would be room if they made room. Maybe it would be awkward for one of the other men to share a bed with Dalton, but there was no reason Jim Rutherford could not bunk with Beaker.

Finally Beaker said, "I can take the couch in the living room."

Michael was also quite aware that his wife did not like the idea of Beaker staying in their home, but before she could protest further he said, "That works. We'll fix you up with some extra blankets and a pillow."

Beaker took a drink of water, heedless of a dribble that worked its way downward through the hairs on his chin. "Tomorrow we can bring my food, water and other supplies over here. Anything we leave at my place will be fair game for burglars."

Michael nodded. "We have a lot of storage space in the garage, and if we need more we can push the BMW and the Avalon out to the driveway."

"Not until we siphon out the gas," said Beaker. "Gasoline is almost as precious as water now. I'll need it to make more runs. And nobody leaves the house alone, even for a few minutes. If we go outside – out front at least – we go in pairs or more."

Spencer ran to the living room and began to bark.

In an instant everyone but Dalton was armed: Beaker with his rifle, Jim with his pistol, Michael with the shotgun and Dena with the revolver that had belonged to Frank the Rapist. Michael hoped that the dog was barking at a pigeon or stray leaf in the front yard, because he had no more experience with a shotgun than Dena did with the revolver.

They heard the front door slam open and Michael mentally kicked himself. He had forgotten to lock it after letting Beaker in earlier.

Spencer backed into the dining room, still barking furiously at the yet unseen intruder.

Then Izzy Franklin stepped in, her eyes wide, searching the room. Even in the candlelight her dark roots were clearly visible beneath the dyed platinum hair that hung limp around a hag-like countenance. She wore nothing but a white, silk slip and hemp sandals.

Izzy's gaze settled on Dalton. Slowly she raised her right hand, pointing at him with a thin, bony finger. "You!" she shrieked. "You are an abomination before the Lord!"

Michael saw Dena lower her revolver. "Izzy—"

The president of the Hugo Drive Neighborhood Association then turned her accusatory finger to Dena. "And you brought him here!"

CHAPTER THIRTEEN

The dining room erupted in chaos. Spencer barked non-stop, positioning himself protectively between the strange, frantic woman and Dalton. Michael and Dena tried to get Izzy to settle down. Izzy continued to point hysterically, shifting her finger from Dena to Dalton and back again, screaming about abominations and God's curse. Jim was shouting for everyone to be quiet, which only added to the cacophony.

Jerry Franklin came in through the dark living room. "Izzy, please..."

"Do not tell me to be tolerant, Jeremy!" Izzy whirled on him. "America has been struck down, just as surely as the Lord struck down Sodom."

Dena wondered when Izzy Franklin had become so extreme in her religious views. She had always known that Izzy did not like homosexuals, just as she did not like "colored" people, Jews or anyone with an accent that she considered peculiar. This Christian spin seemed like more of a convenience, however. It certainly simplified Izzy's position. The woman did not need any rationale for her bigotry so long as Jesus was on her side.

Then Izzy was directing her fury at Dena again. "How could you bring someone like that here, into a decent, God-fearing neighborhood? How could you?"

"He's my brother," said Dena weakly.

"Read your Bible! He is an abomination!"

Beaker slowly placed his rifle on the dining table and stepped towards Izzy. His eyes burned with smoldering umbrage. "If there is an abomination here, it's you, Izzy Franklin. This is not your home, and you've got no right to tell these folks who they can have under their roof."

She glared up at him. "Don't you talk to me like that, Mr. Beaker. The Bible tells us that homosexuality is a sin."

It seemed to Dena that Beaker grew even larger, towering over

Izzy like some primal, immovable force. Dena stepped closer to Michael, not that there was anything Michael could have done to protect her from Beaker. The man's upper arms were as thick as an ordinary man's thighs.

Izzy repeated, "It's a sin, Mr. Beaker. You know that as well as I do." There was less conviction in her voice now.

"I know sin when I see it," growled Beaker. "It's a sin to sit behind your painted windows while your neighbor starves or goes without medicine. Do you know why Jim and Barbara Martin died? Because Jim needed medication and Barbara didn't want to see him suffer. She killed him, Izzy. Barbara Martin killed her husband. But you didn't know that, because you were too worried about yourself. Hiding, like a cockroach slipping through a crack in the floor. That's what has struck us down, Izzy. Not God, not even the aliens, but sinners like you; everyone who gave up and ignored or turned against his neighbors after that night. If you want to see sin, just look in a mirror."

Izzy wheeled around on her husband. "Jerry! Are you going to let him talk to me like that?" she demanded. When Jerry did not answer, she screamed like a madwoman and ran from the house.

Spencer started to chase her, but Dalton called the dog back. Heeding the call, Spencer stopped in his tracks and trotted back to Dalton, who rewarded him with a corn chip.

Jerry Franklin said, "Dena, I'm sorry, really. I don't know where Izzy got this idea about God's judgment and your brother."

Dena frowned. "How did she even know about Dalton? She's never met him, Jerry." She glanced at her brother, who, despite being somewhat androgynous, was not exceptionally effeminate. "How did she know he's gay?"

Jerry's pudgy face reddened as he said, "I don't know…I might have said something…I mean…" He shrugged and started to walk out of the room.

"Jerry!" When he looked back at her, Dena said, "One of the alien ships is supposed to be here in Pennsylvania. Be careful."

He nodded, and a moment later he was gone. Beaker went back to the table, sat down and shoved a piece of ham into his mouth as if nothing unusual had happened.

Dalton said, "Thanks, Mr. Beaker."

"It's just Beaker. If I'm going to be sleeping on your sister's couch we don't have to be formal."

"Okay...Beaker." Dalton sat down at the table. "What's your first name?"

Beaker stared at him for a moment and then turned to Michael. "After we get my stuff over here tomorrow we should make a list of everything in your garage. We need to know exactly what we've got, because eventually it's going to run out. I think we should get the rest of the neighborhood together with us, too. Who is still here?"

Dena took her seat and said, "We really don't have room. The Clarks, the Inghams, the Kellers and the Naras are still here, unless somebody else has left. And of course Izzy and Jerry, although they obviously aren't interested in joining forces."

"The Naras?" asked Beaker. "That's the Indian family, right? I met them at Izzy's house."

Michael said, "I don't think there's any point in trying to talk to Andy Keller."

"Even so," said Dena, "The other families would add six more adults and a child. Where would we put them?"

Jim Rutherford cleared his throat. "I could move into Dalton's room. I can sleep on the floor in there."

Dalton shook his head. "No, I'll take the floor."

Beaker said, "Or both of you could pretend you're adults and just share the same bed."

Jim shrugged, his eyes darting to Dalton for a fraction of a second. "I guess I'm okay with that, if you are."

To the Andersons, Beaker said, "And we can carry over some

extra beds from my house and the Coopers' if we need to. Everyone won't get his own comfy room, but we'll probably be safer if we are all together. We should rig up some way to collect rainwater, too. It's stupid for me to look for bottles of water when the stuff falls out of the sky for free."

Michael said, "Stacy Cooper has those large planters on her patio. I might be able to clean those out and make them water-tight. We can put them under the downspouts."

"I can help you with that, sir," said Jim.

* * *

After dinner, at Michael's suggestion, they all moved out to the patio. The moon was nearly full, and the air felt fresh and clean. There were only four patio chairs. Jim chose to stand, pacing occasionally around the wrought iron table. Michael and Dena placed their chairs close together. Dena saw that Beaker rarely looked in Dalton's direction, and she wondered if, despite his words to Izzy Franklin, Beaker was more uncomfortable with her brother's sexuality than he would readily admit.

"We should use anything that will hold five gallons or more," Beaker was saying. He was still making plans to collect water. "Picnic coolers, old washtubs, pickle barrels. Just as much water comes through my downspouts as yours, and we can install even more containers at the Martins' house. I don't know about the rest of you, but I'd like to have a bath someday."

"A bath sounds lovely," said Dena. She looked up at the moon, swimming in a sea of stars, and remembered the night, that last night of civilization, when she and Michael had showered together.

Michael kicked off his flip-flops and propped his bare feet on the edge of the table. "Beaker, you've said that the aliens might be trying to communicate with us. Do you have any reason to think so, or is that just wishful thinking?"

Beaker ran his fingers through his dark hair, which was longer now even though his jaw line had the same, two-day-growth it always seemed to keep. "Maybe it is just wishful thinking, but it's reasonable enough."

"Reasonable, sir?" Jim stopped his pacing. "Nothing the aliens have done has made any sense at all."

"Exactly," said Beaker, nodding. "Maybe the aliens' actions don't make sense because we're expecting the fuckers to think like us, and not like aliens."

Dena frowned. "I don't follow you."

"Folks always expect others to be just like them. That's why Izzy Franklin gets all twisted up about people like..." His voice trailed off.

"Like Dalton," said Dena. "You can say it."

Beaker leaned forward. "What I'm saying is that people aren't real good about looking at things from the other fellow's perspective. We never have been. And if we can't understand each other, why would we expect to understand a completely different species?"

Michael said, "That's rather cynical, don't you think?"

"Nope, I don't think so at all." Beaker shook his head. "We don't understand the life forms that evolved with us right here on earth. I remember one afternoon, before the aliens came, I was watching a nature show about African lions. The narrator was talking about how, when a male lion takes a new mate, he kills any cubs that the lioness already has so he can pass on his own genes."

"Yeah?"

Beaker grinned in the dark. (Dena did not think it made him look any friendlier.) "I'm pretty sure lions don't know much about genetics. But the narrator couldn't really say why the male lion kills those cubs, because nobody actually knows. So he gave the lion a very human motivation requiring an understanding of advanced science. Nobody knows what the lion is thinking, or if he is thinking at all. Nobody knows the lion's perspective. And we're a lot more closely related to lions than we are to these space creatures. They may not even realize that we humans are the ones they should be talking to. Maybe, from their perspective, grass is the dominant life form on earth."

Dena said, "Grass? Oh, come on!"

"Think about it. Look at how much time people spend – or used to spend – mowing their lawns, and fertilizing and watering. Any alien watching us down here on Hugo Drive, without knowing anything about our world, could have perceived us as slaves to the grasses; humans as a servant race. The competitors of grass are the trees and bushes that we faithfully mow down and trim back for our grass overlords. And then we provide the grass with its basic needs, allowing it to expand its territory, often in regions where grass couldn't survive without the labor of its unquestioning servants."

"But we do all that for our own benefit! Or we did, before that night."

Beaker shrugged. "The aliens would have no way of knowing."

Michael said, "He's right, Dena. The same argument could be applied to cattle or any other domesticated animal, right, Beaker? I read somewhere that it is our arrogance leading us to believe domestication is one-sided. The idea was that what we call domestication is really a symbiotic relationship."

"Exactly," said Beaker. "We think we're using poultry, but it could as easily be said that poultry – especially chickens – uses us for its own ends."

Dalton, who had been scratching Spencer's head, looked up and said, "Do you have any idea of what goes on at a poultry packing plant? We treat chickens horribly."

Beaker nodded, "The individual birds, maybe, but as a species *Gallus gallus* has been wildly successful. Before the aliens came there were more chickens on this planet than any other kind of bird." He looked around at his hosts. "Yeah, okay, I heard about the chicken thing on another nature show. My point is that an alien might see it as the chickens domesticating us humans."

"The needs of the species trumps the needs of the individual?" asked Dalton.

"Maybe." Beaker turned away from Dalton. When he again spoke, it was to Michael and Dena. "This is all just crazy stuff I've thought about. Maybe the aliens haven't tried to communicate at all. Maybe they're looking for some rare element we don't know about. Maybe this is just their version of a vacation in the Bahamas."

Jim, who had been circling the table, stopped pacing. "They must know we're the intelligent species, though. Otherwise they wouldn't have targeted our satellites and power plants. And it wasn't grass or chickens that fought against them."

Beaker said, "They may not have seen it as much of a fight. For all we know, we may have looked like nothing more than monkeys throwing poo. And the aliens destroying our satellites doesn't mean they were impressed by them. When another animal builds something remarkable, like African termite mounds or the Great Barrier Reef, we call it 'instinct'." He shrugged. "We don't laud the intelligence of termites and coral polyps."

Michael muttered, "I can't believe I'm saying this, but I think we're going to have to actively look to the needs of our own species now." He noticed the other four staring at him. "First we need to survive, and then, eventually, we'll need to ensure that another generation is born and survives."

His eyes darted in Dena's direction for just a moment, but she knew what he was thinking. Although he had never questioned her even once, Dena knew in her heart that Michael did not entirely believe she had never used any form of contraceptive. She did not know why she had never become pregnant, but at the age of thirty-two she thought it unlikely that would change.

Perhaps the other three men caught the same glance and

understood. Whatever the reason, the conversation came to a stop. They sat together in silence for several minutes. Then, to change the subject, Dena asked, "Do you have any children, Beaker?"

He pushed himself up from the patio chair. "It's late enough," he said. "Can't waste the whole night here. Do you have a key I can use to get back in?"

Michael retrieved a key from under a stone next to the kitchen door. "This works both the front and back doors. I can go with you, if you need help," he offered.

Beaker glanced at the gate to the privacy fence surrounding the Andersons' back yard. "We need to get a lock of some kind on that gate, too." He pocketed the key and walked to the gate, closing it behind him.

When Beaker was gone, Michael said, "He must have a child. Did you see how he closed up on us? You hit a sore spot there, honey."

Dena folded her arms across her chest. "It was just a question. Why does he always have to be so rude? I don't like the idea of him staying here."

"Because he's rude?" asked Michael.

"No, it's more than that. What if he gets up in the middle of the night and kills us all in our sleep."

Michael laughed softly. "His house is next door, Dena. If he wanted to kill us, it's not as if he didn't know how to find us."

"I'm glad he's staying here," Dalton suddenly blurted out. "He stood up to that woman for me, Dena."

"Yes, he did," she said quietly. Beaker was intimidating, but he had done for her brother what she herself could not. He had stood up to Izzy Franklin, even as Dena should have stood up to her parents six years earlier.

They heard the engine of Beaker's Silverado turn over, and then the sound of the truck faded as he drove away into the night.

CHAPTER FOURTEEN

When Dalton Holt, Jim Rutherford and the Andersons woke the next morning, they found Beaker asleep on the living room couch. Stacked on the kitchen floor were boxes of canned foods and two bottles of cheap wine.

Michael and Dena changed in to fresh – if not really clean – clothes and went out together to see which of their neighbors would join them in what was rapidly turning into a commune. While they were gone, Jim Rutherford and Dalton took inventory of all their food and supplies, including Beaker's newest contribution.

Later that morning Michael and Dena returned with Rajinder Nara, his wife Asha and their eight-year-old son Jadu. Dalton had not yet met the Naras, but he was taken aback by how emaciated they looked. Michael carried the boy in his arms, and Asha leaned against Dena for support. They brought the Indian family into their kitchen, where Dena opened a large jar of applesauce and spooned it into three bowls.

"The Naras didn't have much food in their house, since they'd just moved in," Dena explained to her brother as she fed little Jadu Nara. The boy could barely sit up by himself.

Rajinder swallowed a spoonful of applesauce and moistened his lips with his tongue. "In India there are many people who do not have enough to eat, but I never thought we would suffer so here in America."

Nobody else would be coming to the Andersons' house. The Clarks were gone. According to Asha Nara, the Clarks had packed up their car and left early the previous morning. Maybe they had discovered what happened to the Inghams and the Kellers. It seemed that Andy Keller had gone completely insane. From what Michael could determine, Keller had stabbed his wife to death with a carving knife. He then went over to Ted and Dolly Ingham's house and killed both of them. Finally, still at the

Inghams', he cut his own wrists and bled to death on the sofa in their family room.

The good news, for what it was worth, was that both the Inghams and the Kellers still had some food in their pantries when Andy went on his rampage. Michael said that he and Jim could get the food later, just as soon as he could bring himself to go back into the two houses down by Route 228.

That plan changed when Beaker woke up in the early afternoon. "I'll go get the stuff," he said, sitting in the kitchen with the others. "The Kellers' house can be seen from the highway. You can bet somebody will clean the place out if we leave food there." He looked over at Jim Rutherford and said, "I could use some help, soldier boy."

"Yes sir."

Dalton said, "I can help, too."

Beaker stood and walked to the living room. "Jim and I can handle it."

After the two men left, Michael went up to the attic to find a cot for Jadu. The boy's parents would take the bed that Jim Rutherford had been using up until then; Jim and Dalton would now be sharing the blue room. Dena stayed in the kitchen and talked with the Naras, who kept apologizing for imposing. Asha Nara in particular felt that she and her family would be a burden.

Dalton took Spencer out to the back yard and tossed a worn tennis ball for him to fetch. The dog brought the ball back and Dalton threw it again, a ritual they repeated for the next few minutes.

Yesterday Beaker had defended Dalton. Today the huge man barely acknowledged his existence, and Dalton could not recall anything he might have done to provoke the change. Anyway, he thought to himself, who the hell was Beaker to make him feel like he was useless? Maybe he did not have Jim Rutherford's upper body definition or Beaker's muscular bulk, but loading cans and cartons into the back of Beaker's truck did not require prodigious strength.

Spencer brought the ball to Dalton, and he threw it across the yard again. "I should have told him to go straight to hell," he muttered to himself.

But Dalton knew that he did not have the courage to get into a fight with Beaker. He was pretty sure the man could crush him into a pulp with one hand tied behind his back. And the others – Dena and Michael, Jim and the Naras – knew it too. The house belonged to Dalton's sister and brother-in-law, but in less than a day Beaker had taken over as the dominant male.

Beaker was calling the shots, and if the man did not like Dalton, well, it was not the first time in his life that he had been marginalized. Even his sister had dropped him like a hot potato when it became inconvenient to have her homo brother around. Now Dena was trying to move on, to repair the rift between them, but Dalton knew he would never completely forget that he had been the only member of their family not invited to her wedding. Nor would he ever be able to wipe his memory clean of the excuses and alibis Dena had given since then to keep him from visiting her and Michael, or the phone calls cut short.

"Good boy," said Dalton, taking the tennis ball from Spencer's mouth. "Now take a bow!" Spencer lowered his chest to the ground. "Good boy!" Dalton repeated.

Dogs were better company than people. Dogs accepted Dalton for who he was; not only Spencer, but all dogs, purebred or mixed. People would turn on you when you did not live up to their expectations, no matter what those expectations were or how unreasonable they might be. For his parents and his sister, it had been Dalton's sexual preference. For the men he met at the clubs, Dalton was either too skinny, too quiet or dressed wrong. People would abandon you when you disappointed them, and Dalton always seemed to eventually disappoint people in some way. A dog's affection, however, was constant.

"Spencer, finish."

The dog went to Dalton's left side and sat next to his leg, but not before glancing toward the patio. Dalton turned to see his sister standing on the patio and smiling at him.

Dena said, "I think you missed your calling when you took up grooming. You should have become a trainer."

He walked back to the patio, with Spencer following at his side. "I've done a little training too, you know. I belong to an obedience club up in Butler. Or, I guess I should say, I used to belong to one."

Dena surprised him by hugging him tightly. Dalton put his arms around her awkwardly to return the hug. "Are you okay, Dena?"

Still holding him, she said, "I was going to drive up to Butler that weekend. You know, the weekend of the dog show you invited me to. I just wanted you to know that."

"I know."

"No, really." She looked into his eyes. "I'm not just saying this. I'd told myself that I would get up there and see you."

"I know, Dena." Dalton nodded solemnly. "I don't know how, but after we talked on the phone I knew you were going to try to come up to the show. Maybe we have some kind of psychic thing going on. I've heard of that happening with other twins."

"But even if it's true, we're just fraternal twins." She turned away from him. "I wish the ships hadn't come down when they did. I wish I'd had time to show you, really, that I care about you. I wish a lot of things had been different."

"You've let me move in here." He sat on one of the wrought iron chairs and signaled for Spencer to sit on the patio next to him. "I appreciate that. I know Michael isn't happy about me staying with you."

She sat in the chair next to his. "Michael has his own issues to work through," she said. "He likes you well enough."

As if he could hear them talking about him, Michael came out through the kitchen door. Rajinder Nara followed behind him.

"I have the cot set up," Michael said. "Jadu and Asha are both resting up in their room now. And guess what? Rajinder here is an engineer."

The dark-skinned man nodded to Dena. "I was hired to teach at the University of Pittsburgh. Instead I am a burden on you and your husband."

"Nonsense," said Michael. "Nobody is a burden here. We all pitch in and do what we can."

Unless we're told that we're not needed, thought Dalton.

* * *

Beaker and Jim Rutherford came back later that day with the bed of the Silverado filled with food and supplies taken from the houses down the street. They had also buried the Kellers and the Inghams in shallow graves. Hearing this, Dalton was rather glad that Beaker had rejected his offer of assistance. One day of grave digging had been more than enough for him.

In the evening Dena woke Asha and Jadu, and everyone gathered in the dining room for another meager dinner. Eight-year-old Jadu was wide-eyed and silent throughout the meal, and Dalton wondered if either Beaker or Jim had thought to stop at the Naras' house and get a few of the boy's toys. Dalton had not seen anything for Jadu to play with when the men brought in everything they had collected in Beaker's truck.

After sunset they all stayed up and talked for a while in the dining room, but it had become their custom to go to sleep shortly after it got dark. It was difficult to accomplish much by candlelight, and they needed to conserve what candles they had.

The exception was Beaker, who was going out on another run. Before he left, he nodded in the direction of the living room and said, "That couch is where I'm sleeping, so it had better be empty when I get back." After he left, Dena laid out a pillow and two folded blankets for him, something she had forgotten about the night before.

Dalton took Spencer out to the back yard one last time before going to bed. It was a cool night, and for the first time Dalton wondered what they would do that winter. So far they had been blessed with a lengthy Indian summer. Dalton did not think the small fireplace in the family room would provide much heat, but it would have to suffice. And that meant they would need to chop or gather firewood.

The house was quiet when he came inside. Enough moonlight came through the kitchen window, but the hallway and stairs were completely dark. Making his way alone through the house, with only Spencer at his side, Dalton tripped on the bottom stair.

The upstairs hall was almost as dark, but moonlight provided some illumination in the blue room when he entered. Spencer immediately began to bark at the silhouette of a man standing next to the bed.

"Quiet, Spence!" said Dalton. "It's just Jim, you know him."

Jim said, "You don't mind sharing the bed? Because I can sleep on the floor if you'll give me a blanket."

Dalton shook his head. "No, you don't have to do that. There's plenty of room for both of us." He pulled off his tee shirt, but left his jeans on as he climbed onto the bed.

Jim was less modest. The shirt and dark jeans he had been wearing for the past two days came off, and he tossed them onto the bureau. Wearing nothing but a pair of boxer shorts, he also got into bed and pulled the sheet up.

None of the people staying at Dena and Michael's house had bathed properly since the night the alien ships arrived, and Dalton was used to the constant odor of humanity. But nearly naked and in such close proximity, Jim had a pungent and decidedly musky smell that excited Dalton's senses. He forced himself to remember that the well-built young man next to him was little Jimmy Rutherford, the kid who Dena used to babysit back when they were in high school.

Spencer jumped up on the bed.

"Off, Spencer," said Dalton. The dog hopped to the floor. Jim made no suggestion that they let Spencer sleep with them. Dalton could hear Spencer look around for an area of the carpet that suited him. The dog then flopped down with a disappointed sigh.

Dalton realized he was not breathing. He inhaled deeply. He thought he could feel the heat emanating from Jim's body.

In the dark, Jim asked, "Are you sure you're okay with this?"

"Yeah, I'm fine." Dalton rolled over with his back to the former soldier and tried to lose himself in sleep.

CHAPTER FIFTEEN

Over the next few weeks the Andersons' suburban home began to resemble a rural homestead. Rajinder Nara supervised the installation of containers to collect rainwater, and soon every downspout at the Anderson, Beaker, Cooper and Martin homes emptied into a receptacle of some sort. They salvaged two axes, one from the Clarks' house and one from the Kellers', and Jim Rutherford began chopping down some of the smaller trees in the neighborhood. He stacked the wood in a growing pile just off the patio. Dena and Dalton began digging up the sod in the back yard to make an extensive garden. Beaker had found an assortment of vegetable seed packets on one of his nocturnal runs. They had no plans to plant the seeds until the following spring, but they wanted to have the garden ready.

The Coopers' charcoal grill stood on the Andersons' patio. Dena now often cooked warm meals on the grill rather than serving cold canned goods. She retained control of her kitchen, which extended to include control of the patio outside. Meal planning often required a certain amount of creativity to make the best use of their supplies, and Dena surprised herself with some of her own culinary inventions.

Rajinder and Asha went back to their home one afternoon and gathered some of Jadu's toys. They also retrieved more clothing and a few personal possessions, including a ceramic image of the goddess Lakshmi that Asha set out on a table in their room.

After the first hard autumn rain, when they finally had a decent supply of water, Asha took charge of the laundry. She heated water on the outside grill when Dena was not cooking on it, and afterwards hung the clothing out on a line stretched from the house to the closest oak tree at the back of the yard. Everyone was grateful for clean clothes, something they had always taken for granted before the alien ships came. Asha had to use the water sparingly, even with their new system for collecting it, and personal bathing was limited to sponge baths.

They converted the garage into an attached storehouse. Michael's BMW was pushed out to the driveway with Dalton's Civic to make room for the supplies that Beaker continued to bring in, and Dena's Avalon soon joined it. Food supplies filled the left half of the garage. Dena placed a dozen mousetraps in strategic locations between the cans and bottles and cartons. The right half of the garage held non-food items: bleach, gasoline, detergents, ammunition and candles, as well as some herbicides and pesticides that Beaker had found for the garden that did not yet exist. A plastic bowl filled with disposable lighters sat on a shelf next to the door.

Without any announcement or ceremony, Michael had become Beaker's lieutenant. There was no question that Beaker was in charge. Nobody wished to challenge this, but Beaker slept most of the day and was often uncommunicative even after he woke, so it was Michael who the others turned to for leadership.

Beaker began to come back with fewer supplies from his late night excursions. If a house had been abandoned, more than likely it had also been cleaned out by looters, and Beaker was not going to break into any occupied buildings. The others agreed with him on this. Do unto others, they concurred, even though each of them knew that others might not extend the same kindness unto them. For this reason a round-the-clock watch was established, although, of course, there were no functional clocks. On alternate days Dalton would stay up, armed with the shotgun, as late as he reasonably could. Then in the wee hours of the morning he would wake Dena, give her the shotgun and try to climb into bed in the blue room without waking Jim. Dena would be on watch through the morning until Michael felt he could take over until sunset.

The next day this pattern would repeat with Jim, Asha and Rajinder taking the shifts.

They chose the shotgun because Jim Rutherford and Beaker

were the only two among them who had any skill with firearms. If somebody needed to aim the shotgun, all he or she would have to do is point it generally in the right direction.

Although Jim and Dalton still shared a bed, because of the new schedule they no longer got into that bed at the same time, which, for Dalton at least, was less awkward.

Several times now Beaker had been gone for more than one night. He was traveling farther in his search for supplies, usually moving north or west. Michael had offered to go with him, an idea Dena did not like at all, but Beaker said he would only be in the way.

* * *

Dena was caught in the misty haze between consciousness and sleep when there was a knock on her bedroom door. Michael's arm was draped over her breasts and shoulder, but he pulled away from her and she could feel his body tense.

Then Jim Rutherford's voice came from the other side of the door. "It's me. Are either of you awake?"

Dena sat up and reached for her robe at the foot of the bed. "We're up now, Jimmy. What is it?"

The door opened. There was just enough light coming through the window to see that Jim had the shotgun, reminding Dena that he was on watch. Which meant she and Michael should have been getting a full night's sleep, but that did not seem to be happening.

Jim said, "It looks like those crazy people across the street are leaving. The Franklins. I thought you would want to know."

Dena threw back the sheet, heedless that she wore only panties and a bra. It was too dark for Jim to see much anyway. She pulled on her terrycloth robe. "We're coming, Jimmy."

Michael was also out of the bed. He was in pajama pants and did not bother to reach for anything else. He and Dena brushed past Jim and hurried down the dark hallway.

The front door was locked and Michael fumbled with it long enough for Jim to catch up with them. Once outside they could see somebody moving around in the Franklins' dark garage. They had not seen or heard anything from either of the Franklins since the night Izzy had marched into their dining room and accused Dalton of being an abomination. Dena felt bad about the estrangement. As rude and judgmental as Izzy Franklin could be, she was still a human being and had been a friend, or at least a close acquaintance, for as long as Dena and Michael had lived on Hugo Drive.

Dena, Michael and Jim stopped next to Michael's BMW, using it for cover. It was impossible to tell who was in the Franklins' garage. Izzy and Jerry never left the garage door up, not before the alien ships arrived and certainly not afterwards. Izzy had once commented to Dena that leaving one's garage door open was as slovenly as leaving the toilet seat up.

Michael caught Jim's eye and looked down at the shotgun. Jim understood. He aimed the double barrels at the garage across the street.

"Jerry, is that you?" called Michael.

'The person in the garage froze, and then they saw the dark shape of a man step closer to the entrance. Dena did not think it looked like Jerry Franklin. The figure in the garage doorway was not stout enough.

But it was Jerry's voice that said, "Yes, Michael, it's me." His voice sounded dry and harsh.

Jim lowered the shotgun and the three of them crossed the street. Even in the dark they could see how overgrown and weedy the Franklins' lawn had become.

The night was cool, but Jerry wore only a pair of walking shorts, house slippers and black socks. He had lost at least twenty pounds, and his naked chest and belly sagged around him like a deflated balloon. Even in the night Dena could see the dark shadows under his eyes. She wondered if he had been sick.

"Are you leaving?" she asked.

Jerry opened the back door to his Audi and the glow of the car's interior light filled the garage. The back seat was already piled with several suitcases. Jerry picked up a laundry basket stuffed with blankets and put it on top of the suitcases. "We're going to try to get down to Pittsburgh," he said.

Michael said, "I don't think that's a good idea, Jerry. Beaker tells us that things are worse in the city."

"It can't be any worse than here." Jerry slammed the door shut, causing the car light to turn off. The darkness fell over them like a weight. "We don't have any food left. Izzy and I haven't had anything to eat for days, and we ran out of water yesterday morning."

The door at the back of the garage opened and, although Dena could not make out any details, she knew the woman standing there was Izzy. Unlike her husband, Izzy Franklin actually looked bulkier. After a moment Dena realized it was because she was wearing a heavy winter coat. The garment was out of season and seemed a little strange, but in a couple of months it would be extremely practical.

Without speaking to them, Izzy made her way around the front of the Audi towards the passenger door.

"You don't understand," said Dena. "There have been riots and fires in the city...think about what happened over in Caldonia, and then multiply that to match Pittsburgh's population."

Michael nodded. "It's not safe out there, Jerry."

Izzy grasped the door handle. "And it's safe here?" she asked. "Is it safe here, where people who you thought were your friends will turn against you?"

Dena said, "Izzy, we didn't—"

"Is it safe where your neighbors will let you starve like rats?"

"You should have said something to—"

"Don't tell me what I should have done, Dena Anderson." Izzy opened the Audi's door then, and as the light came on again Dena could see the cold fury in the woman's eyes. The dark roots of Izzy's hair were even more pronounced now. "Don't lecture me, Dena, not when you're harboring sodomites and colored heathens, but you turn your back on God-fearing Christians."

Dena started to protest, but Michael grasped her arm and pulled her back next to him. He took a step backward, out of the garage, drawing Dena with him. Jim stepped back with them.

"Goodbye, Izzy," said Michael. His words were sharp and final.

Izzy got into the car and closed the door. Jerry stared at the Audi as if he was unsure of what to do. Then, slowly, he looked up at Michael and Dena and said, "She's my wife."

Dena nodded. "We know, Jerry. Be safe."

Jerry Franklin got in on the driver's side of the car. Dena, Michael and Jim stepped back to give the Audi plenty of room as it backed out of the garage and driveway. They watched the red taillights retreat down Hugo Drive, growing smaller and smaller until the car turned right onto Route 228.

Dena slipped her left arm around Michael's waist and her right arm around Jim's. "I guess we should get back to our sodomites and heathens." There was no amusement in her voice.

They walked back to the house together. Jim locked the front door and stayed downstairs, where he would remain on guard for the next few hours.

* * *

Dena was at her parents' house, in their front room, talking with her mother and father. Dalton was somewhere upstairs, Dena knew, and she was glad that her parents had patched things up with him. She even went so far as to say so.

"You know we couldn't stay angry with him," said Dena's mother.

"It's not Dalton's fault that he's a sodomite any more than it's his fault that he's colored."

"But he's not..." Dena wondered why her mother had used those words. She had never heard her mother say 'colored' before in reference to someone's race, nor refer to a homosexual as a 'sodomite'. She glanced over at the cat and kitten figurines on the fireplace mantle and noticed that the calico cat was missing.

Dena's father smiled. "He's not? That's great news. I knew no son of mine could be a queer."

"No, I mean Dalton's not colored. You know that, Dad."

The calico cat was at Dena's feet, but it was a real cat, not a figurine, rubbing against her ankles.

She was jerked out of her dream by an explosion that seemed to shake the whole house. Spencer was barking, and Dena could hear Jadu Nara screaming downstairs. Michael sat up next to her in the bed, looking around the room with an expression of surprise.

"What the hell was that?" asked Dena. The room was still dark, but it was the welcoming shadow of early dawn.

They met up with Dalton, Jim and Rajinder in the upstairs hall; each of the men was in a varied state of undress. Jim wore nothing more than his boxers, but he had his pistol with him. Dalton and Rajinder both wore jeans. Spencer raced down the stairs where they could still hear him barking frantically. Michael led the way as all five of them hurried after the dog.

Spencer was on the living room couch barking at the closed curtains. Eight-year-old Jadu cowered behind one of the end tables, screaming loudly. The pillow and two of the blankets that Beaker was using were strewn across the floor. Next to the couch stood Asha Nara, holding the shotgun in trembling hands. Asha stared at the front door, which now had a sizeable hole in it. Dena could hear voices outside.

Asha turned to them as they came into the room. "There is somebody outside!" she said. "Mr. Beaker is out there now. I am sorry about the door, I was so scared!"

Rajinder hurried to his wife and gently took the shotgun from her. Dalton told Spencer to hush even as he went to Jadu and tried to comfort the child. The dog released several more yelps, but then ceased its barking. With his pistol ready, Jim Rutherford opened the front door. Michael and Dena followed the young soldier.

Beaker stood on their front lawn wearing nothing but a frayed pair of white cotton briefs. He had his rifle, but had lowered the barrel. Jerry Franklin's dark green Audi was parked in the drive behind Dalton's Civic, and next to this stood Jerry and Izzy, wide-eyed and shaking. Jerry now wore a light jacket.

"What are you doing back here?" Dena asked sharply.

"It's just Izzy and Jerry," said Beaker. He turned to Dena as he pointed out the obvious.

An unintentional glance at Beaker's briefs answered any question Dena may have had as to whether his excessive size was proportionate all over. She forced herself to look up at his unshaven face. "They left last night for Pittsburgh," she said.

"But we didn't make it there," said Jerry.

Izzy nodded. She was shivering despite her heavy coat. "We only got to the exit down on the interstate where that super-market is. You know the one."

Dena did know the supermarket Izzy meant. She had shopped there occasionally when making a trip to or back from Pittsburgh. What she did not know was why that was relevant to anything. "You aren't welcome here," she said.

"No, you're not," agreed Michael.

Beaker stared at the Andersons. "People can't come back to Hugo Drive once they've left? Who came up with that rule?"

Michael said, "They can go back to their own home, I can't stop them from doing that. But they aren't welcome in our house or our yard."

Izzy doubled over, clutching her stomach as she choked on

deep, wet sobs.

Jerry said, "Please, Michael, you know she didn't mean what she said."

Dena said, "We know she meant it, and so do you." She shook her head. "I'm sorry, but I don't have the strength or patience to put up with her attitude anymore."

In answer to Beaker's confused expression, Michael said, "Izzy made some inappropriate comments about Dalton and the Naras last night."

"To say the least," added Dena. She stepped closer to Izzy. "Dalton is my brother, and Rajinder and Asha are our guests as well as our neighbors. That – and the fact that they are all decent human beings – should be reason enough for you to show them a little respect." Dena turned abruptly away from her. "Go on home, and don't come around looking for handouts from the sodomites and heathens who are staying here."

In a hoarse voice Jerry said, "We can't go home alone, Dena. Please, Michael, we just can't do it. You have to let us stay here at your place."

Dena whirled back around and stared at him with a look of disbelief. "Here? With the way Izzy feels about Rajinder and Asha? After what she called my brother?"

Jerry turned to Michael, who only said, "Don't look to me for support, Jerry. I agree with Dena. With everything that has happened, there isn't any place for your wife's prejudices in our home."

Izzy wiped tears away from her bloodshot eyes. "We have to stay here," she said, her voice weak.

"Why?" asked Dena. "Why would you even want to stay here under the same roof with Dalton and the Naras?"

"Because they're here!" screamed Izzy.

"Of course they're here," snapped Dena. She glanced back at the house, hoping Asha and Dalton could not hear everything that was being said. "They're our guests."

Jerry shook his head. "No, Izzy doesn't mean the Naras or your brother. She means the UFOs. The aliens are here now!"

CHAPTER SIXTEEN

Still in her winter coat, Izzy Franklin huddled next to her husband Jerry on the loveseat in the Andersons' family room. A single candle on the Chippendale table provided most of the light in the room. Beaker stood like the Colossus of Rhodes in front of the dark rectangle of the television screen. He still wore nothing but his cotton briefs. Michael and Jim Rutherford stood to either side of the much larger man; Michael in his pajama pants, and Jim in his boxers. They were listening as Jerry recounted his brief excursion that night. Dena came in with two glasses of water for the Franklins, and then sat in her terrycloth robe on the adjacent couch with Rajinder and Asha Nara.

"There wasn't anything left on the shelves in the super-market," Jerry was saying. "I told Izzy it would be a waste of time to stop there."

Beaker said. "Of course there wouldn't be anything. That store is right off the interstate. Anyway, supermarkets are the worst places to look for food now. You do better at abandoned houses."

Jerry took a drink of water and coughed. "There were a couple of dumpsters on the far side of the building, so I went to see if I could find anything inside them. That's when I heard Harry."

"Harry?" asked Michael.

Beaker looked sharply at Izzy. "Where were you all this time?"

"I was waiting in the car, obviously."

Jerry said, "Harry is the man I found by the dumpster. Harry Lawson. He didn't look too good. He was shaking, as if he was sick, and there were open sores on his arms and neck."

Dalton came into the family room with Jadu. The man and the boy each had a couple of small plastic action figures. Dalton sat on the floor next to the couch and beckoned for Jadu to join him.

The dog followed them in and tried to mouth one of the toys in Dalton's hand, but then found a place behind them to lie down.

"Sores?" asked Beaker. His attention suddenly focused on Jerry. He reached out and took Jerry's wrist, turning it and examining the skin on Jerry's palm and the back of his hand.

"It wasn't a disease," said Jerry, pulling his hand away. "Not any normal disease, anyway. I saw another sore open up on Harry's cheek while he was talking to me. It was like...it was like his skin was dissolving. He said that he was a volunteer at the no-kill animal shelter, wherever that is."

Dalton looked up. "I know where it's at. It's just down the road from that supermarket. I got Spencer from the shelter. It's one of the best in Pennsylvania. The volunteers there are very dedicated."

Jerry stared at him. "I'd say so. Harry told me that he and two other volunteers were still at the shelter taking care of the animals."

Michael looked skeptical. "People were staying at the animal shelter? What were they living on?"

"Oh no!" Dena leaned forward. "Don't tell me they were eating the dogs and cats."

Dalton shook his head. "They wouldn't do that."

"They were probably eating dog and cat food," said Beaker. "I don't know where they were getting water, but they could easily live on dog and cat kibble. And a place like that could have a lot of pet food in storage."

Rajinder looked around at the others. "Does it matter now what they were eating? I want to know about the aliens." He put his arm around Asha.

Beaker nodded and turned back to Jerry. "So you said this guy was sick."

"No, I said he was shaking like he was sick, but it wasn't from any illness." Jerry shook his head. "He was wounded. I think it's their wands."

Dena remembered the odd wand-like devices that the three televised aliens had been holding when they came out of the ship in St. Louis.

Jerry continued, saying, "Harry didn't even know the ship was there until the aliens broke into the shelter. The aliens took them by surprise."

"They were on the ground?" asked Beaker. "The aliens left the ship?"

"Yes, they came into the animal shelter. Harry said they had those wands, like we saw on television. One of the aliens saw Harry and his friend, I don't remember what he said her name was, but she was a woman. The alien pointed its wand at them and Harry dropped behind the front desk. He saw his friend – the woman – fall to the floor. Then three of the aliens walked past him and down the hall."

Dena asked, "Did they kill the woman?"

Jerry nodded. "Harry went to her, but she was already dead. He told me that he ran out of the building and then he saw the ship in the parking lot, just floating there, over the entire parking lot and part of the grounds around it. And so he ran." He looked from Beaker to Michael. "You have to believe me. I'm not making this up."

"Were they still in their spacesuits?" asked Beaker. "What did they look like?"

"I've told you everything, honestly." Jerry rubbed his hand across his face, as if he could somehow wipe away the memory of that night. "Harry said the alien missed him when it used its wand, but I don't think it did. He just didn't take a direct hit. Like I said, another sore opened on Harry's cheek while he was talking to me. I watched it open up!" He took another drink of water. "Then a few minutes later he began to scream and jerk around, and the next thing I knew, he was dead."

Michael asked, "Did something shoot out of the wand? Did it make any kind of noise?"

"No." Jerry shook his head. "At least, Harry didn't say so, and I think he would have. All he said was that the alien pointed the wand."

"So they're killing us with magic wands," said Dena. She shrugged. "I'm sorry, but how am I supposed to believe something like this? It sounds more like a fairy tale."

Dalton put down the action figure he had been entertaining Jadu with. "Arthur C. Clarke said that an advanced technology is indistinguishable from magic."

Jim Rutherford frowned. "Advanced technology? So we're like cavemen to the aliens?"

"Maybe worse," said Beaker. "They might think no more of us than we do of insects. Look at how they acted at the animal shelter, if we believe Jerry's story. The fuckers didn't stop to see if the man behind the desk was dead. They just swatted at a couple of flies and went on their way."

Rajinder enfolded Asha completely in his arms then and held her close.

Jim Rutherford looked up at Beaker and quietly said, "Sir, we don't have a chance against an enemy like this."

Beaker nodded. "But you knew that when they shut down Oakdale. The United States Army just doesn't close up shop and go home."

"But Oakdale is just a support—" Jim shook his head and stared at his feet. "No sir, the Army doesn't do that."

Izzy Franklin pushed her bony fingers into the dark roots of her hair. "We're going to die," she said. "I know we're all going to die!"

"And we've always known that, too," said Beaker. "Even before the alien ships came. We're all mortal. The question has never been whether we're going to die, but when and how. The aliens may kill us tomorrow, but today, right now, we need to do something about that front door."

Asha said, "I am sorry about that. I did not mean to ruin the door."

Beaker shrugged off the apology. "There are plenty of extra doors here on Hugo Drive. Rajinder needs to take watch. Michael and Jim can help me take the door off my house and bring it over here."

Dalton said, "I can help."

"You're watching the kid," said Beaker, nodding to Jadu. "Anyway, we don't need a whole committee to take a door off its hinges."

Dena stood and tightened her robe's matching terrycloth belt around her waist. "Dalton, you and Asha can help me get breakfast."

Beaker's matter-of-fact attitude renewed their confidence. The aliens would either come or not, and there was nothing to be done about that. The best they could do was live in the present. In truth, it had always been the best they could do; only now they were acutely aware of it. Beaker, Michael and Jim Rutherford dressed and went over to Beaker's house to get his front door. Since those three would be alert at the front of the house, Rajinder took up the shotgun and patrolled the back yard. Dena, Dalton and Asha mixed water with powdered milk to pour over bowls of Cap'n Crunch, leaving Jadu to entertain himself with his toys in the family room. The dog Spencer, of course, followed Dalton into the kitchen and stayed mostly by his side, eagerly accepting a few pieces of cereal when Dena offered them to him.

By their actions, they all knew that they shared an unspoken conviction. They might not have much longer to live, but they were going to make the most of each moment.

Only two people were left out of this. Jerry and Izzy Franklin remained sitting quietly on the family room loveseat, saying nothing, staring at the television as if they could scry some meaning in the dark reflections across its flat, blank screen. They remained there when Dena came in and handed each a bowl of cereal and a spoon.

From the kitchen Asha called to Jadu, who put down his toys and went in to have his breakfast. By then the men had come back with Beaker's door, and they joined the others around the small kitchen island. It had become their habit to have breakfast there, with most of them standing, instead of in the dining room where they usually ate dinner.

Beaker glanced in the direction of the family room. "We need to figure out where Jerry and Izzy are going to sleep," he said, scooping a spoonful of cereal into his mouth. A trickle of milk dribbled into the stubble on his chin. "That's your job today, Dena."

Michael said, "Maybe we can rearrange things in the family room."

"And make them sleep on the floor?" asked Dena. She tried to keep a tone of disapproval in her voice, but a part of her was not entirely opposed to the idea. She was still angry with Izzy.

Swallowing a mouthful of cereal, Michael said, "There's a sofa in there, and Izzy is small enough to make do with the loveseat."

Beaker shook his head. "Beds are as plentiful as doors. Just clear a space, Dena. Jim and I can take my bed apart and bring it over here after we get the door up. Nobody has to sleep on a sofa."

Dalton stirred at his cereal. "You don't either, Beaker."

"What?"

"You don't have to sleep on the living room couch." Dalton pointed to Jim Rutherford with his spoon. "One of us is on watch most of the night. You could share the bed with us, if Jim doesn't mind."

"The couch is fine," said Beaker.

Dalton said, "It would work out okay. Jim and I would have to take turns on the couch after our shifts are over, but it would only be every other night for us, instead of—"

"It's not going to happen. I said the couch is fine for me."

Beaker put his half finished bowl of cereal down on the island and looked at Michael. "I'm going to get the door up. Go ahead and finish your breakfast."

The atmosphere in the kitchen thickened with awkward tension as Beaker strode out. Dalton's cheeks were bright red. Asha had taken a renewed interest in her bowl of Cap'n Crunch. Only Jadu seemed unaffected by the exchange between Beaker and Dalton. He hummed a tuneless, childish melody while trying to submerge a piece of cereal with the back of his spoon.

Staring at his own bowl of cereal, Jim Rutherford said, "Some guys have a problem..." His voice trailed off. Then he looked at Dalton. "Don't let him get to you."

"I thought he'd be okay with it," said Dalton. He stood and went to the back door. "Come on, Spencer, let's go out."

Outside, Rajinder was coming across the lawn. He smiled when he saw Dalton come from the kitchen with Spencer, and was surprised when the smile went unacknowledged. Spencer ran across the yard and lifted his leg on one of the oaks. Ignoring Rajinder, Dalton stood on the patio and watched his dog, his arms folded defensively around his chest.

Jim Rutherford came out of the house and caught Rajinder's eye. He hooked his thumb towards the back door. Catching the message, Rajinder nodded almost imperceptibly, walked past Dalton and went inside.

Spencer went to each of the trees at the back of the lot, inspecting the bark to see if any other dogs had somehow entered the fenced yard and left a urine marker while he wasn't looking. Jim went over to Dalton and stood next to him.

"You okay?"

Dalton shrugged. "It's not like I was trying to hook up with him."

"Nobody thinks that," said Jim.

"Beaker obviously does."

"Beaker's an ass. The rest of us know you wouldn't try

anything with him."

Dalton relaxed a little. "You're putting a lot of faith in me, aren't you? I mean, I *am* gay, and Beaker could be a good-looking man if he cleaned up a little."

"Maybe so, but you aren't stupid." Jim shrugged. "Face it, Dalton, even if you wanted Beaker, it would be suicidal to make a pass at him. He's built like a bull. Sort of smells like one, too, but then so do the rest of us."

Both of the men laughed.

Spencer ran up to them and barked playfully. Stooping down, Dalton rubbed the dog's withers. "You're right," he said. "I could never force that man to do anything he doesn't want to do. So why would Beaker be afraid to sleep in the same bed with me?"

Jim shrugged his shoulders and said, "Guys like that put on a show of being tough to impress other people."

"Except with Beaker I don't think it's just a show," said Dalton.

"Yeah." Jim grinned. He sat on the patio next to Dalton and both of them stroked Spencer's shoulders and ribcage. "Beaker scared the hell out of me when he shot those men who broke in."

Dalton nodded. "I'm surprised Dena let him move in here. I know he makes her as nervous as he makes me."

Jim asked, "If you were Dena, would you have told him no?" He pursed his lips and looked out over the back lawn. "Dalton…I want you to know…if anyone says they think you were trying to hook up with Beaker, tell them to talk to me. I'll set them straight."

"Thanks, Jim."

Dalton noticed that Spencer's attention was focused on the house behind them. He turned to see Beaker standing in the open kitchen doorway. Then Jim looked around and scrambled to his feet.

Beaker looked pointedly at the soldier. "Were you going to help me take the bed apart or not?"

"Yes sir." Jim hurried across the patio and followed Beaker

into the house.

Alone on the patio with Spencer, Dalton continued to pet the dog. Once again Beaker had not acknowledged him in any way. Dalton was getting used to the rebuffs, but he could not help but wonder how much Beaker had heard.

He also wondered which he was more afraid of, the aliens or the burly man from next door.

CHAPTER SEVENTEEN

It was a warm autumn that year. They were still enjoying an Indian summer and had not yet needed to use the wood Jim was cutting to heat the family room. Where the Franklins would sleep after winter's cold set in had yet to be decided. Dena was sure the communal living arrangements would need to be adjusted, but she did not yet know how. It would depend, in part, on how well their small fireplace in the family room could provide heat without the assistance of an electric furnace. Beaker had liberated a dozen sleeping bags from a sporting goods store over in Cranberry Township, and Dena thought they could use the bedrooms upstairs throughout the winter if everyone made use of the sleeping bags.

Beaker was often gone for two or three days in a row, and the rewards of his excursions were diminishing. That morning Dena had found two boxes of macaroni noodles, a jar of olives and three bottles of ketchup on the kitchen island. It was Beaker's habit to leave everything in the kitchen to be inventoried before it was stored in the garage. This was the most discouraging cache Dena had seen.

Rather than store the bottles of ketchup, Dena kept them in the kitchen. That afternoon Dalton and Izzy joined her on the patio and helped her transform the ketchup into something vaguely reminiscent of tomato soup. The soup was watery and had a peculiar flavor, but it would fill their stomachs and, according to the label, provide them with some Vitamin A and carbohydrates. It was Asha's day to keep watch. Her shift with the shotgun was over, but it meant she did not have kitchen duty. Instead she was reading one of Dena's novels to her son Jadu up in the guestroom that her family was using. There were no children's books anywhere in the house.

On the patio, Dena and Dalton tasted the pale soup repeatedly, adding a dash of salt or a pinch of dried basil. They had an assortment of spices in containers on a card table that Dena had set up next to the grill. Izzy watched and made suggestions. She had a head cold and claimed that she could not taste anything. Any disdain she had for Dalton or for Rajinder and his family had been put aside, or at least was now well hidden.

Spencer was curled up in the corner next to the kitchen step. He was so quiet that he could have been sleeping, but his eyes followed Dalton's every move.

Izzy dabbed at her nose with a small rumpled handkerchief that she had found somewhere. "It's too bad we don't have any crackers to go with it," she said.

Dalton tasted the ersatz soup. "I don't think crackers could salvage this."

Dena laughed and said, "It's not that bad."

"It is that bad. In fact, it's worse."

Izzy said, "I guess it's a good thing I can't taste anything right now." She looked at Dalton, her dark eyebrows furrowing into a frown. "You need to ask Beaker to keep an eye out for more canned soup. Even cold, it has to be better than watered down ketchup."

Dalton turned away from her and picked up a plastic container of dried oregano, pretending to read the label.

"Did you hear me?" asked Izzy sharply.

Dena stirred the soup. "I'm sure Beaker would have brought more soup back if he'd found any. It's not like he's picking and choosing, Izzy. He takes everything he can get, whatever that turns out to be, which is why Mama Anderson's Homemade Tomato Soup is mostly ketchup."

Dalton put down the oregano and began to examine the container of tarragon.

After a moment, Dena said, "He's rude to everyone, Dalton."

Izzy looked up. "Who?"

Dalton put down the herb container. "Not the way he is with me."

"You mean Beaker?" asked Izzy. "That's because you're—" She caught the look in Dena's eyes and wisely bit off the end of her sentence. "I think he's had a very hard life."

Dena shook her head. "Even if he has, that's not an excuse for his behavior." She set her spoon on the card table next to the herbs. "He's decent enough one minute, and then crawls back into his shell the next. And he is openly mean to Dalton."

"But we need him," said Izzy.

"I know." Dena sat down in one of the patio chairs. "He goes out almost every night, risking his own life to keep us in food and necessities. He even may have saved my life. He works as hard as any of us, and asks less in return. Believe me, I'm aware of everything he has done for us."

Dalton muttered, "Yeah, Beaker's a real saint."

"He is, in his own way," said Dena. "I just wish he'd act nicer. I know his size shouldn't matter, but he's too damn *big* to be so mean. Izzy, what do you really know about him?"

Izzy Franklin sat in another chair and thought for a minute. "Well, he's widowed, of course."

"Everyone knows that."

"He must have money." Izzy nodded, completely in agreement with herself. "Yes, I'm sure he has money, because he doesn't work at a regular job."

Dena shook her head. "That doesn't mean anything. He could be a writer, or maybe some kind of consultant. There are a number of occupations that would allow him to work out of his home."

"I don't think so," said Izzy. "I mean, I think I would have noticed if Mr. Beaker had been working. He used to watch a lot of television, before that night, and he often spent his afternoons at the Caldonia Library."

"Doing research, maybe."

Izzy shook her head. "Not unless he was researching contemporary fiction. That's almost the only thing he checked out."

Dena asked, "And just how do you know that?"

"I asked the librarian. The short woman, Debbie Whatever-Her-Name-Was."

"Was he in the military? Maybe he suffers from post traumatic stress."

"No," said Izzy. "He doesn't have any service record."

"Did the librarian know that, too?"

"Of course not!" Izzy laughed. "I asked him once. Mr. Beaker and I did talk now and then. He has never been very outgoing, but you know I've always tried to understand the needs of everyone in the neighborhood."

It was true that Izzy Franklin had always been the nosiest busybody on Hugo Drive, always eager to sniff out a closeted skeleton.

Dena glanced at her brother, her own skeleton, now out of her closet and adding another sprinkle of pepper to the soup. She stretched out in the iron patio chair, feeling her muscles tighten and release. "Well, whatever Beaker's problem is, he needs to stop acting like a jerk around Dalton. I'm going to say something to him."

"No!" Dalton wheeled around, sprinkling soup from the end of the spoon across the patio.

"Somebody needs to."

"No, nobody needs to say anything to him." He shook his head emphatically. "I don't need you to defend me, Dena. I've gotten by just fine for years now without your help, and I don't need it now."

Spencer was suddenly on his feet, barking in the staccato way he did when excited. At first Dalton thought it was because they were arguing. "It's okay, Spence."

The barking did not stop or even pause.

The kitchen door flew open and Rajinder Nara came out with the shotgun. He looked around at them and asked, "Are you all right?"

"Listen!" said Dena.

In the distance, to the west, they heard the barking of dogs. The sound was faint at first, but it was clear that this was what had caught Spencer's attention. He ran to the fence, adding his voice to a harsh symphony that was growing in volume.

Jim Rutherford came out on the patio. Then all of them followed Dalton's dog over to the fence. It was built of solid cedar planks, but was only five feet high, and they were not exceptionally short people – although Izzy had to stand on her toes to see clearly.

The land beyond the Andersons' lot dipped down into a gulch, and running towards them across the gulch were dozens of dogs. Pit bulls and terriers ran alongside hounds and mixed-breed dogs, long and short coats, curly haired and wire haired, all of them barking and baying as they raced across the land. They ran up the gulch and across the Coopers' overgrown back lawn and patio. A few dogs stopped on the patio, sniffing at the cement, perhaps catching a lingering scent from years of Don Cooper's barbeques. These few were bowled over, yelping in protest, by their companions coming up behind them.

The massive pack poured over the patio and around the Coopers' house, disappearing from view as they ran to the street. The barking continued, but quickly began to fade.

Spencer continued to bark, warning off the intruders who had gone on their way. Dalton knelt next to the dog and tried to calm him.

Dena asked nobody in particular, "Where did they all come from?"

"Maybe the animal shelter," suggested Jim. "The Franklins don't know what happened down there. If the dogs at the shelter got loose, would they come this far north?" He looked at Izzy, but she only shrugged.

Dalton said, "They could have come from anywhere, or every-where. People often dump their dogs if they become inconvenient. There's nothing new about that."

Rajinder nodded solemnly and said, "A dog would indeed be inconvenient in these times." Although he did not mean anything by it, he glanced at Spencer for just an instant.

Putting his arms around the dog, Dalton said, "We aren't dumping Spence off somewhere. If he goes, then I go, too."

Dena shook her head. "Nobody is getting rid of Spencer. Don't worry about that. We have plenty of other things to worry about, but that's one item not on the list."

* * *

The subject of the feral dogs came up during dinner that evening. Despite Dalton's concern, none of the others even hinted that Spencer might need to go. Jim Rutherford even went so far as to point out that it had been Dalton's dog that first sensed the feral pack. There seemed to be a general agreement that Spencer was a useful member of their extended household.

Jim said, "He's not a bad watchdog. Dena and I should have reacted sooner when Spencer tried to alert us about those burglars, but now we know better."

Michael swallowed a spoonful of his faux tomato soup and tried not to grimace at its taste. "We'll need to be aware of wild dogs, though. That's going to be a problem. And cats, too. We haven't seen many yet, but you can be sure there are a lot of cats fending for themselves now."

Izzy frowned. "The Kellers had a cat."

Michael looked across the table at her. "That's one we won't see around the neighborhood anymore," he said grimly. He did not need to elaborate. The Kellers' tabby had met with the same fate as Charlotte Keller and Ted and Dolly Ingham.

"How can cats possibly be a danger?" asked Dena.

"These animals are going to be hungry, and dogs and cats aren't wary of humans the way wild animals are. They're going to want food, and we have food."

Rajinder said, "And there is rabies."

"That's right," said Michael, nodding. "The animals aren't getting veterinary care. We're going to see a lot of disease. I don't think there are many diseases we can get from dogs and cats, but rabies will almost surely become a problem."

"Exactly, sir," said Jim. "That's why we need our own dog to let us know when other animals come around."

After dinner Beaker left the house earlier than usual. Dena asked if he thought he would be back that night, but his response was an unintelligible grunt. Asha Nara cleared away the dinner dishes. Rajinder handed the shotgun over to Dalton, who would be on watch that night, and people began to wander off to their beds: Jerry and Izzy Franklin downstairs in the family room, the Nara family in the guestroom, Michael and Dena in the master bedroom.

Dalton caught up with Jim Rutherford as the former soldier was starting up the stairs.

"It was nice of you to put in a good word for Spencer at dinner tonight," he said. "It would kill me if I had to give up Spence. I know it sounds nuts, but he's like family to me."

Jim smiled. "It doesn't sound nuts. It sounds like you have a really great dog." He went up the stairs and made his way through the dark hallway to the blue room.

Closing the bedroom door, Jim pulled off his shirt and shorts and kicked off his shoes. He knew how much the dog meant to Dalton Holt, and at the dinner table he had wanted to squelch any proposal to get rid of Spencer. Jim had thought Beaker might make that proposal – but from Beaker it would have come as more of an ultimatum.

Stripped down to his boxers, Jim climbed into bed. He would be asleep long before Dalton came upstairs and joined him in the wee hours of the morning. So far Dalton had not once tried to make a pass at him even though they were sharing the same bed.

Although Jim was not at all attracted to Dena's brother, he did not think he would be upset if Dalton were to hit on him, and he wondered if he would have the same restraint sharing the bed with an attractive young woman.

* * *

Jim woke the next morning to the sound of Dalton snoring loudly next to him. Spencer was curled on the floor, but sat up as soon as Jim threw his legs over the side of the bed.

"Need to go out?" he asked the dog. He pulled on his clothes and went out to the hallway, motioning for Spencer to follow him.

Asha and Jerry were talking in the kitchen when Jim and Spencer came downstairs. Asha was soaking dried pinto beans in a large bowl of water while telling Jerry Franklin how she had met Rajinder. Jim nodded to them, but continued on to the kitchen door to let Spencer out to the back yard.

Dena was walking slowly across the yard, most of it now bare soil, with Jadu at her side. The boy's little brown fist clutched firmly to Dena's right hand; in her left hand she held the shotgun. Spencer ran across the dirt, circled them twice, and then went to urinate on the oak trees. The cotton clothesline held a row of jeans, shirts, Asha's emerald green saree and an assortment of underwear.

Jim walked across the patio and cocked his head to one side. "You did laundry this morning? I thought that was Asha's job."

"Izzy did it," said Dena. "She told me she couldn't sleep. She was up while Dalton was still on watch."

"Jerry's in the kitchen with Asha."

Dena nodded. "I know."

"I guess the Franklins have moved on from their racism."

"Jerry, maybe. But I don't think it's ever been as much of an issue for him." Dena looked down at Jadu and squeezed his hand. "I can tell that Izzy still has a problem with the Naras staying here."

Beaker had not come home that night. His blankets were still neatly folded on the living room couch. There was some speculation as to when he might return, but his absence did not interrupt the day's routines. Around noon Michael took the shotgun from Dena and began his shift. Relieved from that duty, Dena helped Asha heat water on the grill for washing a second load of laundry. Jim and Dalton spent the afternoon cutting firewood from trees in the Grahams' back yard. Jim did most of the chopping, while Dalton stacked the wood in the wheelbarrow they had salvaged from the Clarks' garage.

They all gathered around the dining room table that night and ate by candlelight. Jerry Franklin commented on how sunset was coming earlier, and Rajinder said he hoped the winter would not be too cold.

After dinner Michael handed the shotgun over to Jim. He and Dena then went upstairs to their bedroom. Soon Rajinder and Asha took Jadu upstairs, and the Franklins went to their bed in the family room.

Dalton took Spencer out to the back yard and, with nothing better to do, Jim followed with the shotgun. It would be another long night for Jim, trying to stay awake and alert, making the occasional trip from the back yard through the house to the living room. For hours he would be watching for an intruder or threat, but mostly fighting off boredom.

Spencer was making his rounds to the trees while Dalton watched from the patio. Although the sky was clear enough, the moon was little more than a crescent and the back yard was shrouded under night's dark veil. Jim sat down on one of the patio chairs and laid the shotgun on the wrought iron table. Dalton joined him, taking another chair, and the two men talked late into the night, with Spencer lying between them on the patio.

Like Michael, Jim Rutherford was very much aware of the

physical resemblance between Dalton Holt and his sister. They could have been identical twins were it not for their difference in gender. Dalton had Dena's eyes and lips and cheek bones. In the dark it was easy for Jim to look across the table and see Dena sitting there.

"Huh?" Jim sat upright when he realize Dalton was speaking to him.

"I said I'm going up to bed." Dalton grinned. "You aren't falling asleep out here, are you?"

"No." Jim shook his head. "No, I'm good."

Dalton took Spencer into the house. Jim could hear them as they made their way through the kitchen and upstairs.

Jim Rutherford had never thought of himself as bisexual, but it had been more than six months since he had been with a woman. There were not many prospects for a single, hetero-sexual man on Hugo Drive, and Jim was beginning to realize that this might never change. Beaker did not have to describe what was going on in the outside world; what Beaker did not say spoke volumes. The man no longer mentioned other groups, like the people who once gathered at the church in Wexford.

Jim looked up at the stars and wondered how many survivors were still out there, roaming the countryside, searching for suste-nance or medicine or shelter.

"All the Martians had to do was shut down the power," he said quietly. With no phones, no lights, no computers or tablets, no reality television or Facebook or email, humankind had ripped itself to shreds.

Jim grabbed the shotgun when he heard a vehicle coming up Hugo Drive, but relaxed a moment later as he recognized the sound of the Silverado's engine. He stood and went into the house. Despite the dark, Jim could now maneuver through the Andersons' house with ease. It was a skill he had developed from night after night of keeping watch. He heard the Silverado pull up and park in front of the house as he walked into the living room.

Unlocking the front door, Jim went out to see if Beaker needed any help carrying things in. The large man got out of the truck, closed the door and then walked around to the passenger side. That was unusual. Beaker usually threw everything into the bed of the truck. But then Jim saw that Beaker had another person with him. It was a small person, not really a child, but smaller even than Izzy Franklin, who was the shortest adult in the house.

In a whisper, Jim called out, "Hey, Beaker." Beaker nodded, but said nothing.

Jim walked across the front lawn towards them. As he came closer, he saw that this new person was a very young woman, a teenager at least a few years younger than himself. She was filthy and nervous, but Jim thought she was the most beautiful girl he had ever seen.

CHAPTER EIGHTEEN

Beaker had found Emma Bouchard hiding in the basement of a farmhouse outside of Armandale. The girl had been living there for weeks and did not know where the original residents were. Like Dalton Holt, the Franklins and the Nara family, many people in western Pennsylvania had left their homes after the arrival of the aliens to congregate with others for their mutual support and protection. Beaker thought the owners of the farmhouse might have done this. In any event, there were no signs of violence and the only dead body on the property was that of Emma's boyfriend, Cody Jennings, in a bedroom on the second floor.

"I thought he was dead, but I wasn't sure," said Emma. She took another bite of apple pie filling that Dena had poured out of a can for her.

Dena and Izzy had rallied around Emma, feeding the half-starved girl the most comforting foods they could find in the garage. Jim Rutherford was just as solicitous. He had not left Emma's side since she arrived in the early hours of morning. Asha was on watch in the back yard where her son Jadu was playing with Dalton's dog, and Beaker had fallen asleep in the living room.

The other men wanted to question Emma immediately, but Jim defended her like a mother hen. Now, however, it seemed that the girl wanted to talk.

"Cody wouldn't eat anything," she said. "He'd been sick, you see. I think he was sick when we moved into that house. He didn't want me to know, but I could tell something was wrong."

Dena nodded sympathetically and glanced briefly at Michael. Turning back to the girl, she asked, "Emma, honey, where does your grandmother live?" She had told Emma that her family was gone.

"Silver Springs."

"In Maryland?" Of course in Maryland, Dena chided herself. What other Silver Springs was there?

Emma asked, "Did they say when they're coming back?"

"I'm sure it will be soon." Dena frowned and shook her head. "No, you're old enough to know the truth, and the truth is that we have no idea when your parents will be coming back. We don't know if they'll be back at all."

Fresh tears glistened in Emma's eyes. "I shouldn't have left them! All of this is my fault. If I hadn't left, Cody would still be alive and I'd be with my family." She choked on a bit of apple and began to cough.

When the coughing subsided, Michael said, "You have us, Emma, and we aren't going anywhere."

She nodded and wiped at her eyes. Jim, was sitting next to Emma in his camouflage fatigue pants. He watched her carefully as if he were afraid she would shatter.

Emma said, "I heard Mom say that we might go to Mema's if the power and phones didn't come back on. I didn't want to lose Cody. We are...we were...in love."

Jim reached out and gently rubbed her back. "It's okay, you don't have to talk about it."

"But I want to," said Emma. She looked around at them. "I need to."

Dena said, "Maybe it would be easier if you were to start at the beginning. You say that you were in love with Cody. Where did the two of you plan to go?"

* * *

Emma Bouchard had no plans at all when she got into Cody's beat-up Dodge Neon, and neither did he. They knew that the Jennings family was packing to take an extended vacation at Cody's uncle's house in Tennessee, and Emma had heard her own parents talking about Maryland. Rather than be parted, they eloped, although there was no happy ending at the other end of their rainbow, nor would there ever be.

Their dreams of a future together soon proved to be a nightmare. Cody drove up to Oil City where one of his internet friends – before the aliens came – had told him he could find work at a bottling plant. But without power the bottling plant was closed, and by the time Cody and Emma arrived money was rapidly becoming a meaningless abstraction anyway. There were rumors of the aliens attacking outlying areas around the town. The rumors were false, but no less effective at inciting panic. Retail outlets selling vital necessities – grocery stores, pharmacies, hardware stores – had been raided and stripped of their wares.

And of course Cody had no way to contact his internet friend in Oil City. They had never met in person. Cody did not know the other boy's address or even his real name.

They drove around western Pennsylvania, sleeping in the Neon and begging for food and water. A few people helped them, but usually they were ignored and several times they found themselves at the wrong end of a gun.

One afternoon they came across two men who had just shot a deer. The men refused to let them have any of the venison, but they were welcome to the guts. The men even started a little campfire for them to cook it over. Cody sharpened a stick with his pocket knife and used that to hold pieces of liver over the flames. It was the first animal protein that Emma had eaten in days.

When they found the abandoned farmhouse it was Cody who suggested they take up residence until the owners returned. That was when Emma first suspected something was wrong. Before that, they had knocked on the doors to other houses and received no answer, and Cody had never suggested they break in, much less move in.

This house still had food in a basement pantry. Mason jars of pickles, tomatoes and green beans stood on the shelves in neat rows. There were also several cases of Diet Pepsi, which they had to drink warm, but it was palatable enough. Emma found a little stream and collected water in a bucket. For several days they lived as husband and wife in a youthful fantasy where time seemed to have no meaning. But soon Cody could no longer ignore or conceal his discomfort. He stayed in bed, waiting for the sickness to pass, and Emma waited with him.

She waited until he no longer answered when she spoke to him. Until he no longer stirred, and his fingers only entwined with hers when she held them in place. And still she waited.

Emma waited until the night she heard the truck outside and looked through the window to see that the big, unshaven man who lived up the street had come looking for her. She ran down to the basement then, feeling guilty about leaving Cody alone upstairs, but certain that her parents had sent Mr. Beaker to find her. He would take her back with him to her parents' house on Hugo Drive and she would never see Cody again.

It was only then that Emma's heart broke, her mind opened and she fully accepted that Cody Jennings was dead.

That was how Beaker found her in the basement, crying for a boy and a dream, both gone forever. He wrapped a blanket around her and carried her out to the truck. She cried throughout the long drive back to Caldonia. Beaker said nothing at all until he had parked the Silverado in front of the Anderson's house and come around to open her door. Even then he only had two words for her. "We're here."

* * *

With a sympathetic nod, Dena said, "Beaker is not very good at expressing his feelings."

"Do you want to wash up?" asked Izzy. "We have a grill on the patio that we use for heating water."

Jim said, "I'll get a fire started." When none of the others objected, he stood and went to the garage to get one of the disposable lighters.

Michael cupped Emma's chin with his hand and lifted her face until she was looking into his eyes. "You aren't responsible for anything that has happened. I want you to understand that. Cody is dead, but it isn't because of something you did. Your family has gone to Maryland, but they would have gone anyway."

"Okay." Emma's voice sounded weak and tired.

Releasing her chin, Michael said, "We don't have any time for people to feel sorry for themselves or to take on the blame for things that aren't under their control."

After water was heated, Izzy Franklin helped Emma get cleaned up. She gave the girl one of her blouses and a pair of Capri pants to wear. The two women were close enough in size that the clothes fit fairly well. Bathed and dressed, Emma stretched out on the sofa in the family room, now pushed against the wall to make space for the Franklins' bed. She was soon sleeping fitfully.

Later that day Dena caught Michael alone in their bedroom where he was putting away some of their freshly washed clothing that Asha had taken off the line outdoors.

"Where is she going to sleep, Michael?"

"Emma?" He closed a bureau drawer. "In the family room, I guess, if Izzy and Jerry don't mind. She should be fine on the couch."

"For now, maybe, but she's a young woman. She needs her own room."

"And I need a sirloin steak, but that's not happening either." He went to his wife and kissed her on the forehead. "We've all had to make a lot of sacrifices, and Emma is no different. Did you see the way Jim was looking at her?"

"That's another reason she needs her own room. So do Jimmy

and Dalton. We have these people sharing beds and rooms, and eventually there's going to be a problem. The guys will just have to deal with their urges, and with each other, but Emma's very young. And she just lost somebody who was very important to her. She doesn't need Jimmy Rutherford's attention right now."

"Or maybe it's the medicine she really does need," said Michael.

"He's thinking with his penis."

"Maybe he is." Michael shrugged. "But considering Emma's current list of potential suitors, Jim's penis may be pointing him in the right direction."

"Michael!" She couldn't help laughing.

"Come on, Dena, it's not like Jim's done anything wrong. He obviously likes Emma, and she could do a lot worse."

Izzy Franklin woke Emma that evening in time for dinner. Beaker was already awake and sitting at the dining table. The table had been built to accommodate six people, but now nearly twice that many were trying to gather around it. Dena had made an interesting if indefinable meal of warmed-up canned refried beans seasoned with taco sauce and crushed coriander. To celebrate Emma's first day with them, Michael brought in a bottle of expensive wine from the garage to accompany the beans. Elbows jostled as six men, four women and the Naras' little boy ate by the faint, flickering light of the single taper burning in the center of the table.

Michael was outlining an idea he had for fencing off the Coopers' back yard and expanding their future garden when they saw random flashing lights behind the closed dining room curtain. Leaving the table, Michael went to the window and pulled the curtain aside.

They all shouted as a flash of light, no longer filtered by the curtain, burned against their retinas. Spencer began to bark. Michael dropped the curtain back. Everyone blinked repeatedly while their eyes slowly readjusted to the dark room. There was another flash behind the curtain, followed by two more, and then the lights stopped.

"Did something explode?" asked Jerry.

Jim said, "I don't think so, sir. I didn't hear anything like an explosion."

Michael cautiously drew the curtain aside again, just a crack, while shielding his eyes with his other hand. "Whatever it was, it came from the south."

Izzy grasped Jerry's hand and squeezed it tightly. "It's the aliens!"

"You don't know that," said Michael. Then he shrugged with an almost helpless gesture. "But it probably is."

Izzy stood, pulling on her husband's arm. "We have to go, Jerry. We have to go now!"

"Go where?" Jerry asked her. He stood and held her by the wrist. "There isn't any place to go, Izzy."

"We're just going to sit here?"

Dena stood and went to her. "Yes, that's exactly what we're going to do. We know that we can't fight these things, so we are going to stay right here and be here for each other. That's the best we can do."

"The lights might not be anything to worry about," said Michael.

Asha picked up Jadu. "Do you really think that?"

"No, but I can hope. Beaker, do you have any idea what…" Michael looked around the room. "Where's Beaker?"

They heard the engine of the Silverado start up and then fade into the distance.

CHAPTER NINETEEN

Dalton Holt went to the living room and peered through the front window again. The night sky was overcast; with no starlight or moonlight he could not even see the spirea by the porch. In his mind Dalton could envision the juniper bushes in the center of the cul de sac and, beyond those, the other houses, now empty. But his imagination was alive that night, and in the vision he also saw men in spacesuits lurking between the houses and behind every bush.

There had been something terrible about the flashing lights they had seen earlier that evening. Something violent. Something that forced Dalton to remember why he was patrolling his sister's home with a shotgun instead of sleeping peacefully in his Butler apartment with Spencer curled up by his side.

It was Spencer's presence that kept Dalton relatively calm. The dog looked up at him curiously and then went over to sniff at the corner of the couch. Unconcerned. That was reassuring. If Spencer was relaxed, Dalton knew nothing was seriously amiss.

Spencer looked again to Dalton. It was a look that would have prompted Michael to ask "what do you want, boy?", repeating the question at least twice and then losing interest when Spencer did not give him a verbal reply. Izzy would ask Spencer if he wanted to go out, and then open the kitchen's back door, and of course Spencer always went out because that is what he thought *Izzy* wanted him to do.

But Dalton recognized the look for what it was. Spencer was just checking in with him, seeking guidance.

"Good boy," said Dalton, assuring the dog that everything was fine between them. There was no further need for words. Dalton nodded towards the kitchen and began walking through the dark house, and Spencer followed.

Over the years dogs had collectively become a protective barrier shielding Dalton Holt from the less benevolent behaviors of his own species. Eventually, long after Dalton's sister and parents wanted no more to do with him, Spencer had become his closest companion. The dogs that were brought to his grooming salon became an ever-growing circle of friends. For Dalton, humankind was little more than an inconvenient annoyance. At the salon a dog would nip Dalton now and then if it was frightened by his clippers or the dryer, but dogs never hurt him senselessly the way people had hurt him time and again.

That was how it had been before the aliens came, anyway. Now, to survive, people had to put their differences aside and stand together, but Dalton did not believe it would last. Not for him. His tenuous bond with the other people staying in Dena's home would almost certainly end soon. He was sure of it.

In some ways he felt even more isolated now than he had before the aliens came. The other single men – Jim Rutherford and Beaker – may have thought their prospects were slim, but Dalton could see that the dating pool for a thirty-two-year-old gay man had evaporated. He had never been successful at relationships, but always before there had been the possibility, the hope, that he might meet somebody.

"I'll always have you, Spence," he said, opening the back door in the dark kitchen and stepping outside. The dog followed him onto the patio.

Dalton's new friendship with Jim Rutherford had given him a feeling of a platonic connection, but how long would that last if Jim and Emma Bouchard became a couple? Where would that leave Dalton? Jim would become preoccupied with his new love, and Dalton would be the odd man out. He thought of leaving with Spencer and making his own way in the world. That would probably be better than staying at Dena's house after the others finally realized that he did not fit in with them.

Spencer ran out to what used to be the back lawn and pawed at the dirt. Dalton stepped onto the turned soil and walked over to the dog.

"No, Spence, leave it." The dog stopped digging and looked to Dalton.

Spencer had to learn not to dig before they planted seed in the spring. That would be easy enough; assuming Dalton remained at the house. Spencer was both intelligent and responsive. For the people now living together at Michael and Dena's home, surviving until spring would probably be a more difficult challenge. Even with Beaker bringing supplies from the surrounding region there were a thousand things that could threaten their existence. Winter in western Pennsylvania was nothing if not inconsistent. They might have a mild, gentle winter, but it was equally possible that they would be buried in hip-deep snow and suffer weeks of bitter cold temperatures. If the frost and freeze did not kill them, there were men who would be less hesitant than Beaker to take their lives for the foods and supplies they had collected. There would be hungry animals, too, possibly driven to desperate aggression. There would be disease.

And of course the aliens still presented a terrifying danger, even though Dalton had yet to see one.

As a child he had watched as many science-fiction movies and television series as any other boy. He had seen his planet ravaged by reptilian humanoids, giant robots, big-eyed squatty creatures and huge bugs, but the one common denominator was that the aliens always confronted the people of earth directly and aggressively. The exception that proved the rule was the benevolent and cuddly alien, but that was a different kind of story altogether. Evil aliens attacked; they did not just brush off the world's militia and governments as if these were of no consequence. They did not shut down human civilization the way a person might switch off a ceiling light.

God, he missed electric lighting.

Dalton looked down at Spencer and, despite the darkness, he saw the sudden change in the dog's demeanor. Spencer stiffened. Then the dog's ears lifted slightly and the hairs over his neck and withers stood up.

Realizing a bark would alert any intruders, Dalton put the tip of his finger to Spencer's mouth. It was the sign he used to indicate that Spencer should remain quiet. Watching Spencer's line of sight, he motioned for the dog to follow him and walked slowly and quietly to the gate, now padlocked at Beaker's insistence. The padlock was on the outside of the gate, but that did not matter because Dalton had no intention of opening it just then.

Something was on the other side of the fence. More than one something, he thought. There were at least two of them, moving along the outside of the fence, and from the sound of their movements Dalton could tell they were not human.

CHAPTER TWENTY

Michael shook his head emphatically. "I'm sorry, but you can't keep them."

"You wouldn't say that if they were people." Sitting on the patio, Dalton used his fingers to comb loose bits of dirt and a small twig from the black poodle's wooly coat. Next to him, Emma Bouchard and Jim Rutherford were doing the same with a chocolate-brown poodle. Both dogs were considerably larger than Spencer, who was stretched out lazily next to Dalton's thigh. The Naras and the Franklins had also come out to the patio.

"But they aren't people, Dalton, they're dogs."

"Michael, you take in any human who walks past the house. I'm just asking you to have a little compassion for these animals."

Dena now had the shotgun and was standing on the opposite side of the patio. She looked over at her brother with an expression that she hoped conveyed compassion. "Michael's right, Dalton. We need to make our food last as long as we can. And the people we have 'taken in' are our neighbors."

"Jim isn't," Dalton said stubbornly. He immediately wished he had not said that.

Jim looked up. "Neither are you."

"I'm family."

"We're *all* family," said Michael. He glanced around at his wife and brother-in-law, at Jim Rutherford and young Emma, at Rajinder, Asha, Izzy, Jerry and little Jadu. "And that includes Beaker as well. It also includes Spencer, but we have to draw the line somewhere, Dalton. We don't have the resources to take in stray dogs. Don't you see that?"

Emma Bouchard began to cry.

Michael sighed and threw his head back. "Oh for God's sake, Emma, don't start on me, too."

"Please, Mr. Anderson..." She swallowed. "Let me keep Hershey. He can have half of my food."

"Hershey?"

Dalton looked up at him. "Emma named that dog Hershey, because he's the color of a chocolate bar. This one is Ebony."

Jerry Franklin said, "I'm not giving up any food for these damn dogs. Having one dog makes some sense, but we don't need three."

"Nobody is giving up their food," said Michael. "The dogs aren't staying."

Emma broke into loud wails. She buried her face in the chocolate poodle's matted coat to muffle her crying.

Michael looked from Emma to Dalton. He opened his mouth several times as if to speak, and then finally said, "We'll see what Beaker says. If he's okay with you keeping the dogs then I guess they can stay."

He walked past Dalton quickly and went into the house. There were few places where Michael could be alone anymore. Neither of the toilets was functional, so the bathrooms were only used for storage now. The second-floor bathroom seemed as good a place as any to collect his thoughts. He went up the stairs, taking the steps two at a time, and locked himself in the room.

Two large economy packages of paper towels were on the toilet seat. Michael pushed these off and sat on the lid. He buried his face in his hands and wondered when Beaker was going to come back.

He did not like Beaker any more than anybody else did. For the past year, until the aliens came, he had happily ignored his misanthropic neighbor. Then he had to tolerate the man. But now Michael found that he missed Beaker whenever he went away. The night excursions were not so bad, but more and more often Beaker was gone during the day, and when Beaker was gone the weight of their circumstances fell squarely on Michael's shoulders.

They would not see him cry. He would not let them see him cry.

He was still telling himself that when Dena knocked softly on the door.

"Go away," he said, wiping his tear-moistened palms on his jeans.

"Michael, it's me. Are you okay?" The doorknob turned, but of course it was locked. "Open the door," said Dena.

He turned the lock and let Dena in. She held the shotgun with the barrel pointed to the ceiling.

"Do you want me to take over?" he asked, nodding to the gun. The next shift was his.

Dena shook her head. "Not unless you want to."

"If you see any more stray dogs, shoot them before Dalton tries to adopt them." He was only half kidding.

"Why did you say they could keep those dogs if it's okay with Beaker?" Dena asked. "You know it isn't going to be okay."

"Yes, but then it will be Beaker's problem." Michael held his hands out helplessly. "I can't do this, Dena. If you or anybody else has some insurance contracts to sort through, then I'm your man. Otherwise I don't know what I'm doing. I've buried our neighbors, ransacked their houses, carried water, chopped wood and tried to keep the peace around here. I've reached my limit. I can't tell Dalton that he has to get rid of those dogs. Not with Emma crying her heart out."

"It's going to be harder on them the longer the dogs are here."

Michael sighed heavily. "I wish I knew where Beaker went, and when he'll come back. If he's coming back at all."

Dena went to the bathroom window. It looked out over the brown soil that had once been her back yard. Asha was now taking dry laundry down from the line.

"Beaker will be back," she said.

"You don't know that."

"It's what I choose to believe." She turned and faced him. "Beaker will be back, and he will know what caused those flashes of light."

* * *

That afternoon the Silverado came back up Hugo Drive. By then Dalton had removed the visible dirt from the poodles' coats and trimmed them both with a pair of Dena's scissors. He stayed in the back yard with them, standing protectively between all three dogs and the house. Emma and Jim stood with him. If Jim had any hard feelings about what Dalton had said earlier, he did not show it.

Michael met Beaker at the front door. It was Michael's shift, so he had the shotgun. Beaker stopped halfway across the yard, his Browning rifle in hand, and stared at Michael curiously. "What the hell is wrong with you?" he demanded.

It was then that Michael realized he was in a defensive stance. He relaxed and said, "We need to talk."

"We sure do," replied Beaker. He strode past Michael and into the house.

Michael followed him through the living room and into the kitchen, where Beaker put the rifle on the counter well out of Jadu's reach. The women, except for Emma, were in the kitchen. Rajinder and Jerry were sorting through supplies in the garage.

Beaker turned to Michael then and said, "I need everybody together."

"Beaker, Dalton is outside with—" Michael began to explain the situation to Beaker, but the other man opened the back door and was gone. "—two dogs that he found last night."

Michael and the women hurried after the huge man. Beaker was standing at the edge of the patio, staring at Dalton, Jim, Emma and the three dogs. Spencer started towards the patio and then noticed a difference in Beaker's body posture. Beaker held himself stiffly, his shoulders slightly hunched as if he was ready for a fight. The dog looked back at Dalton, unsure of what to do.

Izzy said, "Now don't be upset, Mr. Beaker."

Beaker stared at her for a moment, and then back at the

poodles. "Why are those dogs in the yard?"

Dalton walked towards the patio. "They're mine, Beaker." The black poodle, Ebony, followed him, but Emma Bouchard held her arm around Hershey's neck. "I found them by the gate last night. They aren't as well trained as Spencer, but both know how to sit and come, and they'll get better. And I'm keeping them, whether you like it or not."

By the time he finished his speech, Dalton was less than a yard from Beaker, looking almost child-like in stature, frail and slender, as he stood in the larger man's shadow. Spencer pawed at the dirt nervously, but Ebony seemed oblivious to the tension between the two humans.

Beaker's fists clenched and relaxed several times.

Michael's own hands tightened on the shotgun. He hoped that he would not have to threaten Beaker with it. The thought frightened him, even though he was armed and Beaker was not.

With his eyes fixed on Dalton, Beaker asked, "Where are Jerry and Rajinder?"

"They're in the garage," said Izzy. She looked around at Michael and Dena nervously. "Should I get them?"

Dena asked, "Beaker, did you find out what the lights were last night?"

Beaker turned from Dalton and walked over to the wrought iron table. "I said that I want everybody together. I don't want to repeat this."

Izzy went to get the two other men. Dena and Asha sat in two of the patio chairs; Asha had Jadu on her lap. By this time Emma had released Hershey. Everyone congregated around the table. The dogs paced between them, but then went over to Dalton when he sat by himself on the edge of the patio.

Folding his massive arms over his chest, Beaker quietly said, "Pittsburgh is gone."

Rajinder asked, "What do you mean it is gone?"

"I mean it doesn't exist anymore, not in any recognizable

form." He looked at Dena. "That's what the flashing lights were. Millvale and everything south of that has been destroyed."

Dena clenched her fists against her temples, refusing to believe what she was hearing. "But why Pittsburgh?"

Beaker said, "We all know it hasn't just been Pittsburgh. It's the same thing that happened to St. Louis and Chicago. I think the aliens have been systematically destroying our cities, probably all over the world. I think they perceive the cities as nests or breeding grounds."

"Nests of what?" asked Izzy. Her eyes suddenly widened with comprehension. "Oh. You mean us."

Beaker nodded.

Jim Rutherford said, "But they haven't just been attacking the cities, sir. At Oakdale we had intelligence that one of the ships was attacking farms in Missouri."

Dena said, "And remember the Amish settlements they've supposedly destroyed. That doesn't fit the pattern either, Beaker."

Jerry Franklin shook his head. "No, but I think we need to accept that the aliens' intention is to exterminate us." He reached for Izzy's hand.

Michael was finding it difficult to breathe. "I'm not ready to give up," he said. "We have worked so hard…"

Beaker leaned on the table. "Who said anything about giving up? You people are still doing that same thing, imposing your own perceptions on a species that we know nothing about. Yeah, I think the fucking aliens are probably cleaning out what they see as our breeding grounds, but that doesn't mean they want us extinct."

"What other reason would they have?" asked Dena.

"How the hell should I know? Do I look like an alien to you?"

Dena thought that deserved a sarcastic reply, but she decided to keep it to herself. "We need to understand their motives, Beaker."

"And that isn't going to happen until we figure out how to communicate with them." Beaker pushed away from the table, stood up and paced the length of the patio with long strides. "They seem to be focused on the cities, with notable exceptions, so I think we may have a chance yet. I say we hunker down and try to wait this out. No more cooking on the grill; we'll have to eat our food cold. Nobody goes outside without a good reason. I saw their ship, probably the one that destroyed the city. It was moving slowly over Sewickley. Damned if I can tell how it's powered. The stores in Sewickley have all been looted, and any people still there are hiding out just like us, but the ship wasn't attacking the town. If we can stay inconspicuous and non-threatening, maybe they'll pass us by, too."

Michael slowly nodded. "That sounds like as good a plan as any. Hide and pray."

Beaker said, "I'm going out on one last run. I'll leave tonight, but we need to empty the truck first. I didn't get much this time, so that won't take long. Then I want to get something to eat before I go."

Dalton looked up at him. "Driving around Pennsylvania doesn't really fit into the 'hunker down' plan, Beaker."

Michael inwardly groaned, and again he wondered if he would have to threaten Beaker with the shotgun. The large man slowly walked around the table and stood in front of Dalton, who still sat on the patio's cement surface. Dena stiffened and started to rise.

In a low voice Beaker said, "No, it doesn't fit the plan, but we have to eat." He chewed on his upper lip and considered saying something more to Dalton, but then he took a deep breath and looked around at the others. "The ship is south of here, and I'll be going north and east. I'll probably be gone for at least two or three days. I want to salvage as much as I can, and then, when I get back, we should be able to hold out for a while."

"But not indefinitely," said Jerry.

"No, eventually we will run out of food." Beaker turned back to Dalton with a sudden movement. "Which brings us back to these dogs you've got."

Dalton held his ground, meeting Beaker's gaze. "I'm not giving them up."

"I heard you the first time," said Beaker. "But if you're going to keep them here, you're going to have to help feed them."

"I...I'm going to take care of them. I've always taken care of Spencer."

Beaker shook his head. "I didn't say take care of them, I said feed them. If you're keeping the dogs, then you're going out with me this time and helping me look for food."

Michael caught the look of alarm in Dena's eye. Stepping towards Beaker he said, "Maybe I should go with you, or Jim could."

"No," said Beaker. He pointed to Dalton. "They're his dogs, so they're his responsibility. He's coming with me tonight."

CHAPTER TWENTY-ONE

Dena cornered Dalton alone upstairs in the blue room, although at that point in the afternoon it was rapidly fading into a gray room. The sun would be setting soon. The days were growing shorter and cooler.

"You don't have to do this," she said. "I'll tell Beaker you aren't going."

Dalton was shoving extra clothes into the canvas duffel he had brought with him from his apartment in Butler. "That's what he wants one of us to do. If I don't go with him it will look like I'm afraid."

"Or it will look like you're smart. Dalton, it's dangerous out there."

He shrugged and pushed a handful of folded socks into the duffel. "It's dangerous here, too."

"At least here you won't have to worry about Beaker." Dena sat on the edge of the bed. "Why does he want you to go with him? He never did before. I think he's planning something."

Dalton said, "Then let's hope he thinks his plan all the way through. If I don't come back with him, he's not going to get a very warm welcome. Nobody wants to harbor a murderer here."

"No, but he could make up a story easily enough. Accidents happen."

"Would you believe him if he told you I died in an accident?" Dalton closed up the duffel. "Beaker isn't stupid. Even if something did happen to me – accidentally – nobody would believe him, and he knows it."

"I still don't like it," said Dena.

"I don't either, but I'm not going to let him win. And he's right, anyway. Because of me, we have two more dogs to feed." He sat next to her on the bed. "I want you to promise me that you'll take care of all three of them while I'm gone. I know Spencer won't give you any trouble, but Hershey and Ebony don't know the house rules yet."

Dena nodded. "I promise. I'll have to ask Michael about whether they can stay in our bedroom, though, unless you think they'll be okay in here with Jimmy."

"I don't know," Dalton admitted. "Spencer will be fine, but Hershey and Ebony have been living on their own for a while. I don't know how they'll react to being confined in the house. That's why I want you to promise you'll take care of them, even if they give you some trouble."

"The dogs will all be here, alive and well, when you get back." She kissed his cheek gently. "I swear to God, I'll kill him if he lays a hand on you."

When Dena and Dalton emerged from the blue room, Spencer met them at the doorway. They went downstairs with Spencer following at their heels. Asha had just put a white taper candle in the center of the dining table. The nightly candle had become their signal that dinner was ready.

They had their first cold dinner in weeks. Breakfast was often served uncooked in the form of cereal or canned fruits, but Dena had been using the grill consistently to prepare warm, if sometimes unusual, meals. This evening's fare was cold chili. There was little conversation. Dena sat between Dalton and Michael. Beaker sat directly across from them, dwarfing Jim Rutherford on his right and Rajinder Nara on his left. Jadu tried to talk to his mother, and Asha responded with a quiet tone that was barely more than a whisper.

Beaker's decision to take Dalton with him that night had cast a somber mood over everyone, and Dena did not think it was out of concern for her brother. Not for some of them, anyway. Izzy tolerated Dalton now, but she had no genuine affection for him. To Emma Bouchard he was little more than a stranger. Even Michael, by his own admission, was sometimes uncomfortable around Dalton. It was Beaker who worried the others. Beaker had changed in some fundamental way when Dalton stood up to him that afternoon.

Dena tried to focus on eating her chili while simultaneously keeping one eye on the huge man sitting across from her. She wanted to believe that the subtle change in Beaker's demeanor had nothing to do with her brother, that it was something else: seeing the alien spaceship up close, or just the weight of the stress they had all been under. But it was when Dalton had quipped about Beaker hunkering down that something changed. Dena did not know what had happened, but she knew exactly when.

Her voice sounded loud and forced as she said, "Dalton should take the revolver."

Beaker's dark eyes looked across the table. "I'll have my rifle and plenty of bullets. That's all we need."

"Maybe so, but I want him to have the revolver anyway." She nodded to the shotgun leaning against the wall behind her. "We have this gun and, if that's not enough, Jimmy has his pistol. If you're going to take Dalton with you, he might as well carry the revolver."

The two of them stared at each other silently, and Dena thought Beaker was going to refuse what sounded to her like a reasonable suggestion. But he shrugged his enormous shoulders and said, "Okay, then, he can bring it along, for all the good it will do."

At least he'll be armed, she thought.

Beaker stood and looked down at Dalton. "We need to get going. Finish up and get your stuff." He started to turn to the living room, but paused and added, "Be sure to get some ammo from the garage. An empty revolver is just a fancy paperweight."

Within a few minutes Dalton had gathered his duffel, the revolver and a box of bullets. By then Beaker was already waiting in the cab of the Silverado.

Dena and Michael walked with Dalton to the truck. A light rain had started to fall, and clouds completely obscured the stars.

Leaning close to her brother, Dena whispered, "Keep one

hand on your gun."

Dalton nodded. He pulled open the truck's passenger door. The interior light illuminated Beaker's scowling, unshaven face and the Browning rifle now in its rack behind the seat. Beaker did not look at Dalton or acknowledge him in any way as he tossed his duffel behind the truck's seat. When the door closed Beaker started the engine.

Dena began to cry when the Silverado drove off.

Michael put his arm around her. "They'll be fine, honey. You know Beaker can take care of himself."

"That's what scares me, Michael." She leaned against him for support. "Dalton doesn't stand a chance against Beaker; not in a physical fight."

"But he has that revolver."

"Yeah, well, Dalton can't use a gun any better than I can."

"Then why were you insistent that he take it with him?" asked Michael. "Did you see how pissed Beaker looked?"

Dena shrugged. "I wanted to improve Dalton's odds a little. But I can still worry. What I saw was the way Beaker kept sneaking looks at Dalton while we were eating. Something is different about him, Michael. I know it."

"Beaker has only done good things for us since all of this began. We have to trust him. He may be strange, and not very friendly, but he has never tried to hurt any of us."

"No," admitted Dena. "Not yet."

* * *

When the Silverado reached the end of Hugo Drive, Beaker turned left onto Route 228. The windshield wipers squeaked rhythmically as they brushed away the raindrops that spattered against the glass. The truck's headlights pierced the night.

In the dark cab, Beaker said, "We'll go east of Butler. I haven't been through that area yet."

Dalton nodded. "And the ship is south of here, over Sewickley." That, at least, was reassuring.

There was a long pause, and then Beaker said, "It was."

"It was?" asked Dalton. "What do you mean by that?"

"I mean it's a goddam spaceship. It was flying over Sewickley this morning, but by tomorrow it could be anywhere."

Dalton slouched down in the seat. "By tomorrow we'll be back at Dena's."

"Not unless we come across a lot more food than I think we will."

"We're not going back in the morning?"

Beaker shook his head, "I told you and everyone else that we'll be gone for two or three days. And that was just a guess. I'm not going back until I've filled up the bed of the truck."

"But that could take weeks!"

Beaker said nothing. They drove on through the night, eventually turning onto a highway that took them north. It was the first time Dalton had left his sister's neighborhood since he arrived there. There were no other vehicles on the highway. No lights illuminating billboards or the interiors of bars and residences. It seemed to Dalton that they would be very conspicuous to anyone lurking in the darkness.

Eventually Dalton asked, "Do you think everybody is dead?"

"No," said Beaker. "A lot of people have died, either murdered or by suicide, but not everybody. The others are like us, hiding and waiting."

Dalton looked over at him. "Where did you live before you bought your house on Hugo Drive? You don't sound like you're from around here."

The question was met with silence. Dalton turned and looked out the window, but he could not see much more than the headlights reflecting off the wet pavement. He told himself, quite truthfully, that he did not really care where Beaker had moved from. The query had only been a halfhearted attempt to make conversation. Now Dalton remembered Beaker saying that he planned to be gone for a few days. In retrospect, Dalton wished he had taken Dena's advice and refused to come along.

When they were almost to Butler, Beaker turned off the highway and onto a two lane road. Soon after this he asked, "Do you know how to use that gun?"

"Yeah," Dalton lied. "Of course I do."

"Show me how to take the safety off."

Dalton lifted the revolver and turned it in his hands as if considering this. Then he said, "I don't want to mess with it in the dark."

Beaker chuckled softly. "I know why Dena wanted you to take a gun with you."

"For protection," said Dalton.

"I reckon you could say so. Protection against me, right?" Another chuckle. "But a revolver isn't very useful if you don't know how to use it."

Dalton felt a knot tighten in his stomach.

CHAPTER TWENTY-TWO

"Ebony!"

The black poodle dropped her paws from the kitchen counter, but the mixing bowl she had been licking fell with the movement and clattered on the floor.

Dena stooped to pick up the bowl. "I swear, if Michael sees you doing anything like this I won't be able to keep you in the house." Flecks of vanilla pudding – or what Dena hoped would pass for vanilla pudding – dotted the floor and the side of the counter.

Over the past two days Hershey, the brown poodle, had started to fit into the household (thanks in no small part to Emma Bouchard's efforts) but Ebony was still a bundle of chaotic tension.

As Dena picked up the bowl, she saw Izzy Franklin standing in the kitchen doorway. Izzy went to the opposite side of the room and found a cotton dishcloth. "Did she eat the pudding?"

Dena shook her head. "No, it's in that serving bowl." She nodded at a ceramic bowl on the opposite counter. "Anyway, I'm not sure that it will become pudding. It's supposed to be refrigerated after mixing it with the milk, and I'm pretty sure the directions mean cold milk, not powdered milk and water."

Izzy began to wipe up the flecks on the side of the counter. That caught Ebony's attention, and the poodle pushed Izzy's hand aside to lick up the remains of her crime.

"Don't let her do that," said Dena. "You're just rewarding her for getting into the pudding in the first place."

Izzy put the cloth on the countertop. "But she didn't get into the pudding. She was just licking the empty bowl."

Whether or not Ebony should lick up the spilled pudding became a moot point as the dog finished the job and then, when an idea for some new bit of mischief had entered her head, she dashed out of the kitchen and up the stairs.

Dena said, "That poodle is driving me crazy."

"The pudding looks good though," said Izzy, glancing at the ceramic serving bowl.

"It will keep us alive." Dena shrugged. "I already miss hot dinners. I may fire up the grill tomorrow and heat some of those canned tamales. I can't imagine eating tamales cold right out of the can."

Izzy said, "You'd better do it before Mr. Beaker comes back if you—" She caught herself when she saw the sudden change in Dena's expression. "I mean when your brother and Mr. Beaker come back."

Dena turned from her. "They've been gone for two days," she said quietly.

"Well, Mr. Beaker said that he – that they – would be away for two or three days." Izzy went to Dena and put a hand on her shoulder. "I'm sure your brother is fine. Mr. Beaker will take care of him."

"It's Beaker that worries me." She shook off Izzy's hand and stepped away. "You've seen how he ignores Dalton. He's as bad as you, and he's dangerous."

"But it was Mr. Beaker who stood up for your brother when I…" Izzy found that she could not look at Dena directly in the eyes. "I suppose you think I'm a horrible person."

Dena sighed. "No, Izzy, I've always known you were a horrible person. It just became more obvious when everything went to shit."

"I've only wanted everything to be right. That's all I've *ever* wanted; for everything to be like it was before."

"Before what, for God's sake?"

"We haven't seen her in more than ten years, Dena." Tears suddenly filled Izzy's eyes.

"Seen who?" asked Dena. She helped Izzy sit down on one of the kitchen chairs.

"Kylie, our daughter." Izzy wiped the palm of her hand

across her nose. "We still talk to J.J., of course, but even he doesn't visit anymore."

Her children. Dena remembered that Izzy and Jerry had two grown children.

Izzy said, "We told everyone that Kylie went off to college. We had to, don't you see?"

"No, Izzy, I'm sorry, but I don't see. Did something happen to her?"

Izzy nodded. Taking a deep breath, she said, "We found out that she was dating a…black man." When it became obvious that Dena was not making a connection, she reiterated, "A black man! I tried to talk some sense into her, but she wouldn't listen. And we couldn't let people know that our own daughter was involved with…with a…"

"A black man," Dena said helpfully.

"Well, yes. I told her that she couldn't bring him here, to Hugo Drive, but I never thought she would choose him over her own parents. But she did. They moved away; I don't know where. That was the last time I saw Kylie, and now I don't think I'll ever see her again."

"I'm sorry, Izzy, really. But that's not a reason to treat other people the way you do."

"We aren't supposed to mix with those people."

"What people?"

"People who aren't like us. Blacks and Asians, Jews, Muslims and gays. That's what happened to our Kylie. She would—"

"No, *you're* what happened to Kylie," said Dena. "It was you who drove her away."

Izzy glared at her. "You wouldn't say that if your brother wasn't a gay."

Dena was ready with a hot retort, but she checked herself. After a moment, she said, "No, maybe I wouldn't. It took a long time for me to accept Dalton for who he is. If he wasn't gay, maybe my mind would still be as narrow and closed as yours."

"Is it so terrible that I want to associate with my own kind?"

They both froze as they heard Asha's voice from the upstairs foyer, saying, "No, it is not." Dena wondered how much Asha Nara had overheard.

A few moments later the small, dark-skinned woman came into the kitchen wearing a saffron saree. "Mrs. Franklin," she said, "if you are offended by me and my family, you are welcome to leave at any time. I am not a Christian and I am not white, and neither of those things is going to change. And another thing that will not change is where I am staying now with my husband and my son. The Andersons have very kindly opened their home to us, and we have accepted their invitation. But you are not a prisoner here, Mrs. Franklin. If my beliefs or my accent or the sight of my skin is not acceptable to you, I will not be offended if you choose to look elsewhere for your own kind, as you say."

"I didn't mean—"

"Yes, you did, Mrs. Franklin." Asha's eyes were hard and cold.

Izzy turned to Dena for support. "Of course we have to band together now, under these circumstances."

Dena shook her head. "Dalton isn't going to change either, Izzy. So if anyone *is* going to change, I think it needs to be you."

Michael came in through the back door. He held the shotgun firmly . Looking around at the three women, he asked, "Is everything all right?"

"Everything's fine, Michael," said Dena. "Isn't it, Izzy?"

Izzy Franklin slowly nodded her head.

Going over to Izzy, Michael said, "You've been crying."

Dena said, "It's nothing to worry about. We've all been under a lot of stress. You know that."

"Okay, then." He gave Izzy another puzzled look. "I'll be in the living room if you need me for anything."

After her husband left the room, Dena asked Izzy, "Are you okay?"

"I guess I don't have much choice."

"No." Dena smiled as she shook her head. "No, you don't. But I want us to be friends."

Asha nodded. "I would like to be friends, too, Mrs. Franklin."

Izzy smiled at Asha Nara, but Dena could see in the woman's eyes that there was no affection behind the expression. There might be friendship someday, but not now. For now it was enough to have tolerance and at least a superficial veneer of respect.

Asha turned suddenly to Dena. "I almost forgot why I came down here. There is a problem."

"What is it?" asked Dena.

"It is your brother's dog, the new black one."

"Ebony? What has she done now?"

Asha said, "It seems that she has pooped on our bedroom floor."

CHAPTER TWENTY-THREE

Dalton woke to Beaker shaking his shoulder roughly.

"Get up," growled the large man. He picked up Dalton's jeans from where they were hanging over the back of a chair and tossed them onto the bed. Finished with social amenities, Beaker took up his rifle and crept down the stairs of the abandoned farmhouse.

Dalton threw back the covers and pulled on his jeans. Apparently murder was not part of Beaker's immediate plan. They had spent the past two nights looking for food and supplies, but with little success. There seemed to be two kinds of residences in the Pennsylvania countryside. Most of the homes were of the first kind; abandoned and looted of anything worth taking. In two nights they had only found half a dozen cans of tuna, an unopened jar of Miracle Whip and a plastic bottle of chocolate syrup. Beaker was determined to fill up the bed of the Silverado before they returned to Caldonia, and at this rate it was a feat that would take months to accomplish.

They also had to watch carefully for the other kind of residence. Some buildings were occupied, just like the Andersons' home at Number Twenty-Two Hugo Drive. Beaker and Dalton had no intention of attacking these homes, but the occupants did not know this, and most of them had found some way to arm themselves. Beaker was adept at giving the occupied buildings a wide berth, but the Silverado was nevertheless shot at twice during their second night of scavenging. Fortunately Beaker was also adept at beating a hasty retreat.

Dalton's sweatshirt was on the floor next to his canvas running shoes. He picked up the shirt and pulled it over his head.

Twice now they had spent the daylight hours sleeping in abandoned houses. Beaker believed it was safer to hide out during the day, and Dalton had no reason to dispute this. Not any house would do. Beaker looked for buildings that, in his mind, would not attract anyone who might be moving about in the day. The residence also needed a suitable place to hide the Silverado. As an added precaution, Beaker insisted that they sleep together. This had surprised Dalton the first morning.

"You don't mind sleeping in the same bed with me?"

Beaker had given him a hard look. "There isn't much I can do if I'm not there when somebody comes in and tries to slice you open with a carving knife."

In Dena's guest bedroom Dalton had always slept in his jeans when he shared the bed with Jim Rutherford, but now he climbed into bed wearing only his boxer briefs. It was Dalton's little passive-aggressive challenge that he hoped would make Beaker uncomfortable, but the other man stripped down to his own briefs, got into the bed and turned his wide, massive back to Dalton. And this is how they slept that first day. Not that Dalton slept much at all. The thought of someone coming in and killing him in his sleep kept him awake late into the afternoon.

By the second morning, though, he was exhausted and sleep overcame him almost as soon as he pulled up the bed's covers.

Dalton finished dressing in the dark room, picked up his revolver and hurried downstairs. Beaker had shown him how to use the gun the night before. The sun had already set and Dalton could not remember how the house was laid out, but he could hear Beaker fumbling around in another room. Following the sounds, he found Beaker in the kitchen. Faint moonlight coming through the kitchen windows silhouetted the tall, muscular man. He was next to a refrigerator that stood open and empty. This house, like almost all of the abandoned houses, had been emptied of all foods.

Beaker's shadow moved forward and Dalton felt the man put something in his hand. It was a small can, and the smell arising from it instantly revealed its contents.

"Tuna fish?" asked Dalton, although he knew exactly what it

was. "We only have six cans of this."

"You have to eat something."

"Is there a fork?"

A cold chuckle came out of the dark. "Do you want a napkin, too, Princess?"

Dalton was glad that Beaker could not see him blush. He reached into the can with his fingers and realized that half of the tuna was gone. Beaker had eaten it, and saved the rest of it for him. It only took a minute for Dalton to finish off the rest of the can.

On the way out to the truck, when Beaker was not looking, Dalton wiped his fingers clean on one of the kitchen window curtains.

* * *

The Silverado was parked on the far side of the house, hidden behind a row of tall rhododendrons. The bed of the truck still held the jar of Miracle Whip, the bottle of chocolate syrup and five of their cans of tuna.

Beaker put the rifle in the gun rack and started the truck. Dalton tried to be optimistic as they renewed their search for supplies, but their quest seemed more and more futile. They rummaged through three other abandoned houses and found nothing more than a can of sauerkraut and two boxes of laundry detergent. After this they came to a farmstead where candlelight glowed behind drawn curtains. Beaker drove the Silverado quickly by the farm, and then on past the next few abandoned houses. When Dalton asked why, Beaker responded curtly that the people in the occupied farmhouse would have already taken anything from the surrounding properties.

Five miles farther down the road Beaker decided to explore yet another abandoned home. They each had a flashlight, but Beaker had insisted these be used only when necessary. The light could attract attention, he said, and their supply of batteries would not last forever. And so once again Dalton found himself stumbling around in a strange, dark house, hoping to find something – anything – worth carrying back to his sister's home.

This was an older house with high ceilings. Beaker was rummaging through the kitchen, opening drawers and cabinets, trying to feel a box or bottle but only touching plates, cups and utensils. Dalton watched him for a few minutes. Then, more to have something to do, he went into the next room.

Clouds now covered most of the night sky, blotting out any moonlight and starlight that might have otherwise come through the windows. Dalton was not sure, but he thought he might be in a dining room. He collided against a table standing in the center of the room, and his fingertips reached out to feel a cloth covering over the table.

"What was that?" grunted Beaker from the kitchen.

Dalton nodded. Then, realizing that Beaker could not see him, he called out, "I just bumped into a table. I'm fine. I think this is the dining room."

There was no response, but then Dalton had not expected one. With occasional lapses, Beaker was not a man who indulged in lengthy conversations.

Moving with more caution, Dalton edged around the table. Now he could feel the back of a dining chair, and then another. There were woven placemats arranged on the table, too, one in front of each chair. Whoever had lived in the house had been a tidy homemaker.

From the kitchen, Beaker said, "We aren't going to find anything here. This place has already been cleaned out."

Dalton stepped back from the table and nearly stumbled over another chair tipped onto its side. At the same time his arm brushed against something heavy that moved away from him, and a moment later he felt the sweep of cold fingertips caressing his shoulder.

Startled, he turned on the flashlight and cried out when the narrow shaft of light revealed a woman's corpse hanging from a noose. The body swung back and forth, turning slowly until the empty, dead eyes were looking down at him. She was not a young woman, perhaps in her sixties, her gray hair clipped short. The rope she hung from had been thrown across an overhead beam; its opposite end was tied to the knob on a door just behind her.

A second shaft of light fell on the woman as Beaker came into the room. Dalton reached out with one hand and steadied himself against the dining room table.

"It's all right," said Beaker, coming up to him. "She's dead."

"All right?" Dalton turned to face Beaker. "How is this fucking all right?" His voice cracked from a combination of fear and fury.

"I mean she can't hurt you." Beaker looked over the corpse. "And nobody can hurt her now, either. I think this was a suicide. Look how she used the rope. She couldn't reach high enough to tie it around that beam, so she tied the end to the doorknob and threw the rest of it over."

Dalton wanted to throw up, and he was sure that he would have if he had eaten anything more than half a can of tuna fish over the past twenty-four hours. He turned his flashlight across the rest of the room. In the center of the table was a vase of flowers as dead and desiccated as the woman hanging from the ceiling. Framed photographs on the wall displayed the smiling faces of children.

"Help me get her down," said Beaker.

"What's the point?" Dalton turned off his flashlight. "Let's just get out of here."

"The point is, I want to find out what's behind that door." Beaker set his own flashlight on the dining table and began to untie the rope from the doorknob.

Dalton asked, "What do you want me to do?"

"Hold onto her."

"No!"

"Okay, then, don't." With a final pull, Beaker released the knot. The rope flew up and out of his hands, and the dead woman collapsed in a heap on the floor.

"Jesus, Beaker!"

"I told you to hold her." Beaker set his rifle on the table and picked up his flashlight. Looking back at Dalton, he said, "Cover me."

"Huh?"

"With your revolver, dumbass. I can't hold my flashlight and the rifle at the same time. Not very well, anyway."

Nodding, Dalton clutched his revolver in both of his hands. Beaker turned back and tried the door. Nothing happened.

"It's locked," he announced more to himself than to Dalton.

"So we can't get in?"

"I didn't say that. I just said it's locked." Beaker threw himself at the door, hitting it with his shoulder and hip. Pieces of wood broke off from the frame as the door collapsed inward, and Beaker seemed to suddenly shrink until he was no taller than Dalton.

Then Dalton saw that Beaker, breaking through the door, had fallen down a couple of steps.

"Are you okay?" asked Dalton.

"I'm better than okay." Beaker looked back at him, but in the flashlight's illumination all Dalton could see was the aquiline shape of Beaker's nose. Then the larger man said, "We've hit the jackpot."

* * *

Dalton had never known a hoarder personally. Apparently Mrs. Rebecca Fine had been a compulsive food hoarder. Her body hanging in front of what looked like a closet door would have discouraged scavengers, and Beaker suspected that the first people who emptied out the kitchen thought they had collected everything.

They were wrong.

The stairs that Beaker nearly fell down led to a basement filled with food. Shelving along the walls held jars of peanut butter, cans of fruits and vegetables, boxes of cereal and containers of jam and honey. Mice had attacked the boxes of cereal, but most of the rest of it was still good. Beaker left his flashlight on in the basement as they carried armloads of food out to the truck: peas, canned salmon, green beans, corn, sorghum, peaches, olives, pickles and more. There were bottles of soy sauce and bottles of Worcestershire sauce, cans of baked beans and cans of tomato soup.

Within this cornucopia they came across some old letters and a misplaced utility bill that gave them the name of their benefactor.

The rifle and revolver were set aside as they made one trip after another carrying the food to the truck. Mrs. Fine also hoarded old magazines and newpapers and, while these did not interest the two men, Beaker dumped the periodicals out of their boxes and then packed those boxes with canned foods for easier transportation.

Dalton felt a twinge of discomfort every time he carried a box of food past the corpse on the dining room floor. He told himself that Rebecca Fine no longer needed any of this food, and they certainly did. On one trip he stopped and put his box of food – this one filled with cans of baked beans – on the dining table. Taking up his flashlight he looked more closely at the framed photographs. Most of the pictures were of three children, all of them probably Mrs. Fine's offspring. One photograph was of an infant held by a woman who Dalton was sure was a younger Rebecca Fine. He took that picture from the wall and put it in the box with the canned beans.

"We won't forget you, Rebecca," he whispered. Dalton did not know what he would do with the photograph, but it seemed important to him that the woman be remembered in some way.

They propped the front door to the house with a rock so they would not have to open and close it with each trip to the truck. The bed of the Silverado soon filled up and they had to stack boxes on top of boxes. The work went slower then, because few of the boxes fit well on top of the others, and they did not want the jars and cans to burst open on the drive back to Caldonia.

Beaker said little to Dalton as they worked. Occasionally he would tell Dalton which box to carry up next, or caution him to be careful of a carton threatening to break open at the bottom, but as morning approached Beaker seemed to grow even more distant and aloof.

The sun had come over the horizon by the time they came to the last of the food. Dalton had a box with two dozen cans of cream of mushroom soup to take up. Beaker was loading odds and ends into a large, final box that he would carry out.

Hoisting his box of canned soup, Dalton said, "We still need to find a place to sleep today."

"What's wrong with this place?" asked Beaker.

"If you don't remember, there's a dead body upstairs in the dining room."

Beaker nodded brusquely. "That's the beauty of it. Did you see where the stairs to the second floor are? Anybody coming in will have to almost step over her to get to us."

Dalton felt something threaten to come up from his stomach. "Beaker, I am not sleeping in a house where a woman killed herself."

"Where are you sleeping then?"

Beaker's words were an overt challenge, but Dalton was in no mood to back down. "I mean it, Beaker. I'll hike down the road by myself if I have to, but I'm not staying here."

Without waiting for an argument, Dalton stomped up the

stairs with his box of soup. Twenty-four cans of it. That one armload was more than they had collected the previous two nights.

A trio of goldfinches fluttered across the unkempt lawn as Dalton walked over to the Silverado and added the soup to the stacks of food they had brought up from Mrs. Fine's basement. The air felt fresh and clean, and Dalton realized it had been days since he had felt the warmth of the sun on his face.

The truck sat in the gravel driveway that led to a detached garage behind the Fine residence, and to one side of the garage grew a large birch tree. Dalton leaned against the truck and relaxed. Surely Beaker would come out in a minute with that last box. But if he did not, Dalton was determined to stand by what he had said. He wished he had the keys to the Silverado. Walking down a strange road by himself was not something he was looking forward to.

He jerked to attention as he heard a branch snap. Somebody was on the other side of the garage. At least one person, and perhaps more. Dalton mentally kicked himself for leaving the revolver in the house. He had no means of defense unless there was some way he could suddenly develop super-powers.

"Wh-who's that?" he called out softly.

Dalton took a step away from the truck and toward the house, but he realized that there was no way he could get to the house before the other person came from around the side of the garage. And then that other person came into Dalton's line of sight, walking with quick, purposeful steps.

The alien stopped when it noticed Dalton, and turned towards him.

CHAPTER TWENTY-FOUR

The creature was fully encased in its suit, but its body proportions revealed that this was no terrestrial man or woman. Standing slightly taller than Dalton, its torso was inhumanly long, its arms and legs inhumanly short. In the stubby fingers of its gloved hand it held one of the strange wands that Dalton knew could mean instant death.

He wondered for a moment if the alien had already used its death ray wand on him. He felt as if his guts had turned to ice, but the sensation was only a symptom of his terror.

The oddly proportioned creature stood forty feet away. Although Dalton could not make out any details beneath its opaque helmet, he could tell from the creature's posture that it was aware of him. The alien faced him, but at the same time the front of its helmet remained slightly averted.

Dalton did not retreat or cringe. Every muscle in his body wanted to flee, but he held his ground, only turning his head slightly to avoid direct eye contact. Not that he could see the creature's eyes. Not that he was sure if the thing even *had* eyes.

For a predator, direct eye contact was usually a challenge. Dalton was fully aware that the alien was not any terrestrial predator, but it was certainly not a human being either.

As if to confirm this, a second alien came from around the side of the garage, and this one walked on all fours. There was nothing awkward in its movement, but the posture gave it the semblance of an animal rather than a man. The first alien held up its free hand, apparently signaling to the other, which immediately stopped in its tracks.

Then the second alien rose to its hind legs. The movement seemed to come naturally and easily. Like the first, this one was clad completely in a full suit and helmet.

Through his peripheral vision Dalton saw the two aliens turn to each other. It looked as if they were conversing, but there was no sound. He might have thought he had temporarily lost his hearing, but a bird was singing clearly in the branches of the birch tree.

Of course there would be no external sound, he thought to himself, not with those helmets. If they were communicating with words or music or whatever passed for a language, it would be through some kind of radio transmission.

Then from over the trees beyond the garage came one of the enormous tear-shaped vessels. It was larger than it had appeared in the televised broadcast from St. Louis. Dalton wondered if the Chicago ship was a bigger craft, or if the alien ships just seemed much larger in real life. It was flying lower as it approached. Dalton was not familiar with the land behind the house, but from where he stood next to the truck it looked like there was a large meadow or clearing between the garage and the more distant woodland.

The close encounter with the two aliens ended as abruptly as it began. They turned away from him, and the first alien held its wand to the side of its suit, where it disappeared into a pocket or compartment that Dalton could not see. Then both of the creatures dropped to all fours and trotted – Dalton could not think of any other word to describe their gait – past the garage and into the meadow beyond.

He should have felt relief, but he did not. The worst of it was the casual way the aliens dismissed him. Dalton Holt had never fit in well with others, but even when he had been teased or taunted or threatened, some part of him had still been acknowledged as a *person*. Even when someone like Beaker ignored him, there was a sense of something in his existence to be ignored. To the aliens, Dalton had been no more important than the bird singing in the birch tree, or the stink bug that landed on his shoulder as he forced himself to keep from collapsing onto the gravel drive.

The tear-shaped vessel was now close to the ground in the

large clearing behind the garage, and a ramp was lowered to admit the two aliens.

From the house he heard Beaker growling, "I'm only doing this because I don't—"

Beaker stopped on the porch and stared at the alien ship. Wearing the sweat pants and a wool hoodie he had put on that morning, he was holding the box packed with the last of the food that the mice had not ruined. Slowly, as if any sudden movement might prove fatal, Beaker set the box on the floor of the porch.

The aliens trotted up the ramp and disappeared into the ship.

Beaker walked slowly over to Dalton and asked, "Did they see you?"

Dalton nodded. "It doesn't matter, though. We're nothing to them." His voice was barely more than a whisper.

"We're enough for them to destroy our cities," said Beaker.

"Maybe, but they don't care about us as individuals."

The ship was rising again, its tapered end turning to the southwest. Dalton and Beaker watched as it moved away from them.

Beaker went to the porch and retrieved the last box. Returning to the Silverado, he stacked it on top of the rest of their collection. Then they both went back into Rebecca Fine's house one last time to get their guns and flashlights.

Dalton said nothing more about where they would be staying, and Beaker made no comment at all until they were both in the cab of the Silverado. Even then it was a simple inquiry as to Dalton's current condition, expressed in a single word that sounded like "Y'okay?"

"No, not really," Dalton replied weakly.

The Silverado's engine rumbled to life and Beaker pulled the truck out of the driveway. He turned right, returning the way they had come. After they had driven half a mile, he said, "We'll stay at the same house we were at last night. I think we'll be safe enough there and I don't have time to hunt around for another place."

Dalton asked, "Are we going back to Caldonia then?"

"The truck's full, isn't it?" said Beaker roughly. Then he shrugged an apology. "Besides, the ship was heading in that direction. We should get back in case the others need our help."

"I don't know what you think we could do."

"Neither do I," said Beaker.

* * *

It was still early morning when they came to the two-storey house where they had slept the day before. It was on a side road, and Dalton thought there probably had not been much traffic on that road even before the aliens came. Beaker pulled the Silverado around the house and parked it behind the tall row of rhododendrons. Although the woody bushes were far past their bloom, the leaves effectively hid the truck from the sight of anyone who might drive by. In the daylight they saw a ravaged vegetable garden to one side of the house. What remained of the tomato vines and cornstalks had been trampled into the soil. Beyond the ruined garden was a whitewashed propane tank.

With his revolver in hand, Dalton followed Beaker onto the back porch and through the door leading into the kitchen. It did not seem as if anybody else had been there, but everything looked different with the morning sunlight streaming through the windows. Dalton noticed the stain on the curtain where he had wiped his fingers. Beaker went through every room and closet downstairs, and then checked out the upstairs rooms. There was nobody hiding in the recesses of the house. Nor were there any foods or useful supplies, something they already knew. It was one of the reasons this house was relatively safe. Like so many others, it had already been stripped of everything of value.

Throughout the search, Beaker said nothing to Dalton. The huge man then went to the bedroom they had slept in the day before. Dalton went to the same room. This was their third day out, and he knew the protocol. They had to stay together at all times. Now it seemed almost an imperative. It was in the few moments when Dalton had been separated from Beaker that the aliens had confronted him, and that was an experience he did not want to repeat.

"We're just bugs to them," he said, setting his revolver on the top of an oak bureau.

Beaker had propped the Browning rifle by the door and was pulling his hoodie over his head. He threw that to one side and kicked off his shoes. "You don't know what they're thinking about us."

"You weren't there." Dalton went to the bedroom window and looked out at the surrounding landscape. From the second floor he could see quite a distance, but there was no sign of a spaceship. Looking back at Beaker, he said, "Maybe they don't care about us because – from their point of view – we're as good as extinct. They know that they've already won."

"So now you can see things from their point of view." Beaker stepped out of his sweat pants, tossing them in the general direction of his hoodie.

Dalton turned away from Beaker as the man, now in nothing but his cotton briefs, climbed into the bed they were sharing. As much as he did not want to admit it, Dalton knew that he found Beaker physically attractive. This was a new development – Dalton did not even know when the attraction had been kindled – and one that he dared not let the huge man suspect. It did not matter that the Browning rifle was out of reach. Dalton was sure that Beaker would be able to break him into pieces like a dry twig before he could aim his revolver.

He pulled his sweatshirt over his head. "I don't know everything about them, no. But I know what they think of us. You didn't see them, Beaker."

"Nobody is going to know what the aliens are thinking unless they try to communicate with us – or unless we finally learn to listen." Beaker was facing the opposite direction, speaking over his shoulder.

Dalton finished undressing and slipped into bed. In the sunlight Beaker's broad, naked back seemed almost like a wall separating them.

"I know what they were thinking," Dalton said stubbornly.

"You don't even know what *I'm* thinking," Beaker muttered. He pulled the bedclothes more tightly around his waist. "You don't know me at all."

"No, I don't," admitted Dalton. He resisted an unexpected urge to put his arm around Beaker's chest. It had been a long time since he had been with another man. He rolled onto his back and folded his arms over his own chest, holding himself against temptation.

Dalton knew very little about the man lying next to him, but was that Beaker's fault or his own? Beaker never said anything about his personal life or his past. To be fair, though, Dalton had never asked, either. He did remember one thing that Dena had told him; something she had heard from Izzy Franklin.

Looking up at the ceiling, Dalton said, "I know you lost your wife. I'm sorry about that."

"Go to sleep." Still facing away, Beaker pulled the bed covers up to his armpits.

Dalton closed his eyes, but he knew sleep would not come quickly. Despite his exhaustion, his encounter with the aliens had given him a burst of adrenalin that would probably keep him awake most of the day. Fifteen minutes later he was still fully conscious, and he could tell from the rhythm of Beaker's breathing that the other man was, too.

"What was her name?" he asked quietly.

Dalton felt Beaker's body grow rigid next to him, and he wondered if he had crossed a line. Beaker had never mentioned his wife, or much of anything else.

Then Beaker, in an uncharacteristically soft voice, said a name.

Dalton turned to the man, even though this only meant he was staring again at Beaker's back. "What did Dawn look like?"

There was another stretch of silence between them before Beaker spoke again. "I didn't say 'Dawn'. I said Don, as in Donald." He rolled over then to face Dalton, and his eyes were filled with a mix of anger and sorrow. "Are you happy now? Is that what you wanted to hear?"

"You're—" Dalton did not finish. "Dena told me you were widowed."

"I was. I am." Beaker fell onto his back. He no longer faced Dalton, but he was no longer turned away from him. "His name was Donald Hamilton," he said. "We were together for ten years. Izzy asked me one day if there was a woman in my life, and all I said was that I was widowed."

Dalton impulsively balled up his fist and punched Beaker in the chest. It was like punching a cement block, and Dalton reflected that it probably was not the wisest thing to do just then, but any caution was stripped away by his own sudden anger. "That's why you've been such a douche to me! You're trying to make everyone think that you're straight."

"I don't give a damn what they think about me. I'd just as soon they not think about me at all. All I wanted was to live out the rest of my life in peace, without people harassing me." Beaker shrugged. "Don had a lot of insurance. I was doing fine by myself before that night the aliens came."

"That's why you don't...didn't...have a nine-to-five job," said Dalton.

Beaker nodded.

Dalton thought about this. "I won't tell anybody."

"About the insurance? Money's worthless now."

"No, I mean I won't tell them that you're gay."

"I don't care if they know," said Beaker. "If they don't like it, I'll take all of the food I've collected and go somewhere else.

Anyway, it wouldn't bother Dena and Michael."

"If you don't care, then why are you always avoiding me?" Irritation tinged Dalton's words. "You ignore me, and you never let me help with anything you're involved in."

"Yeah, well, I guess I was afraid."

Dalton said, "So you did care if they found out."

Beaker scratched at his armpit. "No, doofus, I was afraid that *you* would find out. I've wanted you since I first saw you at Michael and Dena's house, but I'm not ready to let anybody else into my life. At least I wasn't then, and I don't know if I am now. Can you understand that? I've worked a long time to keep everybody out. It's hard to open that door again."

Hearing this, Dalton did put his arm around Beaker and felt the coarse but soft hairs covering the larger man's chest against his skin. At the same time he sensed Beaker tensing up. "It's all right," he said. "I want you, too."

Beaker put a massive arm around Dalton's shoulder. "I couldn't stand losing someone again. Losing Don was the worst thing that has ever happened to me."

"Then hold me close," said Dalton. He kissed Beaker's chest, then slowly shifted his position and moved his head lower across Beaker's torso, to his belly and then lower still.

"No." Beaker reached out with his other hand and stopped Dalton. "Not now. I haven't bathed in days."

"Okay," Dalton whispered. He let his hand drift under the covers and down until he could feel the soft cotton briefs and the hardness beneath. He grasped it. Suddenly Beaker's entire body shuddered violently as he let out a hoarse cry. A moistness seeped through the briefs.

Dalton drew his hand away. "Sorry."

"I'm not," said Beaker. He relaxed with Dalton cradled in the crook of his arm, and less than a minute later he began to snore.

CHAPTER TWENTY-FIVE

Another day had come with no sign of Beaker or Dalton. Dena reminded herself repeatedly that Izzy was right, that Beaker had told them up front he would be gone for several days, but she could not help worrying. What would she do if Beaker returned alone? Even if some accident did take her brother's life, she would never believe it. Either Beaker would come back with Dalton – alive and well – or he would no longer be welcome in Dena's home.

Asha Nara had the shotgun when Dena awoke that morning. In the early afternoon Asha handed the gun over to Rajinder. Dena did not have a shift that day, which would make the day go by easier for her. There was not much to do while standing guard other than agonize over something she could do nothing about.

She spent part of the afternoon on the patio, picking burrs and bits of dirt from Ebony's coat. Emma did the same with Hershey, although the chocolate-brown poodle did not need it as much. The black poodle always seemed to be into something or other. The smallest things excited Ebony; earlier in the day she had nearly cleared the five-foot privacy fence when she saw a squirrel on the roof of the Coopers' house. She was certainly an athletic dog.

Spencer rested on the patio and watched as they worked. His coat did not collect nearly as much dirt as the poodles' wooly coats did. The grooming attention seemed to help calm Ebony down a little, and Dena wondered what had happened to the dog to make her so excitable and troublesome. Dena did not know dogs nearly so well as Dalton did, but she had read in a magazine somewhere that poodles were one of the most intelligent and easily trainable breeds.

Ebony had obviously never read that magazine article.

Running her fingers through the curly hair on the top of Ebony's head, Dena said, "Okay, girl, you're on your own for a while. I need to start dinner." She looked over at Emma. "Do you want to help?"

"Sure." The teenager stood up, smiling as Hershey licked at her ankle. "Are we really going to cook tonight?"

"Yes, but remember that you can't say anything about it to Beaker when he gets back."

Emma grinned. "I won't, Mrs. Anderson." As the two turned and walked across the patio to the back door, she said, "Jim asked me if I'll go steady with him."

That took Dena by surprise, but she tried not to show it. Stepping into the kitchen, she said, "Jimmy's a nice young man." A nice young man who was nevertheless too old to date a high-school girl. Or he would have been too old if the world were not turned upside down.

"And he's good looking," said Emma. "But how can we go steady when we can't really go anywhere?"

"I don't know, Emma. Right now we all have to make do as well as possible." Dena looked over the cans of potatoes and vegetables that she had brought in from the garage earlier. "Let's open these and mix them together, and then we'll get a fire going outside in the grill."

Emma went to the utensil drawer and took out a can opener. "What are we making?"

"I hope it will be a vegetable stew." Through the kitchen window she saw Michael and Jim Rutherford come in through the back gate. Jim was pushing a wheelbarrow stacked with another load of wood they had cut. The two men stopped and spoke to Rajinder, who was standing with the shotgun at the far end of the yard. All three dogs were in the yard also. Spencer and Hershey were lying together near the edge of the patio, both of them watching Ebony as she raced around the inside perimeter of the fence by herself.

Dena wondered what Missy and Dave Bouchard would think about their daughter dating Jim Rutherford. They might not approve, but Emma was a healthy young woman, and who else was there for her to date?

With a glance at the teenager, Dena took a large clean pot out of a cabinet and set it on the counter. "I don't think you actually have to go anywhere physically to go steady," she said. "It's more of an agreement between you and him. I know it's crowded around here. If you need privacy, let me know and I'll make sure the rest of us give you some space."

Dena felt a little awkward hinting at the need for physical intimacy, but Emma responded by asking, "Do I just empty the cans into the pot?"

When Dena nodded, Emma poured peas into the metal pot and then turned her attention back to opening more cans. "I also don't want Jim to think I'm easy," she said. "I mean, I just met him. Do you think it's too early to go steady?"

Dena smiled. There was nothing tawdry about Emma's affection for Jim Rutherford. "Perhaps it would have been too early if you'd asked me last summer," she said, "but these are unusual times. If you think that you can find some happiness with Jimmy, even for a while, I say you should go for it."

Emma emptied a can of corn into the pot. Her expression clouded over and she set the can down a little too hard. "I don't know if that's a good idea, Mrs. Anderson. That's what Cody and I were trying to do, and he's dead now."

Taking the can opener from the girl's hands, Dena opened a can of potatoes, and then another, adding them to the pot of vegetables. Emma sat quietly, her mind weighed down by thoughts and emotions that no teenage girl should have had to suffer.

"I know you miss Cody," said Dena. "And that's not a bad thing. He meant a lot to you, and you should hold his memory in your heart. But you can't blame yourself for Cody getting sick. Bad things happen sometimes."

Emma nodded. "I know."

"The important thing is that we're still alive, and that we have something to look forward to."

"What do I have to look forward to?"

Dena emptied a third can of potatoes into the pot. "Well, there's a handsome boy in the back yard right now who likes you very much. I think that holds some promise."

A smile played at the corners of Emma's mouth. "Yeah, I suppose you're right."

The sound of all three dogs barking frantically caught their attention. They looked up just as Rajinder came in through the kitchen door. Without so much as glancing at the women, Rajinder ran through kitchen and disappeared into the living room, clutching the shotgun as he ran.

Next Michael and Jim Rutherford ran in from the patio.

The grip of fear clutched at Dena's chest. "What is it, Michael?"

"Stay here," he said tersely. "Both of you, stay right here." And then he was following Rajinder. Jim also hurried through the kitchen, but instead ran up the stairs, taking them several at a time.

Ignoring her husband, Dena ran to the hall and looked up the stairs. "Jimmy, what's going on?"

Then she could hear the source of their anxiety. The roar of engines, not automobiles, but a similar sound; the slightly higher pitch of motorcycle engines.

Michael and Rajinder were in the living room squatting under the front window. As usual, the living room curtains were closed. Rajinder had the shotgun ready. From outside the noise of the engines grew louder. Although Dena could not see how many bikes there were, she could tell it was more than a few. She could also hear Jadu crying upstairs and Asha trying to quiet him.

The Franklins came running in from the family room. "What is it?" asked Jerry.

"Road wolves!" said Jim, leaping down the last few stairs, his pistol in hand.

To punctuate this, the front window imploded as a bullet came through. Izzy Franklin screamed and ran back to the family room. Jadu's cries increased in volume.

Jim Rutherford dove to the window and dropped down next to Rajinder and Michael. Gunshot sounded again from outside. With a practiced motion, Jim raised himself just long enough to respond by firing the pistol at their assailants through the broken window, and then dropped back beneath the windowsill.

Michael shouted, "Dena, get back to the kitchen now!"

When the window shattered, bits of glass had pushed the curtain back enough for Dena to see a horde of men on motorcycles circling the cul de sac. Each man had a hand gun.

Exchanging a silent agreement with their eyes, Jim and Rajinder both raised up and fired at the bikers. One of the men toppled off of his bike and fell to the pavement. The motorcycle continued forward, running halfway across the Martins' overgrown front lawn before falling over.

More bullets came through the window. Dena dropped to the carpet. She saw Jerry Franklin grab his upper arm, and blood seeped through his fingers as he fled to join Izzy in the family room.

"There are too many of them!" shouted Jim. "We can't hold them off!"

A portrait of Dena's parents hanging on the wall exploded as a bullet hit it.

Dena said, "Michael, get away from the damn window! You don't have a gun."

Michael crawled towards her, ducking as two more bullet holes suddenly appeared in the opposite wall. Jim and Rajinder continued to fire at the bikers, but they were clearly outnumbered.

As Michael came closer, Dena said, "We have to get out of here!"

"We can't outrun them, honey. They're on bikes, we're on foot."

"Oh God, Michael, what are we going to do?"

Michael looked over his shoulder at Jim and Rajinder. "How many are there, Jim?"

"Haven't really been able to count them, sir," Jim replied. He fired another shot and dropped down. "More than we can handle."

Turning back to Dena, Michael said, "You can get Emma, the Naras and the Franklins out through the back while I help Jim and Rajinder hold them off."

Dena shook her head. "I'm not going without you."

"Then everybody is going to die," he snapped. "Asha! Come down here with Jadu!"

Rajinder shouted, "Do as he says, Asha! Come down now!" To Michael, he said, "I have the shotgun. It is my responsibility. See that my family is safe."

"Something's happening out there!" shouted Jim.

The bikers had stopped shooting at the house. Rajinder raised up enough to look over the windowsill. Dena and Michael also cautiously raised up enough to see what was happening.

Still circling the cul de sac on their bikes, the men were now staring up at the roof of the house. Some were pointing. There were at least two dozen motorcycles, not including four that had lost their riders and now lay on the Martins' and the Grahams' lawns.

Asha came down the stairs carrying Jadu on her hip. "You have seen it, then?" she asked.

"Seen what?" asked Michael. "The road wolves?"

"The ship. It is over the house."

"Ship..." Michael repeated. "The *spaceship?*"

Asha nodded.

Some of the bikers turned and rode off down the street. Then most of the others joined them, but Dena was even more frightened. The alien ship – one of them – was directly over her home. She remembered what Beaker had said about the city of Pittsburgh. *It doesn't exist anymore, not in any recognizable form.*

It terrified her to think the same thing was about to happen to all of the houses up and down Hugo Drive.

Eight bikers were still circling the cul de sac when something else caught Dena's eye.

"Oh my God, Michael, Ebony got out of the yard!"

The black poodle ran from around the side of the house, crossing the front yard, jubilantly circling the cul de sac with the bikers as if she had discovered a festive party.

"She must have jumped the fence," said Michael.

Whether frightened by the dog or just out of callousness, one of the bikers pointed his gun at Ebony and fired. She jerked suddenly and then fell, twitching several times before her body relaxed on the pavement.

Dena screamed, not so much for Ebony but because the first flash of light startled her when it came a fraction of a second later. The brilliant, blinding flash left two green orbs floating in her vision.

She scrunched her eyes shut. Even so, she was aware of three more flashes.

Blinking, Dena opened her eyes. The green orbs from the first burst of light continued to partially blind her, but she could make out a few things. Ebony was still sprawled on the pavement; the eight bikers and their motorcycles were gone. The bikers did not exist anymore, not in any recognizable form. There was nothing left but ashes and several gaping holes in the pavement.

Dena ran to the front door and threw it open.

"Dena!" Michael shouted. "Dena, what are you doing?"

Heedless of the danger, she ran to the street. She had promised Dalton and, once again, it was a promise broken. Perhaps not with intent, but she felt as if she had betrayed him.

She fell to her knees next to Ebony's body, scooping the dog up in her arms. Tears fell into Ebony's dark curls. "I'm sorry, Dalton," she cried. "I am so sorry."

Overhead, the alien ship slowly turned and drifted south, ignoring the distraught woman sobbing in the street.

CHAPTER TWENTY-SIX

Dalton woke to Beaker shaking his shoulder gently. The room was dark; illuminated only by starlight coming in through the windows.

"Get up," said the larger man. Beaker picked up Dalton's jeans and handed them to him. A delicious smell permeated the house.

"What is that?" asked Dalton, referring to the smell.

"Soup." Beaker found Dalton's sweatshirt and set it on the bed.

"It doesn't smell like soup."

"That's because you're used to eating out of cans."

Dalton threw his legs over the side of the bed. The wooden floor was cold against his feet. "Well that's where all the food comes from now."

"Not all of it." Beaker was fully dressed in his hoodie and sweat pants. Apparently he was going commando, because his cotton briefs were wadded up on the top of the bureau next to Dalton's revolver.

Pulling on his jeans, Dalton asked, "You made real soup? Not from a can?"

Beaker nodded. "I woke up a little before sunset and looked around the garden outside."

"But everything was eaten or ruined from what I saw."

"Everything above ground," agreed Beaker. "There were still a lot of potatoes and onions under the soil, and we brought some salt and spices from the other place, so I made potato soup. I packed the rest of the potatoes and onions in boxes. We'll be taking some fresh food back with us along with all the canned stuff."

Dalton slipped his foot into one of his shoes. "You are an amazing boyfriend."

Turning away from him, Beaker said, "I don't know if you'll like the soup or not. I'm not the greatest cook."

"It smells delicious."

"Hurry up and get dressed, then. As soon as you eat, we'll be ready to go." Beaker started for the doorway, but he stopped and came back to kiss Dalton on the forehead. The gesture was incongruous coming from a man who had until then eschewed any expression of familiarity with the people around him. Then Beaker hurried into the dark hallway and down the stairs.

Dalton put on his other shoe, took his revolver from the top of the bureau and felt his way through the hallway. There, with no windows, it was impossible to see where he was going. He moved slowly, keeping one hand on the wall and tapping the floor with his foot before stepping forward.

He found the stairs and descended them. Before he reached the bottom, he could see a faint blue light coming from the kitchen. Beaker was standing at the kitchen stove stirring a pot. The light came from the blue flame underneath the pot.

"There's still some propane," said Dalton, stating the obvious.

Beaker nodded. He filled a bowl and handed it to Dalton. The soup was a little watery, but it was the best thing that Dalton had eaten since leaving his apartment in Butler. There was enough left over for Beaker to have half of a second bowl. They ate by a combination of starlight and the light from the propane flame. When the two men finished, Beaker turned off the stove and they went out to the truck.

"I have enough gas to drive us home tonight," said Beaker, starting the engine and pulling the truck out from behind the rhododendrons. "If I'm counting the days right, Jerry will be watching the place when we get there."

Dalton nodded. It would have been his own shift, but he was gone, and Jerry Franklin had been recruited to fill in. Now that Dalton and Beaker were returning to the house everything would change again.

The Silverado was the only vehicle on the road. The feeling of solitude was something Dalton was growing used to; although he knew that it was not true solitude. There were other people out there, hiding in some of the houses they passed, trying to survive from one day to the next.

"Where are we going to sleep?" he asked. He turned away from Beaker, watching the night landscape as they drove down the highway. Dalton felt a little uncomfortable bringing the subject up despite the brief intimacy they had shared. Talking about anything personal with Beaker still seemed strange.

"I reckon we'll have to work that out," said Beaker. His voice had a strange pitch, as if he were just as uncomfortable discussing their sleeping arrangements.

"Maybe Jim won't mind taking the couch," Dalton suggested.

Beaker nodded, but said nothing. Once again he was silent and distant. Dalton felt closed out. He silently reminded himself that Beaker had dug potatoes and made a soup for him.

They rode in silence for another twenty minutes, and then Dalton said, "You may not think you're the greatest cook, Beaker, but that soup was pretty good. Until now, I didn't know you could cook at all."

"Until now, that wasn't the only thing you didn't know about me."

Dalton looked over at Beaker and saw that the man was grinning in the dark.

"So what's your first name?" asked Dalton.

The grin faded, and at first Beaker said nothing. Then, finally, "Why?"

"It's just something I think that I should know." Dalton shrugged. "When I'm in the throes of passion I don't want to shout, 'Oh, Mr. Beaker!'"

Beaker laughed then, and it was the first time Dalton had heard laughter from him that was not strained or tinged with anger.

"I don't use my first name. Anyway, I don't want you shouting anything at all while we're staying at your sister's house. We're all crammed in there like sardines."

"Okay, I'll just whisper it, then," said Dalton. "But if we're going to be lovers, I should at least know what your name is."

Beaker shook his head. "I don't like to use that word either. Lovers. It sounds like we're doing something illicit. I want you by my side, but let's call it something else."

Dalton checked the safety on his revolver and put it in the glove compartment. It had been Beaker who had shown him two nights earlier how to use the safety and aim the gun. "You're changing the subject, Beaker. I deserve to know your name."

"It's Rafferty."

"No, really."

"That's really my name. Rafferty Beaker." He turned and looked at Dalton. "Go ahead, make a joke now."

"It's different."

Beaker nodded. "And that's the nicest thing anyone can say about it. I hate my name. Always have."

"Then use your middle name," said Dalton. When there was no response, he added, "A lot of people do that. You know, Michael's first name is Jonathon, but that was also his father's name, so he has always gone by Michael."

"My middle name's worse." The Silverado lurched forward as Beaker's foot pressed a little harder on the accelerator.

Dalton asked, "How could it be worse than Rafferty?"

"Easy enough. It's Krishna."

Mulling the name over in his mind, Dalton said, "Yeah, I guess that's worse. Rafferty Krishna Beaker. The names don't even go together. I think Rajinder and Asha would like the name Krishna, though."

"Sure," said Beaker. "It would be a great name if I'd grown up in Delhi. It was a miserable name for a kid in Fayetteville, Arkansas. Rafferty Krishna Beaker." He sighed. "Farty Kiss-my-Beaver; that's what they called me."

Dalton bit down on his lower lip, certain that laughing would not be a good idea just then. After a minute, he said, "Kids are cruel."

"Yeah, well, let's just say I got into more than my share of fights. Then I hit puberty and everything just got worse."

"When the other kids found out you were gay?"

"No, nobody knew." Beaker shook his head. "But it was something I had to hide from everyone. You know how it is."

"Yeah," said Dalton. "I do."

Neither of them spoke for a long time after that. They drove through the dark Pennsylvania night, a darkness that was even deeper with no yard lights or house lights.

When Beaker finally turned onto Route 228, Dalton said, "You're right. Neither Rafferty nor Krishna fit you at all. Beaker is just a better name for you."

"It's worked for me for years."

Dalton thought about this. "Is that what Don called you?"

Beaker nodded.

"Then it's good enough for me."

They were heading west on 228 towards Caldonia when Beaker suddenly turned off the headlights. Dalton grabbed the door handle as the Silverado soared down a black strip of highway that he could barely make out in the dark. Almost as soon as the lights were doused, Beaker gently tapped the brakes, slowing the truck to half its previous speed.

"What's with the lights?" asked Dalton. "Are you trying to wreck the truck?"

"Don't you see it?" Beaker nodded in the direction of a wooded slope to the south of the highway.

Peering into the dark, Dalton made out the shape of a tear-shaped spacecraft just over the trees.

"Is it the same ship?" he asked.

"I don't know," said Beaker. "Probably. We're going to have to go on without lights. We're not that far from Hugo Drive now, and I don't want to lead those fuckers right up to your sister's house."

"How do you know they won't be able to track us anyway?"

"I don't," said Beaker. "But I'm not going to make things worse than they already are. Keep an eye on that thing, will you? Let me know if it looks like it's following us."

Dalton watched the spacecraft, but it did not move as they continued down the highway. Still, he wondered if the aliens were watching the truck somehow, waiting to discern its destination.

It was past midnight when they turned onto Hugo Drive. Dalton found it hard to believe that these homes had been a thriving neighborhood earlier that summer. Many of the decorative trees had been cut down and stacked for firewood behind the Andersons' house. The buildings themselves were obviously vacant and abandoned, the lawns overgrown, the windows dark.

Beaker pulled the truck onto the Andersons' lawn and turned off the engine. They were less than twenty feet from the front door. "There's no point in carrying all of this food any farther than we have to," he said.

Even in the night they could see the broken, gaping sections of pavement in the cul de sac. The front door to the Andersons' house opened and a solitary figure holding a shotgun stepped out. Dalton noticed immediately that it was not Jerry Franklin.

"Beaker?" Jim Rutherford's voice came from the doorway. "What's wrong with your lights? I could have shot you."

"Glad you didn't," said Beaker, stepping out of the cab of the truck. He took his rifle out of its rack and closed the truck door behind him. "How did you know we weren't a couple of road wolves?"

A dog shot past Jim's legs then and ran around to the other side of the truck. With an excited bark, Spencer passed Beaker and sat in front of Dalton, trembling with the excitement that every dog feels when one of its humans returns, no matter how short the absence.

"That's how," said Jim, nodding to the dog. "Spencer wouldn't have been acting like that if it was anyone but you and Dalton."

Dalton came up to them, with Spencer at his side. As all three men and the dog walked toward the house, Beaker said, "I had to turn the lights off because we drove past one of the spaceships. It isn't far from here."

"I know," said Jim. He nodded to the broken gaps in the cul de sac pavement. "We had a little encounter with them earlier today. That's why I'm watching the house tonight. Jerry was shot." He led them to the house and into the living room.

Beaker looked at him sharply. "By the aliens?"

"No, by road wolves. On bikes."

The light of a taper candle was coming down the stairs, illuminating Dena Anderson's face with a ghostly glow. They could see that Michael was close behind her. When Dena saw her twin she hurried her pace.

"Dalton," she said, "I am so sorry. I really am."

Beaker asked, "Is Jerry all right?"

The family room door opened and a large poodle bounded out, followed by Jerry and Izzy Franklin and then by Emma Bouchard. Jerry's arm was in a makeshift sling.

"I'm going to survive," said Jerry. "It hurts like hell, though."

Dena said, "Ebony was shot, too. She's dead, Dalton. I am sorry."

Dalton nodded solemnly.

Michael said, "Rajinder and Jim here were real heroes, though." He related how they had held the bikers off for a while, and then the alien spacecraft had come, and how one of the remaining bikers had shot the black poodle when she jumped over the back fence. "If it weren't for Jim and Rajinder, we'd all probably be dead now. I'm glad you're back, though, Beaker. We could have used you today."

Beaker nodded and propped his rifle against the living room

wall next to the couch. "We should get the food inside. Dalton and I filled up the truck. We can all catch up later."

Michael, Jim and Beaker went out to the Silverado. Dalton started to follow them, but Dena put the candle down and hugged him tightly. "I'm so glad you're back, Dalton." Then she pulled away and looked into his eyes. "What is it? Did Beaker do something to you?"

"Not yet," said Dalton, grinning.

Beaker came back in with a box in his arms. "Both of you need to get out there and carry things in." He looked at the other three people in the room. "You too, Izzy. And Emma. I don't guess you can carry much, Jerry, but we need the rest of you to help. Either we get the food in now, or we'll just have to leave it."

Dalton and Dena went outside, and they immediately saw the reason for Beaker's urgency. The alien ship was slowly moving towards Hugo Drive. It was still several miles off, but there was no question that it was moving in their direction.

On his third trip out to the truck, Beaker said, "I did this. I've led them right to us."

Dalton was pulling a box of canned corn and jars of olives from the bed of the Silverado. He looked up at Beaker and said, "I'm not going to let you take the blame for this. You told me yourself that we don't know what the aliens are thinking or why they do things. We don't understand their perspective, remember? That's what you said. They could be coming this way for a lot of reasons that don't have anything to do with you."

Dena was surprised at Dalton's confidence, and even more so when Beaker nodded complacently. Both men had definitely changed.

They carried the boxes of food through the living room, down the hall and into the garage. Soon they were stacking boxes so high that Izzy and Emma could no longer help.

Meanwhile, the alien ship had stopped just beyond the Franklins' and the Grahams' properties. It hovered there ominously, like a behemoth silently observing them as they worked.

Michael and Beaker went out to get the last two boxes. Looking up at the ship, Michael said, "It reminds me of an ant farm I had when I was a kid. Only now I think we're the ants."

Dena led Dalton to the kitchen where they could be alone for a minute. Looking to see that nobody had followed them, she asked, "What is going on with you and Beaker? And don't tell me it's nothing."

Dalton shrugged. "I guess you could say we're dating." He leaned close to her and whispered, "Beaker's gay."

Dena watched him closely to see if there was any hint of a joke. "*Our* Beaker?"

"Yeah, our Beaker." Dalton nodded. "And I pretty much think he's my Beaker now. I mean, we haven't worked any of the details out yet, and he doesn't want us to describe ourselves as lovers, but that's where we're at." He ran his fingers through his hair. "I just hope we can spend a little time together before...well...you know..."

"We might be fine."

Spencer came into the kitchen and sat at Dalton's feet. Dalton looked down at the dog, but it was his sister who he spoke to. "Dena, the ship is just outside."

"Yes, but it was here yesterday, too, and they left us alone. In fact it was the ship that saved us. We couldn't have held off those bikers much longer when the aliens came. You heard what Michael said; the ship blasted the bikers after they shot Ebony."

Dalton said, "It sounds almost like what happened in St. Louis."

"I was thinking the same thing." Dena nodded. "Just after the police shot that German shepherd. But we don't really know what happened there. Dalton, we put Ebony in the garage. I didn't want to bury her until you came back."

They joined the others in the living room. Rajinder was awake and downstairs also, and they all crowded into the front room together.

Beaker sat on the couch, taking Dalton by the arm and pulling the smaller man down next to him in the same movement. When Dalton sat, Beaker put his massive arm around his shoulder. This elicited a frown from Izzy, a smile from Dena and a look of confusion from Jim Rutherford. Whatever the others were thinking, nobody said anything.

It was Dena who spoke. "Dalton and I think the aliens may have some interest in the dogs."

Michael frowned. "Spencer and Hershey?"

"No, any dogs. All dogs."

Jerry Franklin asked, "Is that why they broke into the animal shelter?"

"Maybe," said Dena. "Remember how the transmission from St. Louis broke off after a dog was shot? And how the ship killed the bikers yesterday after Ebony was shot?"

"That makes no sense," said Michael. "If they are protecting dogs for some reason, then why were they destroying those Amish farms? Or was that just a rumor?"

"And why hit Pittsburgh?" asked Jerry. "Or the other cities?"

"Or farms in Missouri," added Izzy. "Do they like dogs and hate farmers?"

They talked late into the night, and then Jim handed the shotgun to Dena and went upstairs to bed. Not long after that Rajinder excused himself and went to check on Asha and Jadu. Then Jerry and Izzy went back to the family room.

Emma sat in a corner of the living room, with her arm around Hershey. Michael sat at one end of the couch, and Beaker and Dalton at the other. Spencer stretched out on the floor at the feet of the two men. It was almost as if the dog understood that R. K. Beaker held a special place in Dalton's heart now.

Dena stood near the couch. Holding the shotgun, she kept a close eye on the ship outside. A cool breeze came in through the broken window.

Michael was saying, "If there were some way we could just talk to them and let them know we mean them no harm."

"They may not care, Michael," said Beaker. "If you haven't noticed, we aren't really capable of inflicting much harm on them anyway."

"Then if we could just find out what they want. I'm sick of feeling like a prisoner in my own house."

Dalton rested his head on Beaker's shoulder. The first morning rays were coming through the window. He was tired, and, despite the ship's presence, he felt safe and at ease with Beaker's arm around him. He thought it was probably exhaustion that left him with such a sense of peace.

He was almost asleep when his attention was jerked back into consciousness. Beaker had sat up and pulled his arm back, and Michael was standing.

"This is it," said Dena. She inhaled deeply.

Dalton turned and looked out the window. The alien ship had lowered almost out of view behind the houses.

CHAPTER TWENTY-SEVEN

Beaker told Emma to wake Jim Rutherford and have him bring his pistol. "Let the others sleep," he said. "There's nothing they can do if the aliens confront us." Then, after Emma was out of earshot, he added, "Not that there's anything we'll be able to do either." He reached for his rifle, stepped to one side of the window and peered out at the ship.

Michael went to Dena. "I'll take the shotgun."

She shook her head. "No, this is my shift. Having a penis doesn't give you any special skill with firearms, Michael." Dena focused her attention back to the cul de sac. "Besides, we still don't know that they're looking for us, or what they want."

Beaker readied his rifle. "Dalton, where's the revolver?"

Dalton swallowed. "I left it in the truck. It's in the glove compartment. Sorry."

"Three guns or four won't make much difference," said Beaker.

Jim and Emma came downstairs, with Hershey following behind them. Jim had his pistol, and he went to stand next to Dena. He was naked except for his boxers. Spencer went over to Hershey and sniffed at the larger dog. Hershey gave a play bow, lowering her chest, but Spencer seemed to sense the mood of the humans around him. Spencer turned from Hershey and looked up at Dalton, who was eyeing both dogs thoughtfully.

Beaker looked over at Emma. "Take that damn poodle upstairs and wait there."

"I'm not leaving Jim," said Emma.

Lowering his pistol, Jim went to her. "I'd feel better if I knew you weren't in the line of fire. Go on upstairs. I'll be fine."

She kissed him then, an adult kiss, long and lingering. Then she called Hershey to follow her and went upstairs to the bedroom that Jim and Dalton had been sharing.

Dena stiffened. "Look," she said quietly, gesturing with the barrel of the shotgun at the Franklins' house and its painted windows.

Five of the aliens were coming around the side of the Franklins' home. Three stood upright, each holding a lethal wand. The other two trotted along on all fours. All wore their protective suits. The five creatures stopped in the middle of the Franklins' overgrown lawn. From their movements Dalton could tell that they were communicating with each other, and the terror he had felt when last confronted by the aliens threatened to consume him again.

Jim slowly raised his pistol in both hands.

"Don't fire," said Dena. "If there's a fight, we're going to lose. You know that, Jimmy."

He nodded slowly. "But I'm going to take at least at least one of these bastards down with me."

Dena looked at him nervously. "Jimmy, we don't know that they mean to hurt us."

Jim still held the pistol aimed at the aliens on the opposite side of the cul de sac. "Tell that to the Amish."

Dalton looked back down at Spencer. "The Amish..." he muttered.

Beaker noticed the change in Dalton's expression. "Are you all right?"

With a feverish look in his eyes, Dalton said, "It really *is* the dogs. It's been the dogs all along."

Dena saw that one of the aliens, one walking on two feet, had crossed to the center of the cul de sac and was examining the junipers that Mr. Martin once tended so carefully. "What are you talking about, Dalton?"

"A lot of the puppy mills in Pennsylvania are run by Amish people," said Dalton. He looked around at the others. "Everyone talks about the Amish like they're saints, but they're like any other group – they have good people and bad people, and some of them have puppy mills where they breed dogs for pet shops and wholesalers. Don't you see? To an alien who thinks dogs are the dominant species it would look like some kind of concentration camp; which a puppy mill is, in a way."

Michael asked, "But why would they think dogs are the dominant species?"

"Don't you remember what Beaker said about how the aliens could have a completely different perspective?"

Beaker nodded slowly. "We could look like a servant race."

"Easily," said Dalton. "We feed our dogs, we care for their health, we provide shelter. We do it because we want to, but the aliens may see *us* as the domesticated species."

"The other ship went into rural Missouri," said Dena. "Are there a lot of Amish out there?"

"I don't know," Dalton admitted. "I don't think so. But I do know that Missouri has more puppy mills than almost any other state."

One of the quadrapedal aliens crossed to the center of the cul de sac to join its bipedal comrade.

Michael said, "This could still all be coincidence."

"It would explain why they're destroying the cities but aren't trying to attack us as individuals," said Dalton. "They don't hate us – they just think we're out of control. I think Beaker is right, they *have* been trying to communicate, only not with us humans."

Dena looked from her twin to her husband. "That doesn't do us much good, though, if we don't know what they're saying or how to answer."

"But I think that I do," said Dalton.

"How?"

"Well, not me so much, at least not yet. But Spencer probably can, and I'm pretty good at communicating with him." He nodded slowly, looking down at his dog. "I know what I need to do. And I need your help, Spence." He knelt and scratched the dog behind the ears.

With two leaping steps Beaker crossed the room and blocked the front door. He still clutched his rifle. "You aren't going outside, Dalton. Not with those things out there."

"I have to." Dalton smiled at him. "Don't you see? You can come with me, but please don't try to stop me."

Dena shook her head. "No, Dalton, I agree with Beaker. You don't know what you're saying."

Dalton stepped closer to Beaker and looked up into the man's dark eyes. "I want us to have a life together, and what we have here isn't living. We're just surviving. Put the rifle down and come out with Spencer and me. If we die, at least we'll die together."

"Michael, stop him!" cried Dena.

Michael's eyes narrowed. "I'd rather join him. That is, if it's okay with you, Dalton." To Dena he said, "We can't keep on like this. If Dalton thinks he can connect with the aliens, I'm willing to place my bet on him. I don't want to live out the rest of my days hiding from these things."

Dena started to say something, but found herself nodding.

Still holding his pistol, Jim said, "I'll have you covered, Dalton."

Michael clapped Jim Rutherford on the back. "All right, soldier, but don't fire unless they use those wands on us."

Dalton looked up at Beaker. "I'm going out there now. I'd rather have you beside me."

Beaker slowly stepped away from the door. He leaned the rifle against the wall. Dalton pushed open the door and went outside with Spencer at his heel. Beaker and Dena followed a step behind and to either side of him, and Michael walked next to Dena.

The aliens jerked to attention, and the two quadrupeds immediately rose to their hind legs.

"Don't look at them," said Dalton. "Look just past them, or to one side or the other, but don't stare into their faceplates. They might interpret that as a challenge."

After taking a few steps onto the lawn, Dalton stopped walking. Spencer immediately sat next to him. Beaker and Dena came up to either side of him, with Beaker on Spencer's side, and Michael next to his wife.

One of the aliens in the center of the cul de sac – the one that had just been standing on all fours – reached up with its short arms and removed its opaque helmet.

Dalton inhaled sharply. His first impression was of Lon Chaney Jr.'s version of a werewolf. The creature's face was covered with greenish-brown hair. The mouth looked like that of a terrestrial animal, a predator, with long inferior incisors that extended over the alien's upper lip. If the alien had ears or a nose, these were hidden beneath its hair. There were two eyes, or at least Dalton thought they were eyes. They were blank, dark orbs, with no whites.

Then the creature blinked.

The blink was vertical rather than horizontal, with the eyelids (or what Dalton thought were eyelids) coming from the left and right of the orbs.

"Don't smile," he said quietly.

"I wasn't going to," said Dena. "But why not?"

Dalton said, "It may not matter, but they could take it as a threat if you show your teeth."

Barely moving his lips, Michael said, "If we couldn't take them out with nuclear missiles, I don't think biting is going to be very effective."

The wolfman – as Dalton was beginning to think of the alien – handed his helmet to his companion. The other three aliens then came forward, walking slowly on their short legs. Two of these held their wands pointed at the human entourage, and Dalton had no doubt that he would be dead in an instant if they perceived any of his actions as potentially dangerous.

The wolfman took another three steps towards them. Then the creature dropped to all fours in a graceful gesture. His head and forearms lowered even more, and he thrust his right arm forward as his chest came within an inch of the pavement.

It was the same posture that the lead alien had taken in the St. Louis broadcast.

Without daring to move, Dalton said, "Spence, take a bow."

Spencer stood on all fours and then lowered his chest to the ground.

"Stay, boy."

The dog held his position.

From the wolfman came a sound that reminded Dalton of a recording he had once heard of dolphins. But this creature was no dolphin, and they were not underwater.

Michael took a step forward, but froze when Dalton hissed, "Don't move!"

One of the aliens in the Franklins' yard then crossed to the center of cul de sac and lowered itself in the same position that the wolfman had taken. Then a third alien did the same.

Spencer suddenly rose to his feet.

"No, Spence!" said Dalton.

But Spencer had a mind of his own just then. He looked up at Dalton and barked happily. Then he ran to the street and dropped again in a more natural play bow.

Beaker stepped closer to Dalton. "What's happening?"

Watching his dog, Dalton said, "I can't be sure, but I think we may have just said 'hello'."

Two aliens still had wands, but they held these to their sides and the wands disappeared inside their suits. Spencer was bowing and prancing and barking with exuberance. The wolfman raised up on all fours and responded to the dog's antics with a high-pitched keening.

Taking a step forward, away from Beaker and his sister, Dalton faced the aliens and bowed at the waist.

All five aliens froze. The wolfman looked to his companions. They were turning to each other, and then to Dalton and Beaker,

Dena and Michael. The aliens seemed confused by Dalton's gesture.

Then the wolfman rose to its hind feet and stared at Dalton with its dark, blank eyes. Cocking its head to one side, it mimicked Dalton's movement, bending forward slightly from its low-set waist. The movement was both inhuman and at the same time familiar.

"And now *they've* said 'hello'." Dalton bowed in turn to each of the other four aliens.

All of the aliens stood and bowed awkwardly. Spencer ran closer to them, stopped and gave another play bow, and then ran back to Dalton and Beaker.

Dena moved closer to her twin. "What does this mean? Are they okay with us now?"

"It means we have a future. But nothing will ever be the same again."

Dena saw that one of the aliens was bowing to her. She bowed stiffly. Beaker and Michael also bowed to the creatures.

It was both an ending and a beginning, and, as Dalton had said, nothing would ever be the same.

COSMIC
EGG
BOOKS

If you prefer to spend your nights with Vampires and Werewolves rather than the mundane then we publish the books for you. If your preference is for Dragons and Faeries or Angels and Demons – we should be your first stop. Perhaps your perfect partner has artificial skin or comes from another planet – step right this way. Our curiosity shop contains treasures you will enjoy unearthing. If your passion is Fantasy (including magical realism and spiritual fantasy), Horror or Science Fiction (including Steampunk), Cosmic Egg books will feed your hunger.